RESCUE

On an otherwise serene autumn day,
a veteran's beloved service dog vanishes…

Christopher Dant

SHIRES PRESS
Manchester Center, Vermont

RESCUE

SHIRES PRESS
4869 Main Street, P.O. Box 2200
Manchester Center, VT 05255
www.northshire.com

RESCUE
Christopher Dant

ISBN 978-1-60571-425-7
First Trade Paperback Edition: June 2018

Printed in the United States of America

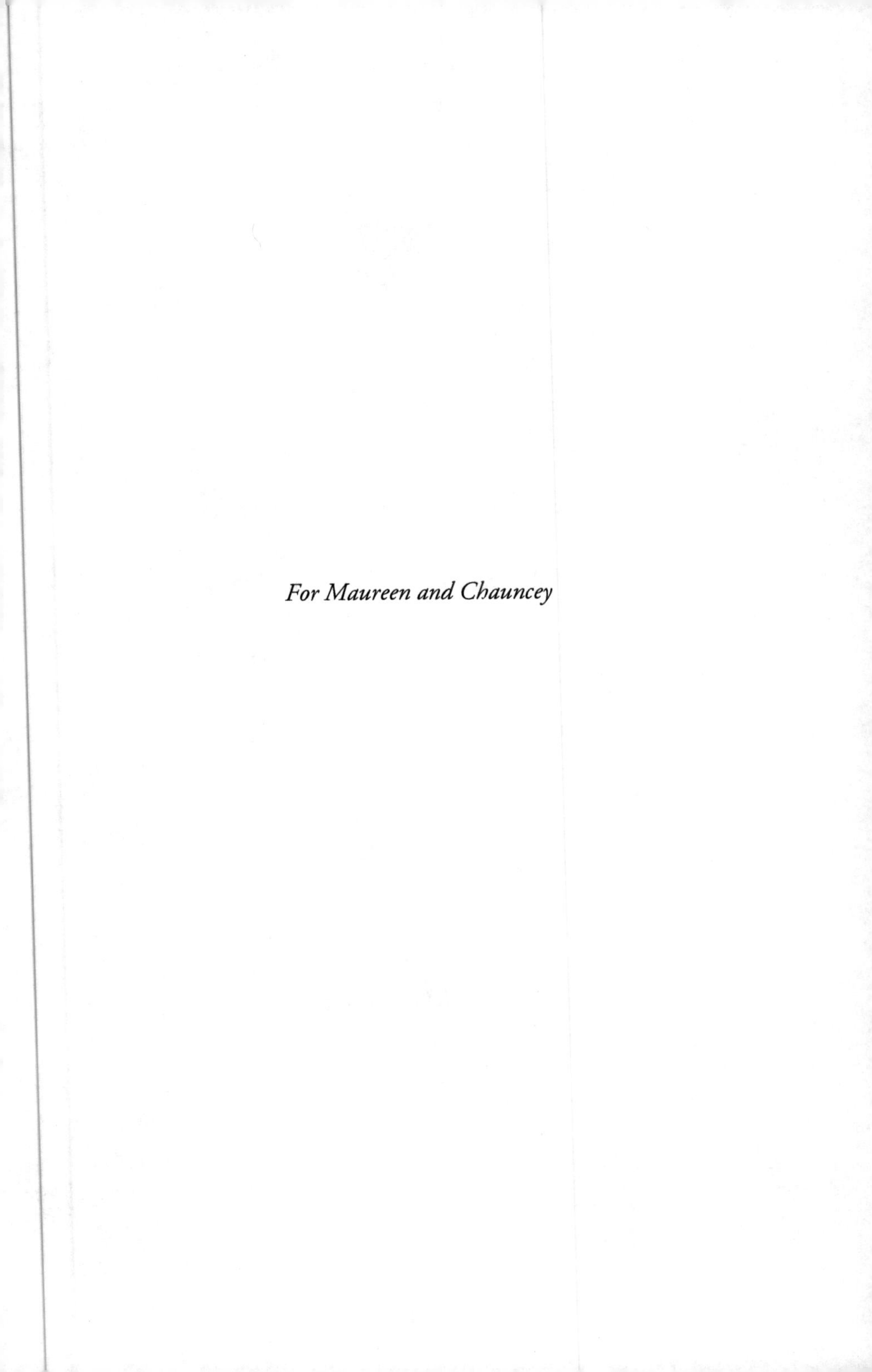

For Maureen and Chauncey

And now the purple dusk of twilight time

steals across the meadows of my heart,

high up in the sky the little stars climb,

always reminding me that we're apart.

Stardust

-H. Carmichael

ACKNOWLEDGEMENTS

I am thankful to the many people who have helped me to transform this work from an idea that began nearly two years ago to the novel it has become today.

First, to my wife, Maureen, who provided me with many inspirations and ideas for the story and sat through endless hours of readings. And to our Golden Retriever, Chauncey, who inspires me every day in many ways. I always looked at her when I got stuck.

Great thanks go out to Paws for Purple Hearts, a terrific national organization that trains and pairs service dogs for U.S. veterans and active-duty military personnel. Especially, I would like to thank the veteran soldiers and dog trainers that reviewed earlier versions of RESCUE, especially United States Army Sergeant Russell Stafford and his dog Major from Paws for Purple Hearts, and United States Army Sergeant Steve Moore, owner and trainer of service dogs with Canine Constitutional.

I wish to acknowledge author and editor Maya Rock of Fresh Ink, formerly with Writer's House in New York, who helped me shape this story. Her early insights and suggestions molded this work and are much appreciated. To my editor, Cathy Taylor, of the Northshire Bookstore, I am grateful for her sharp eye.

To the people of Vermont that motivated the creation of the characters. My tale was driven by their strength, simplicity, and unspoiled spirit. Many of the characters such as Lester Lincoln and Gregory and Grace Swathe were inspired by the wonderful Vermonters I have known over the years.

The quotation, the epigraph at the beginning of RESCUE was taken from the lyrics of the iconic song "Stardust." They reminded me that Dirck and Chauncey, although apart, were drawn together by the stars. It's also a tribute to my father, Charles "Bud" Dant, a highly talented and well-known musician and composer now no longer with us. In a small cafe at Indiana University in Bloomington, he wrote the first arrangement of "Stardust" for Hoagy Carmichael, well before Mitchell Parish wrote the beautiful lyrics. Dad, this is for you.

RESCUE was in part inspired by the service men and women who have sacrificed and continue to sacrifice their lives for our great country and the wonderful service animals that serve those veterans and all those in need. In particular, I was moved by a great man, Luis Carlos Montalván, an Iraq war veteran who owned Tuesday, the Golden Retriever service dog who saved him. At the time he published the New York Times bestseller "Until Tuesday," I became friends with Luis and was moved by his great work with service dogs and veterans. Sadly, Luis is no longer with us. But Tuesday continues his journey.

This is a work of fiction, but every day, in many ways, the dogs that I have known throughout my life have inspired me, particularly our own Chauncey. Although not a service dog, she reminds me daily that the bond between man and dog is unwavering and true—one must start with that.

But here, the hand grows shaky. The relationship between man and his dog is ultimately a mystery, really, one that defies words and can only be experienced. Be it on the hunting fields, on the battlefields, or in service, the many ways that dogs help men and women amaze me.

In this novel, I strived to show that beautiful relationship through a veteran and his beloved service dog. Tested through time and adversity, that bond is indestructible and unspoiled, and revealed in many different ways.

That unwavering loyalty can be seen in the heartbroken dog lying by his soldier's casket; the dog in the lap of a homeless man, protecting him; the faithful dog waiting every day at the train station for his owner to return, years after the man had died; an old, homeless dog taken in by the kindness of a stranger; and the dog at the end of its good life, happy with his final touch.

Dogs are our buddies, our protectors, and ultimately, our saviors. And that is the essence of RESCUE.

1

In the dreadful silence of the foreign land, everything moved in a shadowy, slow-motion hell. Down in a burned-out crater, Captain Dirck Hansen lay in icy numbness, staring into the black oblivion. Ghouls fed upon his limbs as he watched the stealthy approach of his death. A faint cry made him turn.

It was Sergeant Darby, his wide unblinking eyes staring at him. The man's legs had been ripped away and in inaudible gasps, he begged for his commander to end his own misery. Other men tossed into the pit were whispering, holding out their red slippery arms, praying in quiet, grotesque agonies. Then, within the awful stillness, there broke a tremendous clangor of battle, a furnace roar of deafening explosions, loud ghastly screams from men and from children. A crimson roar hurled down, pinning Dirck Hansen under an unending tidal wave of terror. He squeezed rivers of mud through his twisted fingers and lurched back as death seized him in a ferocious vise.

"God, make it stop. Stop, please stop!"

He thrashed between darkness and blinding flashes, between living and dying. He couldn't breathe. His chest, head, and limbs were bound in a heaving tangle. His mortal fear was broadcast, spewing from him an acrid odor like foul cooking meat.

Within the hopeless moments, the moments when he thought the horror would never end, down at the deepest level of his consciousness, Captain Hansen felt a gentle but perceptible warmth upon him. A soft and steady breath pulsed at his face. It smelled of fish.

He opened his eyes to the face of Chauncey, his Golden Retriever. She lay on his chest, moving his head about with her strong muzzle. His murderous mind was eclipsed, and once again, he floated in that dizzy and delicious lightness of being he had come to know with his dog.

He was back. Back again with her in his peaceful Vermont home.

His heart continued to race. Chauncey stayed with him, her warm and watchful eyes steadily at his. She licked his face.

"It's okay," he whispered. "I can breathe now, girl."

Chauncey felt his heartbeat drop, his breathing relax, and now his usual earthy smell had returned. Her job was finished. A job well done, once again. She pulled her head back and panted, her black lips curling toward her ears. It was that perpetual smile he so loved.

They lay close together in silent communion.

"You are my life, Chauncey."

Her tail swished the bedcovers. His dog had given Dirck back everything, everything he had lost in life.

This was only the second such battle nightmare for Dirck in the past months. They were happening less frequently, certainly less in the year since he had brought his service dog home.

The last episode had taken place in their hometown of Glenriver. Along the one-block main street was the Chatham County post office, the Glenriver bank, Mr. Duncan's drugstore, and Gerard's convenience store. They had been on a postal errand that morning. The October air had been crisp, and the town folks were out, enjoying the warm day in the peacefulness of their small Vermont village. Chauncey pranced lively alongside Dirck as they approached the postal building. In the street next to them, Billy Sexton was starting up his old truck. It backfired loudly.

Around Dirck, guns exploded. He dove onto the sidewalk and began thrashing about, reaching for something. Chauncey pushed him over and crawled onto his chest, forming a barrier. Her muzzle nudged his face. He stopped moving. It took only seconds.

She lay on him, licking his cheeks, his nervous hands. His eyes opened. Once she saw him respond, she stood close, guarding him from further dangers. It was a familiar sequence for them both. He lay on the sidewalk staring up at her.

The dog was simply magnificent. Her feathery gold coat flowed over a broad and balanced body that beamed confidence and purpose. She looked cheerful, enthusiastic, eager to work. And, as always in her work, she wore her red vest embroidered in white with **PTSD SERVICE DOG**. One side was pinned with three Iraq War medals, Dirck's medals: the bronze Iraqi Campaign medal, the Three-Deployment Ribbon, and a bright silver Iraqi Freedom Star. The other side was pinned with the lone Purple Heart, the gold-and-purple medal emblazoned with the face of George Washington. The impressive combat decoration "for military merit" had been awarded to Dirck for his extraordinary bravery in an Iraqi battle, the battle that had killed most of his men and left him near death. Chauncey was proud to wear these symbols of Dirck's bravery.

Dirck propped his hand up onto his dog's back and climbed to his feet. She stood firm, giving him the means to stand. No matter how many times his dog had saved him from his tumultuous mind, from the unrelenting anxiety within him, he was still amazed at the simple miracles she brought.

She let out a soft, low moan, a sound she had first made the day Dirck had brought his service dog home. It was a sweet sound, the sound of reassurance, of trust. It signaled to him she would be there. Always.

They stood together alone on the sidewalk.

Across from them, a small crowd had gathered, transfixed by what they had just witnessed. Women wiped away tears. Children held onto their mothers' hands more firmly. An elderly man, a veteran himself, proudly saluted Dirck from across the distance. A young girl couldn't take her eyes off the beautiful, obedient dog. To them, it looked simple.

But they couldn't know what the dog meant to the man. Chauncey held a complexity that defied her actions. She was trained to respond to over one-hundred commands and detect subtle changes in Dirck's smell, his breathing, voice, heartbeat, and movements. Even an otherwise invisible trembling of his foot or hand would arouse her.

She was the barrier against his broken mind, bringing him instant serenity and steady trust. Dirck knew without her, he would lose everything. Again.

He looked down at Chauncey and thought how far they had come together.

2

Before the man, before the war and trauma, before the dog, there had been the young Dirck Hansen, an affable boy who laughed easily and whose heart was full of promise. He had been raised on his family homestead in Vermont by a quiet mother and a strapping father, Douglas. When Dirck was nine, his mother was stricken with leukemia, taking her life quickly, without mercy, leaving him with few memories of her.

Douglas had grabbed their life reins, steering the boy through his formable years until he entered the local college where he met Cynthia Terry, an appealing woman who fell hard for the sweet man. By the time he was a sophomore, they had dropped from school, married, and moved into a one-bedroom New York City apartment belonging to Cindy's mother, who herself had died young. Dirck's outgoing and assured ways attracted everyone he met, and he soon found a strong footing in sales. But it was not long after his first job as a furniture salesman that he became discontent and began drifting from one job to the next.

Even at an early age, Douglas had urged his son to consider the service life, a life he often called his "higher calling." Douglas was a large man with an unmistakable presence. He had risen to the rank of major and served ten years in Vietnam. After the conflict, he had returned to his Vermont homestead in Glenriver, the place he had inherited from his own father.

Dirck spent his early years at the homestead, drawing strength from his father's war stories, the feats of heroism and bravery, the problems back home, and how he had overcome them all with purpose and an endless drive.

Dirck would often look through his father's war trunk, admiring the Distinguished Service Cross, the Silver Star, and the golden oak-leaf major insignias. He endlessly examined the grainy black-and-white photographs of his father's own war heroes, Colonel Dagmar and Brigadier General Muller, asking him about their generation and dedication to country.

Dirck had longed for the same greater purpose and distinction in his own life, a direction he lacked as a husband selling furniture in New York.

One night after returning home from work, Dirck had turned on the television. A large "BREAKING STORY" banner flashed over the newscaster.

"We have learned the Bush Administration has asked Congress for a declaration of war in Iraq to remove a regime that developed and used weapons of mass destruction, harbored and supported terrorists, and committed outrageous human rights abuses, defying the just demands of the United Nations and the world."

There were pictures of Saddam Hussein above video of people rioting in Baghdad. Men were being shot, women and children were wailing, families were running from houses, the streets in chaos. Dirck called his father.

"Dad—wow, are you watching the news? They are declaring war over there. Payback for 9-11, finally. Right, Dad? An opportunity for me. What do you think? Army Infantry Officer School? What about the Marines? Know anyone I can call?"

Douglas's deep, calm voice fired up his son even more. Dirck's heart was racing with possibilities. He was ready.

Douglas Hansen was an impressive man and soldier who stood over 6-foot-3 on a chiseled frame. His officers would often joke that Douglas was not unlike the actor Kirk Douglas, the Viking, the Spartacus.

"Yes, Dirck, I was going to call you when I saw this shit going on," Douglas said. "And, yes, you should call my friend Dick Eccles, retired Army Colonel. Works for a recruiting outfit here in Vermont now. He'll get you into the right hands. I'm proud of you, boy. You'll make a good soldier."

But Douglas had known the Iraq war would be much like the war he had fought in Vietnam: unpopular and deadly, fought in an unpredictable land, home to unpredictable people, and he feared for his son, a fear he never expressed.

They talked about being a patriot, the rewards of a service life, the great men he would come to know, all the things his father held close. After he hung up, Dirck was buzzing with new possibilities, a commitment to a new life.

But his enthusiasm had been met with blank stares from his wife, who feared what the war might bring: losing her husband, becoming a widow, being alone. Still with no children.

Later that week, Dirck worked out the details of his enlistment in the Army Officer Training Headquarters with retired Colonel Eccles. And within two months of his induction into the United States Army, Dirck Hansen stood at the Grand Central Station platform, kissing his sobbing wife goodbye.

His infantry training had lasted six months, after which he was deployed to Iraq as a first lieutenant.

During his first deployment, he fought on the front lines in violent battles.

He came home to Cindy a different man: depressed, erratic, with violent nightmares. Worse, he had become unpredictably angry from daily drinking.

Cindy had maintained an unsuccessful cheerfulness in front of Dirck, a stagy display of failed smiles, half-laughing, half-crying in the face of his unpredictable outbursts. She hesitated getting close to him, and increasingly, they grew apart in the small apartment.

A month after returning home and a week before being shipped off for his second deployment, Dirck staggered home from another night of rambunctious drinking and was met with a dark, empty apartment and a note left on the kitchen table.

Dirck, I moved away to my cousin Terry's place in California. I had to leave, to find some peace within my own life. It was just breaking me up to see you with such anger and depression and I didn't know how to reach you. I couldn't face you or us anymore. Dirck, you know that I loved you from the first day we met in college and wanted so much to give you a family, the family you never had, but I didn't know how to build memories with you when you wouldn't let me close to you. I hope the army will give you what you need but I can't be a part of it anymore. It hurts me to leave but I must. I hope you find a sense of yourself in the service. Cindy

They had been married only three years. Dirck's dreams of building a life and family with his sweetheart had been eclipsed by his drive to serve in a war that would forever change him.

Despite his father's standing and impressive abilities, Dirck's drill sergeants were tough on him, perhaps because of his father, and as time went on, training became nearly impossible for him.

But his father was always with him, his calm, deep voice pushing him harder into seemingly impossible training. And in the end, he had become more of a soldier than his commanders could have imagined.

By the time he reached the rank of first lieutenant, Dirck's attitude and ability had impressed them all, even through the worse battles any man could endure. His courage and lack of fear were traits of his father, characteristics noticed by his commanders, and he rose quickly to the rank of Captain.

With time and in war, Dirck developed an intimidating attitude and look. His rectangular face was defined with a well-chiseled chin, a sturdy jaw line. His face held forward in a steady gaze and had an air of authority that was palpable. It was a manly face, a true face. He appeared ageless, neither young nor old, though in the face was written the memory of things both glad and sorrowful. His hawk-like blue eyes pierced through anyone near him and when he walked into a room, he swept in like a rushing wind, filling everyone with him.

In war, the soldier became a one-man fighting force—over prepared, acting without regard to his own life, confident when all around him were indecisive. He was unpredictable, much like the war he fought. Even when reason dictated caution, he might inexplicably charge into a firefight, acting only on instinct, protecting his men, always. He stayed at the edge of the front for most of the war.

And if you wanted to pinpoint the moment when Dirck Hansen's life changed forever, it was certainly on that bleak winter night in Ramadi outside Fallujah deep within enemy territory.

Captain Hansen and his squad of eighteen American and ten Iraqi soldiers were sleeping, hidden inside two concrete buildings at the edge of town. In the silence of the night, sixty militants had snuck undetected into adjacent buildings and surrounding rooftops. Moments before the attack, a young private in Hansen's group, Billy Dawson, thought he had heard footsteps and jumped out a second-story window, landing on a tin roof below.

Guns exploded everywhere. Dawson was wounded, and in the chaos, Dirck commanded Sergeant Floy to bring him back, thinking Dawson was shielded. But when the man inched out of the building, he was immediately killed. Mike Floy had been one of Hansen's most trusted men, a good man he had trained himself, a friend with two daughters and a young wife from Omaha, Nebraska. He had been only thirty-one. Now he lay lifeless in a pile of rubble.

Throughout the night and into the next day, Captain Hansen saved five of his men with valor, but twenty-three souls perished under his command and Hansen himself lay close to death with the few souls that remained in that small Ramadi village.

Over the following weeks at Walter Reed Hospital, Dirck floated in a hellish purgatory between his dead and living soldiers. He was eventually discharged with honors and decorated with a Purple Heart for bravery, but the battle and the loss of his men became one of the many nightmares that followed him home

After this third and last deployment, Dirck returned to his home in Glenriver, Vermont, but Douglas Hansen wasn't there for his son. Two months before he returned from Iraq, his father had lost his mind in the fog of dementia and had been sent to the local veteran's home, a place Dirck visited twice before his father's death.

On both visits, he had stood next to Douglas, the man he had idolized, the strong, determined man who had inspired him, hoping for some sign, the smallest signal of approval.

Douglas, the great Viking, sat fixed in his wheelchair, staring blankly out the window.

It was Douglas's death that year coupled with the loss of his wife Cindy and the onslaught of savage war nightmares that threw Dirck Hansen into the unknowns of his mind.

Despite his father's promise of rich service rewards, he felt betrayed by what Douglas had held close: duty to country, the honor of the men who served him, the brotherhood they represented. The army had been Dirck's family, his only family.

Now they were gone or lost inside their own fractured minds and he was alone.

He spent the next year in an inexplicable alcoholic haze, unable to leave his house, his prison. His life slid into reliving intense war battles, fought daily within the confines of his mind, wherever he was, continuing to no end, blunted only by increasing amounts of alcohol and narcotics.

Dirck's anger, panic attacks, intense social anxiety drove him inward. At night, he prayed for some peace within himself but his prayers were vague and undirected. He didn't believe in a higher power and he tried to navigate his way through life without support.

Where would he find comfort in the face of such vulnerability? Where would he turn? In the house filled with his father's presence, he felt particularly isolated.

One bleak night, he sat at the desk in his father's old bedroom and wrote him a letter.

Dear Dad,

Sitting in your bedroom tonight thinking about you, wondering why I can only write this letter now that you're gone. I don't have any answers these days. I was looking at the old pictures of you and Colonel Dagmar and General Muller today, thinking about those great stories you used to tell me. I remember you telling me 'son, you've got all those men you're leading into a battle…make sure you bring all of them back home.' But I couldn't, Dad. Nearly all of them died. The war tore me up and now, I can't shake these nightmares. They are in my head wherever I go, especially here at the homestead. Cindy left me after my second deployment and my men are now gone too. I couldn't protect them.

I wish you were here. I am so alone. I'm trying to stay strong in the middle of this shit, but it's overwhelming. I need your encouragement, to hear your voice, to guide me, tell me what to do. I don't feel like I can make it through another day. Sometimes, I just want to join you in peace, Dad.

Dirck

He couldn't think of more. On the envelope, he wrote "Major Douglas G. Hansen, Vermont Veteran's Affairs, Brattlefield, Vermont," the place where Douglas Hansen had taken his last breath. Writing it made Dirck feel mildly better and, as he stared down at the handwritten page, he felt a presence in the room.

He turned and could see his father, Douglas, dressed in his crisp gray-green uniform with its gold oak-leaf insignias, walking around his bedroom in circles, looking up at the interior walls as if they were slowly closing in on him, making him smaller, less relevant, invisible, much like Dirck now felt as he slowly folded the letter and sealed it.

In the middle of that night, he again woke, screaming into the darkness, another battle raging within his riotous mind, this nightmare filled with the unimaginable horror of his own slow death.

He had to end it. He stumbled through his bedroom, ripping open the door to his closet for his weapon. He reached up, pulled the pistol free and dropped to his knees, pointing the gun to his temple. He squeezed the trigger. An empty click. Another click.

"Goddamn it…fire! *Fire*!" he screamed into the wretched darkness.

But he had taken the pistol clips to his safe the week before, a week when he had been lucid, remembering the instructions from his counselor. He collapsed onto the floor, crying, desperate to finish his miserable life.

That week, two psychologists from the Vermont Veterans Affairs visited him to find several empty alcohol bottles, pill containers, and loaded weapons. They labeled Captain Hansen a high suicide risk and immediately assigned him a counselor, Robert Telly, for weekly visits. Telly was an Iraq war veteran who had become a psychologist to make sense of his own war-torn mind.

A day later, Telly showed up at the homestead with a dog. Dirck opened his door, surprised by the alert German Shepherd sitting dutifully at Tully's side. The dog wore a red vest emblazoned with **SERVICE ANIMAL**. It looked up to him as if to ask his permission to enter.

In Iraq, Dirck had admired service dogs that had been used to detect roadside explosives. Some of the dogs had given their lives to protect their handlers. He thought that sacrifice profound.

But he wasn't prepared for his reaction to the dog before him. The young Shepherd continued staring at him, her bright, unblinking brown eyes beaming a warmth he hadn't expected.

Tully signaled the okay to Dirck, and he knelt before the dog and reached out to her. She relaxed and panted, her tail swiping across the welcome mat. As Dirck held her, a powerful calm swept through him.

"This is Tippy," Tully said. "She's my five-year-old German Shepherd. Been with me for two years now. She's my companion, brings me comfort."

"Comfort" was the word vets used to describe a dog that stopped a soldier's PTSD attack.

Dirck felt the Shepherd accepted him, but he sensed something else in the dog—a protector bringing unwavering trust. He loved Tippy.

Tully walked inside, the dog trotting by his side.

"I brought Tippy because I wanted to show you how a service dog might help you. She has protected me through some pretty tough nights, even during my thoughts of suicide. She keeps me focused and in the moment. She is always there for me. Tippy has allowed me to live a pretty normal life," he said.

Tippy looked up at Telly to signal her agreement.

Lieutenant Telly had been in an Iraqi prison for over a year before the conflict ended. He had been tortured and beaten, lost hope of living, and upon being freed and brought home, had been placed in a psychiatric ward. Then Tippy entered his life.

"Let me show you some of her skills," Telly said.

He instructed Dirck to sit opposite him. First, he took his cap and threw it on the floor.

"Tippy...bring."

The dog jumped forward and grabbed the cap and walked to Robert, dropping it in his lap. *Okay, simple enough,* Dirck thought. This was followed by Tippy opening a door, reaching up to turn out a light, and helping Tully off the couch. Then Tippy showed off her main event.

Robert Telly walked to the next room, still visible to his dog. He fell to the floor and began shaking and screaming. Dirck knew those panic screams well. Tippy ran to him and pushed him onto his back with her muzzle. The dog crawled onto his chest and began nudging his head about, letting out soft barks.

Telly opened his eyes and reached for her to signal he was okay. The dog sat back and panted lightly.

Dirck was stunned. He couldn't believe what this dog had just done. He knew he had found his answer, a way through his nightmares, through his despair and isolation.

Tully told him about Canines Assisting Soldiers (CAS), an organization in upstate New York that had trained Tippy. As they talked, Tippy sat next to Robert, looking up at him now and then, waiting for another command. The dog looked happy in her work. Just her presence kept Telly centered.

And for the first time he could remember, Dirck's own mood lifted. He was smiling, engaged, even laughing at Tippy. Telly could see it. He knew a service dog was right for Hansen.

After they left, Dirck was surprised by how much he missed the dog. They had been in his house for three hours, but it seemed like only minutes.

That night, he lay in bed picturing the beautiful Shepherd lying next to him. He talked softly to her, telling her about his day, his fears, his hopes. He closed his eyes and slept in peace that night.

Every Tuesday, Robert Telly returned with Tippy, their visits the highlight of Dirck's week. Increasingly, he found himself filled with anticipation to see the beautiful dog again.

After four weeks, Dirck received the letter that would change his life.

Dear Captain Dirck Hansen (ret.),

Canines Assisting Soldiers (CAS) is most pleased that you have been chosen to receive one of our dogs for your service. Attached find the CAS brochure explaining our program. Please call the number on the brochure as soon as you have read through the information. We look forward to you working with our dogs.

Drury (Dru) Vaughan, Director

The letter was inside a brochure showing the beautiful service dogs with their veterans. At the edge, a punch hole contained a chain and dog tag engraved with "Canines Assisting Soldiers," underneath which was embossed "HANSEN, DIRCK 2298033." On the opposite side was a dog's head etched in relief.

He held tightly onto the tag as he re-read the brochure.

Stress drained from him.

3

Even as a child, Drury Vaughan had loved dogs, growing up with three hunting Labrador Retrievers, a rescue Foxhound, and a small mutt called Milly.

As a teenager, her love of dogs had grown deeper and by seventeen, Dru became a certified dog trainer and handler. When she had turned twenty in the late 1960s, she enrolled in the Marine Corps and was shipped to Vietnam, where she worked as a K-9 military trainer with the dogs that would be used for mascots, detection and tracking, and as sentries to defend marine outposts.

At her own Saigon sentry, Dru first met Bodhi, a three-year-old male Belgian Malinois that guarded the outpost. The black-and-tan dog appeared modest at fifty-five pounds, but his intensity, strength, and speed were deceptive, notoriously fierce. Bodhi's sensitivity to noise and movement was so uncanny that he would leap awake from a deep sleep even if someone had dropped a hairbrush in a far-off tent.

In the first month Bodhi had been on duty, Dru noticed that the soldiers returning from the front would relax when the dog was around. Dru had never seen the men calm and even brighten by simply touching a dog. If they were quiet or moving repetitively,

Bodhi sensed their stress and gently approached them, leaning into them, making them pay attention to him.

Soldiers soon began asking for Bodhi when they started having nightmares or feeling uneasy. Bodhi became known as "the great equalizer" by the men.

On her release from the Marines in 1968, Dru was distraught that many of her fellow veterans had returned home to face a greater threat than the war they left behind—suicide.

After her experience with Bodhi, she decided to raise and train dogs to help soldiers deal with post-war stress. She first bought and trained a young female German Shepherd, "Poola," to assist her veteran friend Abe, who had lost his leg in the Vietnam War and had become a high suicide risk.

She taught Poola in the "anxiety alert," guiding the dog to notice Abe's erratic movements and detect the sharp odor of adrenaline from him during an attack. But in the first week of training, Dru noticed that Poola had begun to recognize Abe's panic even before he knew it was about to hit him. Because of Poola, Abe survived and even thrived, and Dru knew this would become her life's work.

She bought and trained Golden Retrievers, German Shepherds, Labrador Retrievers, Poodles. With her first six dogs, Dru moved to Upstate New York and rented a large kennel, the first headquarters of "Canines Assisting Soldiers (CAS)."

Dru Vaughan stood a lean 5-foot-10 in bare feet. Whether she was wearing combat fatigues or street clothes, her presence and attitude could not be dismissed.

Dru's appearance was best understood through her character: pragmatic, stoic, less preoccupied by gender and instead determined, like her male colleagues, to assert that she was "just doing her job."

Through her discipline and dedication, within ten years, CAS had become one of the most respected service dog organizations in the United States and Dru commanded the highest respect by her dogs and staff. Now, she had turned sixty and her hair had faded to a soft gray, but she was as strong and dedicated to her dogs and fellow veterans as the day she had founded CAS thirty years earlier.

Dru and her trainers maintained twenty dogs in training. When the older dogs had to be removed from service and placed as pets, she purchased promising puppies as young as eight weeks to start the rigorous CAS training.

At one Golden Retriever breeder, Dru noticed one female from a litter of ten that was clearly different from her littermates physically and mentally. The puppy's attitude was directed, mature, her gait and movements strong, her speed and coordination nearly perfect.

Dru purchased the baby Golden on the spot and named her Chauncey, a French baby name meaning "fortune" and "brilliant." From her first month in training, more so than any of the other young service dogs before her, Chauncey learned faster, worked harder and more happily, and quickly grasped the nuances of her training. The puppy possessed an extraordinarily bright disposition and temperament that captivated the CAS trainers. Apropos to her name, Chauncey was simply brilliant in all things.

During her first months at CAS, Chauncey trained in basic obedience and handling, but she showed such promise in her more difficult training that at four months, she was chosen for the "Pups For Prisoners" program, which gave prison inmates meaningful work and skills by training and caring for a young dog.

Inmates would be selected for a dog through their trustworthiness and clean record and would train a chosen puppy for six months.

Chauncey was paired with Jerry Burson, a thirty-eight-year-old man who had already served twenty years of a life sentence for committing murder on his eighteenth birthday. Jerry was a muscular, two-hundred-pound bald man with arms as thick as a linebacker's covered in angry tattoos growing up to his neck like vines. His shoulders stooped as if he carried a great weight there, and he always walked leaning forward. But his frame suited him, and he leaned into his prison tasks, working harder than many of the younger inmates.

Jerry had learned to survive through daily discipline and trust in the guards. But he'd never see life outside of his cell again and would often grow despondent, especially when alone. Most of his fellow inmates had an end date, but Jerry didn't. He was shut down, paralyzed by the hopelessness of prison life forever.

"Lifers like Jerry just cut off their feelings. You got to wall off to survive here, to live another day. It's a daily, hourly nightmare," one younger guard said to his superior.

"Yeah, but I've seen some of these lifers really get turned around when they get to care for these young pups," the older guard said. "It's a big change, too, for the dog. Before coming here, they live in strict discipline and are juggled between trainers so they don't get too attached to anyone. But spending all their days and nights with one prisoner like Jerry for six months, they form powerful bonds. When the dogs leave, it's pretty tough on them both."

Jerry was introduced to Chauncey one afternoon in the empty prison yard. For a month, he had known this would be the day, but hadn't known what to expect.

From the other end of the yard fifty feet away, a CAS trainer led out the puppy. Jerry was told to crouch low and remain still.

The puppy was unleashed and in seconds, scampered the distance to Jerry, wiggling in every direction, squirming and squealing, ready for anything at the other end. She jumped on the big man, unafraid, licking his face, squealing at him.

Jerry wasn't prepared for this. He lay on his back, holding her small body in his large hands.

"Hey little thing—you're pretty friendly," he said.

The puppy's brash forwardness made Jerry laugh. To Chauncey, he was a new friend, someone to love, and she wanted to give him everything.

"You want to stay in this big ol' prison with me, young pup?"

Jerry examined his new dog in curiosity. She was only a twenty-five-pound puppy, but something in her face and the way she carried herself, looked mature, noble. Jerry loved his dog.

Jerry lay on the cement yard, letting the dog have her taste of him. And Chauncey loved how he tasted, how he looked and sounded.

For the first time he could even remember, just for the moment, he forgot where he was. He felt light and free. To the guards watching from the yard, Jerry looked like a lost, withdrawn boy suddenly being awakened.

Through Chauncey's trainer, Jerry learned dog training basics, reinforcing commands, keeping her on schedule, letting her know when it was work time or play time. Jerry's daily tasks of training, feeding, picking up her poop, bathing and brushing the puppy brought purpose to his otherwise bleak life and he put great effort into training Chauncey.

At night when the isolation and desperation was the worst, he would talk with his puppy as she slept under his cot.

The first week they were together, Jerry woke in the night, yelling, crying, slamming his fist into the cement wall. Chauncey jumped onto Jerry's bunk, licking his face, waking him. He opened his eyes to her lying on his chest, staring intently at him. His breathing and heart rate slowed.

"You got me from that bad dream, pup. You're here to take me away from this place, aren't you?" Jerry said. "How do you know when I worry so? How do you know that, Chauncey? When I get nervous and don't know where to go, you're here to make me look at you."

Chauncey had begun training Jerry. She was his counterweight, balancing their relationship by moving in the opposite direction. When he grew nervous, Chauncey remained calm. When he was quiet and withdrawn, she nudged him to pay attention. She taught him to stay in the moment and kept him focused on her.

She especially reminded him that she was always with him without judgment.

Chauncey sensed Jerry's grief and hurt and discovered, for the first time, there could be pain and sorrow in her innocent young world, a world she would come to know as her work.

As the weeks quickly went by, the puppy grew into an impressive young adult. Chauncey was now almost eight months old and nearly fifty pounds, and the pug-nosed puppy face had become squared and noble. The dog was irresistibly beautiful.

By the fifth month of Jerry's program, a new inmate, a young Latino, was housed in the next cell. To this point, the young man had been incarcerated for only three months, two of which had been spent in solitary for attacking guards and a fellow inmate.

Only months earlier on the streets, he had been the fearless leader of a gang and had killed several young men in a rival group.

The morning after the young prisoner arrived, Jerry walked Chauncey past the man's cell. The man reached through the bars to get at them, screaming threats at Jerry and his dog.

But on the second day, things got worse. Despite guards' warnings, in the middle of the night, the inmate erupted in fury feet away from Jerry and his dog.

"That ugly damned dog. I kill that dog of yours. I break its neck and yours, pussy. You're a pussy to have that ugly dog."

Jerry lay awake on his cot, holding Chauncey to his nervous chest.

And, after a second night of cruel threats, Jerry's formidable anger began to surface, anger he hadn't felt in many years. Jerry was twice the younger man's size and strength and knew he could easily kill the inmate if given the chance. But Chauncey smelled Jerry's fear and kept him close and in the present. Over the screams, Jerry whispered into her ear that he was with her, that he was okay.

When Jerry was released each morning for training, he would lead his dog to the right, away from the neighbor's cell, down to the yard. But after two nights of intimidating screams from the inmate, on the following morning, Jerry turned his dog to the left, stopping outside the man's cell.

Two guards stood nearby, ready for certain trouble. Inmates on Block 33 hung anxiously on their cell doors, waiting.

The Latino lay curled on his cell floor and woke when Jerry approached. Chauncey was on her leash, sitting next to Jerry who this morning had worn his clean white prison jumpsuit, the one he had ironed the night before. The young man was surprised to see the large, quiet man and his dog standing before him.

"I know you want to scream and try to overpower it all," Jerry said. "You'll learn to overcome your fear. In time. The anger will pass. My words aren't strong enough to make it go away, to make you see the hope that's still within you."

The man remained balled up as he stared at them. Jerry could see the deep fear and anger that twisted through the man's soul like a thousand black snakes.

So many years before, Jerry saw himself in this man. It was the same anger and despair he had pushed so hard against. Over time, years, the grip of anger, the crushing despair, had loosened.

And now, with Chauncey by his side, Jerry knew nothing, literally nothing, could turn him back to that crippling rage and overwhelming pain. In that moment, Jerry felt great sympathy for the weeping man on the other side of his prison cell.

"If you need someone to talk to, my friend here, Chauncey, will help. And so will I. You can come through that long dark tunnel you're in, friend. Keep trying, just keep trying, every day," Jerry said.

He turned and led his dog away. The only sound in Block 33 that morning was loud sobbing from the man's cell. The guards and inmates were stunned by what they had witnessed.

That day and through the next two nights, Block 33 was quiet, quieter than the guards could remember for a long time. A couple of times, the young Latino ripped into Jerry and his dog, but after each night of threats, Jerry and Chauncey would stop by the man's cell, always with a quiet message of hope.

The following month, the Latino prisoner was moved to another cellblock. And after four years of despair in facing his own life sentence, he too, would receive a puppy in training, one that would transform him like Jerry. And he would never forget the big, kind man and his beautiful dog in Block 33.

The other inmates couldn't believe that a puppy could produce such a profound transformation in a man, especially a man like Jerry. Even Jerry found it difficult to grasp the change within him and sometimes at night, his gratitude would overwhelm him and he would bring his dog up to his bunk, just to lie next to her and feel her slow, easy breath pulse against him.

They were together six months, a short time for a man, but in a dog's life, it was years. As planned, it came time for Chauncey to return for the next phase of her training at CAS.

As the day approached, every night before bed, she would jump on Jerry's bunk and lay next to him. Or she'd sit on his lap in the TV room, frequently looking up at him for reassurance. She knew a change was ahead.

On the final day, Chauncey didn't leave Jerry's side until the guards and a CAS trainer came to his cell. He sat on his cot, holding the dog in his arms, trying to remain strong.

"Young girl, you've got a lot of life ahead of you," he whispered to her, his voice trembling. "You don't know what you've done for me. Your friendship, your love. Everything you've given me. You made me feel the world isn't such a bad place after all. You taught me that. I'll be so lonely without you, girl. I wish I could keep you forever. But I want you to go now, go and help someone like me, someone who has a hard time living."

Even after twenty years inside, Jerry was not a broken man and he had Chauncey to thank for that.

The trainer fixed Chauncey's leash to her collar. Through a blur of tears, Jerry watched his dog being led down the corridor of Block 33. She turned back to look at Jerry, but his expression told her she wouldn't be coming back.

Chauncey had learned about service and experienced her first love but didn't understand why she was being taken away from the man she loved.

When she returned to CAS, Dru could see that the dog was withdrawn and had lost her focus. She knew she'd have to regain the dog's confidence and trust.

Her second day back, Chauncey was brought to a training room and left alone. Dru entered. She knelt in front of the dog and held out her hand.

"Shake." Chauncey's paw rose up but didn't touch Dru's hand. She stared at the wall beyond her.

"Chauncey, look, here," she said, but the dog continued to stare elsewhere.

Dru backed away and knelt, holding out her arms.

"Chauncey, *come*." The dog rose and walked to Dru, but her eyes were diverted.

She led Chauncey back to her crate. The dog's loss would be more difficult to overcome than she had thought and she would have to retrain her from scratch.

Two months passed. Dru reinforced the simple commands: come, down, shake, sit, then moved onto the commands for fetching objects, switching a light, opening a door. She relearned how to navigate around stationary objects, avoid hazards, and recognize the "anxiety alert." But despite the rigor of daily training, Chauncey remained detached. She had to try something different.

Spring had arrived, and after formal indoor training, Dru took her outside to the field behind CAS. Chauncey had not been outdoors since her time in the yard with Jerry.

When she was walked out to the big field, the young dog's eyes brightened.

"Chauncey, let's have fun. Go enjoy the nice day, girl." She said and let her loose.

Chauncey raced through the field, diving into the grass, rolling on her back, biting at the dandelions. Dru called her back, holding out her favorite treats, dried liver. Chauncey's diet was strict, but she had discovered the dog's love of liver treats.

She called for her.

Chauncey raced the distance and stood before Dru, her tail swinging freely, her head up with a big drooling grin. Dru gave her a treat. Chauncey continued pleading.

"Alright, one more, girl, just one more," she cooed.

Every day after indoor formal training, Dru brought her outdoors. Chauncey began to reveal more of her playfulness but through an additional month of training, she remained unfocused. Her moves were perfect but mechanical, and her eyes wandered during training.

Dru knew Chauncey would make an extraordinary service dog for a deserving veteran, but the dog remained withdrawn.

Pairing her would be burdened with uncertainty.

4

Weeks before the long-anticipated day, Dirck dreamed of dogs. German Shepherds running toward him, a black Labrador Retriever waking him from a nightmare, Golden Retrievers wandering through his house.

He was about to cross paths with many dogs at CAS, one that would become his companion for life. But he couldn't imagine the journey that was about to take him there.

Over the coming week, vets and dogs would be introduced in different rooms. The first morning, Dru brought Dirck into an empty CAS training room and told him to sit off to the side in the lone chair. He was not to talk, move or react, only observe.

Pairing was unemotional and exacting. Trainers remained detached to any dogs they favored so as not to influence the vets. Dru watched for the strongest bond between man and dog. Sometimes it was immediate and certain, but more often, pairing was subtle and difficult to exact.

One by one, trainers led dogs into the room. As they entered, everything but the dog stopped. They were extraordinary, their eyes bright, posture perfect, behavior directed, their movements fluid.

The first in was a young white Labrador Retriever wearing a harnessed vest. There was nothing hurried or uncertain about the dog. As the trainer silently trotted the Lab around the room, everything was calm and purposeful. There were no emotions, no wasted movements. The simplicity was alluring. Dirck couldn't take his eyes off the magnificent animal.

Then, the young Lab was quickly led out and another entered. And another. In all, five dogs were introduced to Dirck the first day.

In one introduction, a handler walked in a small male black Labrador Retriever. The trainer put his hand up and said "jump on." The dog jumped onto a platform in the center of the room. The trim black dog froze at attention, his ears forward, his eyes directed at the trainer's arm. Dirck loved this dog. His movements were sleek and elegant.

As quickly as his fascination had fixed upon the Lab, it shifted to German Shepherds, more Labradors, and Golden Retrievers.

Chauncey was one of two Goldens. The other was a statuesque dark blonde male, Toby, larger than Chauncey with a handsome blocky head. Two other vets, Mac and Michael, were brought into the training room with Dirck.

They watched the dogs with nervous anticipation. It was as if their brides were being led down the aisle toward them. At times, Dirck just wanted to get on his knees to the dog and whisper, *let's get out of here, just you and me.*

The first night at their hotel, the vets shared their post-war struggles. Mac Kerr had lost his right arm in Iraq, and while he had trouble negotiating his daily chores, his depression and fear of facing life without his limb had immobilized him. Michael Duncan was a green beret who had led Special Forces and lost his unit in Iraq like Dirck, and, for years, struggled with the same crippling guilt.

Dirck understood these struggles, and they all, in their own way, had discovered how dogs could bring them hope and the promise to transform their hearts and minds. Dirck talked about Tippy and his profound experience with the German Shepherd. Each story was different but ultimately the same—a rescue.

The second day, anticipation mounted. New dogs were brought in, this time with the veterans seated in the center of the room where they could closely observe the dogs move through their routines.

When one male German Shepherd looked over at Mac, the vet began shaking. The dog sensed the man's emotion and was led out. And Michael was so fascinated by one white Labrador that he reached out to touch its back. It was led away without a word.

By the end of the second day, over eight new dogs had been introduced. Like Mac and Michael, Dirck was frustrated and apprehensive by not yet being matched. But pairing was just beginning.

On the third morning, Dru called Dirck back to CAS. His heart was in his throat—maybe this was the day! He was asked to watch other veterans who now had been matched.

Jeff, a vet he hadn't yet met, was paired with a black Labrador Retriever named Riff. In Afghanistan, Jeff had lost his right leg and needed a dog to stabilize him on his newly attached artificial limb.

In the center of the room, Jeff sat in a lone chair while Riff trotted with his handler. The trainer commanded *sit* and the dog sat facing Jeff. The handler dropped the dog's lead and left the room. Jeff sat like a statue, looking at the beautiful black dog before him. He commanded *up*. Riff stood at attention. *Come.* Riff walked to Jeff's side. Jeff reached over for Riff's back to brace himself and rose unsteadily onto his new leg. Riff leaned into Jeff as he attempted to walk forward. Twice he nearly lost his balance, but the strong dog pushed into his side and stabilized him. On *bring*, Riff ran to a corner of the room and retrieved Jeff's belt purposely left on the floor. After each command, Riff returned to Jeff's side, turning his head to meet his new owner.

Jeff looked down at his new dog with tears in his eyes, knowing he would soon take his new dog home. There was silence for a minute before Jeff calmed. Riff's attention remained on Jeff with a steady, unblinking stare, letting him know he was there with no judgement. The bond between Jeff and Riff was unmistakable.

Dirck was transfixed by the pair. That afternoon, Jeff and Riff left the room and Dirck never saw them again.

Even years later, it would be impossible for Dirck to describe the simplicity and beauty of the bond between man and dog he had witnessed that day. He wanted that love, that forever bond. But he also wanted a leader, an energetic and confident dog.

Most of all, he wanted a dog who would accept him and be there for him. For years, he had not touched another living being and wouldn't let anyone near him. But as he watched Riff and Jeff that afternoon, he wanted to throw his arms around the dog, to hold it against his chest and experience the strength that radiated from the beautiful Labrador Retriever.

There were more pairings. Sharon Garcia, a veteran with PTSD, was paired with Tilly, a petite white Labrador Retriever. Mac Kerr was paired with Toby, the two-year-old Golden Retriever that Dirck had seen the first day.

Dru purposely left Dirck's pairing for last. His condition was complex and required a precise match. The subtle interactions were tricky and uncertain, and there was too much at stake.

The next morning, everything came to life. Each dog was brought in and Dirck was asked to hold their leads and move them through simple commands. Each interaction took twenty minutes.

This time, all females were to be brought in—first, Bella, a German Shepherd with a handsome black face, then Molly, a compact white Labrador Retriever and finally, Chauncey, the Golden Retriever Dirck had met the first day. Bella was more reserved than the other two dogs but took her comments of *heel* and *stop* without hesitation.

Then Molly pranced in. She was small for a Labrador but energetic and strong, less controlled than Bella. He moved the small Lab around the room, the dog trotting enthusiastically by his side as she looked up to him for direction. Each time he stopped and commanded *heel*, Molly moved to his left and froze.

He crouched down and looked at the young dog. She stared at Dirck, her front legs shivering in excitement. He could tell the dog wanted to jump on him and began to dance about. He loved Molly's enthusiasm. But a clear bond seemed yet uncertain.

Then Chauncey then pranced in with her trainer. He expected the same enthusiasm as Molly but while she took her commands with ease, something didn't seem right—the dog just didn't exude the same spirit he had loved in Molly.

He knelt in front of the dog and looked at her. Her gaze was fixed over his right shoulder, somewhere on the far wall. He got to his feet and commanded *heel*. Chauncey complied, moving smartly to his left. She glided effortlessly about the room, her feathered tail floating behind her, but her movements seemed automatic, almost robotic.

Chauncey was the most magnificent dog he had ever seen but her detachment confused him. What was the dog thinking? Was this not a connection for her?

After a half-hour break, the trainers brought in the same dogs with the same results and Dirck left that day more uncertain than ever. Molly might be a possible choice for him, but none of them clearly clicked with him. Dru knew they had more work to do.

On the fifth day, Dirck returned with new veterans. One large man, Les, had been recently fitted with two artificial legs. He had been paired with Bella, the female German Shepherd Dirck had admired. It was their first demonstration together.

As Les walked the room, he rocked unsteadily on his prosthetic legs and Bella leaned into him, balancing him at each turn. When he stopped, the Shepherd pushed into his side so he could sit. Each time Les moved, the dog's gaze was fixed at his. Les and Bella were clearly bonded.

By now, Dirck and the two other unpaired vets had lost their initial giddy anticipation and pairing had become hard work. But it was how Dru and the CAS trainers had planned it. They had to be certain that pairing was not impulsive or emotional. The decision was not entirely theirs except in those unusual situations in which a dog clearly bonded with the vet, like Bella with Les.

But that hadn't happened for Dirck. He began to think he wouldn't find a match and would return home alone.

After more formal pairing meetings, Dru took Dirck to the back of CAS's facility to observe the dogs in the open. He hoped Molly would be brought out but the trainer led out Chauncey and handed him her lead. Chauncey sat at his side, not moving, staring to the field. She walked through her paces perfectly but Dirck felt as if he were walking alone.

Then he tried two new commands, *shake* and *kiss*. He knelt in front of her. On *shake*, she brought her paw up to his right hand. Her head was directed at him but her eyes were still fixed off his left shoulder to the field behind him. Dirck looked behind him to see what might be distracting her but they were alone. He didn't understand the dog's detachment.

He moved to the *kiss* command in which Chauncey would be forced to focus on Dirck's face and "kiss" him. He commanded *up* and she stood. Still on his knees, he leaned into her and looked into her eyes. *Kiss!*

Without moving her head, Chauncey's eyes shifted slightly and met Dirck's. For what seemed like a long minute, they silently stared at one another. Now, he could see the sincerity in the young dog's face, in her bright eyes.

She beamed a warmth, the depth of which he couldn't yet appreciate. He sensed she wanted a connection, a forever partner. But he knew this dog was too smart to take just anyone. She sought a companion like she had once had in Jerry. The loss had deeply wounded her. Dirck understood that loss. He would have to build trust back into this sensitive, intelligent dog to earn her love. And he knew the bond would be deep and meaningful.

They continued staring at one another. He leaned in and smiled at her.

"Hey pretty girl, I love you!" he said. *Kiss!*

Chauncey continued staring at him, not moving. She sensed a sincerity in this man's voice and, in what seemed to Dirck like a leap of faith, dove into him with a big sloppy kiss.

It sent chills up Dirck's spine.

Chauncey pulled back and looked at him. Her muzzle curled to her ears. She was smiling!

He burst out laughing, not from amusement, but from happiness. Dru watched them—she knew the dog was checking him out and liked what she had seen.

The last ten minutes of training were walking on air. As Chauncey pranced alongside Dirck, her eyes remained at his. He said *heel* but meant *side*, opposite commands, but nobody cared. The trainers and Dru laughed when Dirck, now giddy, kept bumping into Chauncey as she danced about him, letting out sharp barks.

They fell onto the lawn together, an indistinguishable tangle of man and dog in a world of their own making. This was his dog!

As Chauncey was led back to the facility, Dru approached him.

"Oh, Dru, I choose Chauncey. She's perfect for me!"

'Not yet, Dirck. You have two more dogs to meet this afternoon. It's important we get this right."

There was now too much—an entire life of dog and man—at stake. Dru was a master at matching broken veterans to the right dog. This was no exception.

Dirck went along with Dru's wishes and on this final day, he met two new dogs. Roscoe, the lovable black Portuguese Water Dog, kept bumping into him on their walk around the training room and was not paying attention to him.

Then, Kobe, a big handsome German Shepherd who reminded him of Tippy, kept looking over at Dru and the handlers, focusing on everything but Dirck.

There was clearly no connection with the other dogs.

A week earlier, Dirck wouldn't have known this. After several days watching the dogs, he could see the nuances in them, in their fine movements, expressions, especially, in their eyes.

He understood now how each dog was precisely matched to each vet. It convinced him even more that Chauncey was the right dog.

When the sessions were over, it was playtime in the training field. There were toys and grooming brushes and treats on a table. Most of the dogs were tired and plopped down in the yard here and there.

Chauncey was led out, prancing brightly from around the building, looking anxiously about. Her head snapped around in excitement when she spotted Dirck. She went to the grooming table and picked up a brush and ran to him. She dropped the brush before him and looked up with a tilt of her head and barked. He brushed her smooth coat as she lay on the lawn, her eyes closed. The match was sealed.

All that afternoon, Chauncey followed Dirck around the field, her eyes fixed to his, a smile on her face. This was what Dru and the trainers had been hoping for. But the young Golden Retriever had already made her choice.

Dirck handed her leash back to the handler. He almost couldn't leave her side. As she was led away, she turned and looked back at Dirck. This time, she knew she'd see her man again soon, very soon.

"Chauncey is the perfect dog for you! You knew she was your dog, didn't you?" Dru's lips trembled. "I am so happy this wonderful girl is yours. She's my favorite, one of our most special dogs, you know. I will miss her so very much."

Dirck knew he was about to receive an exceptional service animal. She was his perfect match. They needed one another.

"I do love her, Dru. She's so right for me in many ways, ways I can't even explain right now. It's how she makes me feel when she looks at me. I can tell she wants that same connection. I'm am so happy to be giving her that."

Losing Chauncey would be difficult for Dru but she knew the dog was being led into a life of service, a life she was now prepared for. She hugged Dirck. It was the first time in many years he had touched another human being. He felt as if he were coming back to life.

At that moment, he wanted to get his dog but would have to wait until morning.

That night, Chauncey slept in her crate, drained from the long day but her heart was light. She knew that she would be embarking on her new life, a life of service with someone she could love again.

Early the next morning, Dirck nervously stood in the large CAS lobby. He wore his dark-green U.S. Army captain's uniform pinned with his Iraqi war medals. One was the Purple Heart, the decoration he had earned in the Fallujah battle that had nearly ended his life, the battle that took many of his brave men. The medal was a reminder of the price they all had paid.

That price was now going to be shared with his new service dog, Chauncey.

Dru walked out, Chauncey trotting smartly by her side. Dirck knelt to his dog. She jumped on his shoulders and kissed him and let out a deep, soft moan, an unusual sound for a dog to make. He would come to know that sound—it was the sound of trust, of reassurance, of love. She jumped down and let out a bright bark. Everyone laughed.

Dave Ballard, one of Chauncey's main trainers, took a photograph of Dirck standing proudly by Chauncey. In the months to come, that photograph would be seen by millions of people throughout the world.

"I don't think I've ever seen my girl so happy. She's ready to go home to her new life. Take her proudly into her work, Dirck. She'll give you companionship without judgment. She'll never care why you're having a nightmare. She'll just want to bring you back to her and make your life whole again," Dru said wiping away tears.

"I hope you'll stay in touch and let me know if I can help you with Chauncey. I want to make sure you're both happy."

She bent down and cradled Chauncey's face and kissed her muzzle. Chauncey looked up at her. The dog knew she was leaving behind Dru and CAS for a new life.

The soldier and his service dog walked out of the training facility together in high step. It had taken a year-and-a-half and thirty thousand dollars to train the Golden Retriever, a small price for the lifetime of service she would give Dirck.

They were alone in the parking lot and he was suddenly struck by the power of having his dog with him. Until this point, he could not have imagined what living with a dog would be like.

But now, Dirck knew he couldn't live without this dog.

5

Dirck's family home sat within the great sprawling farmlands of Glenriver, Vermont within a boundless countryside of deeply wooded wilderness with chains of small lonely lakes and meandering rivers lined by miles of less-traveled country roads and unmapped trails that wound through their length and breadth. It was home to the great grey wolf, the woodland coyote, black bears, eastern moose, and many feathered creatures.

Glenriver wasn't on any tourist destination and was known only to the few long-standing, distant neighbors and the local historical society. Theodore Benson, a local magistrate who had founded Glenriver, built the homestead two hundred years earlier and at the homestead's front, the weathered sign read "JUDGE BENSON'S HOUSE 1807."

The homestead was grand. It stood back from the road nearly hidden amongst large, handsome firs and spruce, through which glimpses could be caught of the sprawling yard and meadows beyond. A driveway lined with brilliant white birches meandered through wide-spreading lawns underneath interlacing boughs of weeping willows.

The ride home was quiet but Dirck's head buzzed with the dreams of a child. Every few minutes, he glanced in his mirror to catch sight of his dog.

Chauncey sat quietly in her crate, curiously watching the trees fly by, her nose pointed to the half-open window, sampling the sweet Vermont summer wind. Every half hour, he stopped to let her stretch, but he honestly just missed being close to her. Amongst an otherwise ordinary landscape, she transformed everything. He couldn't take his eyes off the magnificent dog.

They arrived at dusk. Dirck opened his hatch. Chauncey sat at attention, staring out at her new home. The yard and meadows and trees were lit by a majestic golden light.

Here, the world was much bigger than CAS, bigger than even the prison yard. She could barely see the far edge of the woods. She jumped down and zig-zagged about the house in a frenzy. Always mindful of her place, she stopped and looked back at Dirck for direction. He pointed out to the field and yelled *run*. She raced through the yard, diving into the grass, barking into the air with a huge opened-mouth grin. She was full of life.

That first evening, Chauncey roamed the many levels and angles of her new home. She had only ever lived in single-story buildings at CAS and the prison before that but this old house was big and tall, filled with the promise of new adventures.

Dirck followed her up and down three levels in two hours of nonstop movement. He hadn't moved like this since his military days and Chauncey sensed her new master was tired and she plopped down in his lap on the couch.

It was the first time Dirck felt relaxed and free in months, maybe in over a year, he couldn't remember. Chauncey's heart, too, was light. She had a new friend, someone she could love. She knew this man wouldn't abandon her.

That summer night, they sat on Dirck's porch in the pitch-black landscape. Above them stretched out an endless canopy of tiny stars. Chauncey stared at the brilliant sky with wonder and recognition. She now knew this was home, her home.

It was after midnight when he led her to her crate next to his bed. But when he opened the door, she hesitated and looked back at him. He knew what she wanted. It wasn't something Dru had recommended, but it would be only for this night.

He raised his arm and she leapt onto his bed. In the silence of the dark room, Dirck lay with his arm around his dog, feeling her steady breath and strong young heart. This night, the horror of the battlefield, the unending war, was far away, replaced by something more powerful. That night, there was peace.

Even in her early days at the homestead, Chauncey stayed close to Dirck. She would lie by the hour at his feet, eager and alert, watching his face, dwelling upon it, studying it, memorizing his many expressions. She keenly followed each fleeting expression, every nuance of his features, his movements, his sounds, the different smells.

Or she might sit farther out, studying the man's outlines, contemplating his wider gestures. And when he walked into view, the strength of his gaze would draw her head around, and she would return it, her heart shining through her eyes.

Yes, there was loyalty and love, an intense bond, but their relationship transcended explanation. It wasn't simply a sense of himself and a separate being, the dog.

With her by his side, Dirck felt stronger, more powerful, assured. It made him think of men thousands of years ago, ancient men sitting around an open fire, their wild companions nearby, protecting them with some mystical, shamanistic quality. They were heroic, wise, healing in an otherwise brutal and unforgiving world. There was no alpha dog, no dominance or submission, only unspoken and unwavering companionship.

That's how it was for Dirck with Chauncey. He had lost everything that mattered in life: his wife, his father, the fellowship of the men who protected him, and any peace within his own mind.

But with Chauncey, he had been given more than he could ever have imagined.

In the year that followed, Chauncey grew into an adult and her full beauty was revealed. Her twisted straw-colored hair became a flowing and feathered golden-red coat.

Unlike her cousins retrieving birds in the field, her legs were shorter and her prance more delicate. When she ambled about, her hips swayed from side to side almost purposefully alluring.

But it was Chauncey's face that drew everyone's attention. She had a short snout and small pendant ears, giving her an eternal puppy look. Her eyes were a bright and penetrating amber hue that, had it not been for her sweet, captivating way, might have been unnerving when she stared at you. And when spoken to, her eyebrows would bob back and forth in thoughtful expression.

She had now memorized Dirck's subtle expressions, his voice, even his silence, and at night before allowing herself to sleep, she would lie next to him, listening to the pace and depth of his breathing, watching him shift about, smelling him. And when she was assured he was at peace, she'd lay her head down and sleep.

She always woke before him, watching for his eyes to open and his body to signal it was time for the day. Chauncey calmed his nights and steadied his days.

Dirck's neighbors kept dogs for hunting and companionship. Two hunting dogs were particularly fond of Chauncey: a sleek silver Weimaraner boy named Hoppie and a rambunctious, lumbering Bernese Mountain Dog, Chester. Hoppie, the "grey ghost," would mysteriously appear and disappear in and out of the woods near their home, but more often would show up at the kitchen door, conspicuously barking for his companion. Chester was more predictable and boisterous.

But they both shared keen skills learned from hunting in the forests and fields. Chauncey shared these places with them learning all things dog—tracking by smell and sound, moving smartly across land and water, reading the subtle cues of wind, stars, and scents.

Here, at Judge Benson's homestead, the wide fields and meadows were her playground, her domain, and here, she would learn the signs of the equinox and the solstice.

On bright winter mornings, dogs and Dirck set into the white woods, searching for signs of the previous night's travels of a doe or the young black bear fond of traversing through adjacent fields.

Then, almost inexplicably, the twisted fronds of young fiddlehead ferns and the shoots of daffodils and pussy willows erupted through the soft snows, signaling early spring with its damp, evocative smells. Dogs raced through the young-grass fields dotted with wildflowers, stirring up this and that, finding every small creature hidden the night before, barking brightly into the fresh air.

And as fast as they had come, the verdant fields morphed into the heaviness of summer amidst showers of rain and choruses of peeper frogs from endless rushing brooks.

Fields and streams became their markers and they ranged wide and far into the lush Vermont landscapes.

For Chauncey, summer seemed to linger. But by mid-September, the brilliant white light subtly grew into a burnished soft gold and summer greens became muted in the endless canopy of rich flaming maples swaying lazily in the exhilarating northland air.

As the nights became shorter and colder, Chauncey moved increasingly toward Dirck.

6

Autumn marked the end of their first year together and Dirck felt more like he had before the war: full of possibilities, his spirit free and joyful, leaning increasingly toward love.

He made new friends in the small Glenriver community and started a support group for veterans suffering from their own invisible wounds of war. Each week, he brought Chauncey to his meetings, showing off her talents, much like he had first seen with the German Shepherd Tippy.

His world had opened and he took Chauncey anywhere he went, this Saturday being no exception.

"Hey girl. Want to go into town? Got to get those supplies for the porch."

Chauncey knew the routine. She ran to her bin and grabbed a leash. Dirck donned her service vest and grabbed a bag of tennis balls. They drove into Glenriver Township.

He picked up supplies at the general store. The owner Johnathan was always happy to see them. He leaned over the counter toward her.

"Can Chauncey have a biscuit? Just a small one?" he said, always careful to ask but knowing the answer.

"Sure," said Dirck and he nodded and gave her a hand up. Her paws caught the edge of the counter, and she stretched out, her feathery tail swishing in anticipation to the delight of the patrons.

Today, they would travel several miles farther out to Riverdale for supplies he needed.

"Let's go to Riverdale, girl," he said. She sat at attention.

This was a new place for her.

Riverdale Hardware was a city-block-long warehouse, an emerging business. Chauncey knew it was work-time. Builders and farmers stopped to watch the exquisite dog in her bright red vest obediently walking by her owner's side.

He looked at his watch—2 p.m.—still early this autumn day with enough light. Every afternoon was time for Chauncey, an hour of play and exercise, and he asked the clerk if there was a park for his dog.

"Yes, sir. Go out Depot Street and turn left at Riverdale Road and continue about half a mile further. There's the large recreation park there. Dogs are allowed," the girl said.

Riverdale Recreation Park was a mile wide with manicured lawns, tennis courts, and a recreation center building. There were people on the walkway next to the field, one of them with his dog. It looked fine.

Dirck pulled off her service vest, signaling playtime. She wiggled about as he fixed her pink collar and attached the leash. He grabbed the tennis balls.

They walked toward the field. There was older man and his German Shepherd at the edge. He was cautious about Chauncey interacting with other dogs.

He stopped and surveyed the park again. At the field's far side sat the recreation building and a road that curved behind it to another part of the park, maybe an exit, and the woods beyond. It looked safe.

He walked her to the park's grassy edge, removed her leash, and hurled a tennis ball into the distance. Chauncey raced out in a large circle, bobbing the ball in her mouth. This was her unstructured time, so Dirck didn't give her commands unless he needed her back. She always returned without commands.

The older man's Shepherd was running with Chauncey in the field. The dog reminded him of Tippy. He approached Dirck.

"That's Mikey. He's friendly. An eight-year-old boy. Loves to run with other dogs," the man said.

The two dogs chased each other around the wide expanse. Dirck called in Chauncey and threw another ball well out into the field, out toward the far recreation building. She raced the distance for the ball.

"Just last year, I lost my last girl, Tess, to cancer," he continued. "She was a Golden, just like yours. She was only five. It was the worst day of my life when I had to put her down." His face brightened. "Then, Mikey came along. He was a rescue and he ended up saving me. Dogs have been my whole life it seems."

The expression on the man's face made Dirck pause. He could see how the man's spirit had been uplifted by the love of his dog. He thought about his own pain and loss, and how his dog had rescued him from so much suffering.

"My Chauncey is my savior, too. She has returned my life to me."

He wanted to say more, to tell the man more about his despair and the great happiness that had replaced it, but he had momentarily lost track of time.

He looked out toward the field but didn't see Chauncey. He heard her bark. It came from the other side of the recreation building.

He cupped his hands to his mouth. "Chauncey…*Chauncey*!"

His voice carried across the field. Mikey ran back to them but Chauncey didn't appear. Then another bark. Dirck took off across the field toward the building.

She barked again, this one sharper, followed by a short yelp.

The cry from his dog panicked him. He ran toward the recreation building, which was about three hundred yards out, and he reached it in twenty seconds.

He rounded the building and could almost see her bounding around the side of the building, barking in excitement but she wasn't there.

In the distance, he heard a car or truck accelerating on the adjacent road.

"Chauncey! Come! Come, girl!"

His yells echoed panic about the building and into the woods beyond. He ran back to the field, back to the woods. Back to the building.

He stopped and listened. An annoying gentle breeze wafted past him.

The older man and his dog had run into the field toward the building and other people had been alerted by the man and his lost dog. Several of them ran across the field and into woods. They knew her name now. A chorus of voices calling *Chauncey* filled the field.

It was 6 p.m., three hours since they had arrived. He must have run through the park a dozen times now. Some of the people who had helped Dirck were telling him how sorry they were that they couldn't find her and returned to their cars. The old man and his dog, too, had given up and left.

Another hour passed. Time slowed. Then, as darkness began to envelop the park, Dirck was alone.

From the hills beyond, a huge sadness rolled down upon him.

Dirck stood in the middle of the expansive field, looking at the lonely building where he had last heard his dog bark, trying to piece together some sense of the last long hours but his world had turned surreal, immobilizing him, another anguished battle raging inside him, rushing in like those familiar, horrible fields of war, those places from which he had been delivered by the only thing that mattered, his dog, his protector who had given him unwavering trust, his companion who had brought him back from all he had lost, and now, now here in the middle of the Riverdale Recreation Park, a calamitous fear rose in him, broadcasting from him a pungent odor, and in the back of his mind, he thought maybe, just maybe, his familiar acrid smell would alert her and she'd race back to him, and he knelt onto the grass, hoping to God that it would.

But it didn't. She was gone.

7

Jake Tollinger was a bear of a man, his unsteady large frame barely balanced by his thin legs, one of which didn't work well, an injury from years as an infantryman in Afghanistan and he swayed over the uneven wooden planks of his rented woodland cabin that sat within the rural Vermont woods.

Here, Jake made his home with his eleven-year-old daughter, Joannie. The girl's mother had been an alcoholic and her angry, erratic behavior had frightened the young girl.

When she had turned nine, Jake took off with her to live in the woods. Jake had been friends with the local magistrate, who had granted him custody. But soon after he had left his wife and moved to the isolated cabin, Jake had retreated into his own alcohol-laced quarantine, sealing him from Joannie.

Joannie's only real joy in life had been little Mac, her bouncy five-year-old black-and-white Cocker Spaniel boy. But a month after moving, Mac hadn't returned to the cabin after being let out, sending the girl into frantic hours of searching, only for her to discover the young dog lying in a nearby ditch. Mac was nearly unrecognizable except for the small red collar the girl had made him a week before. The speeding truck had not even slowed down.

The girl couldn't comprehend Mac's loss and for weeks, lay curled on her bed with her door closed. When she finally emerged, she spent all her time making a small, elaborate shrine for the dog in the woods behind the cabin, a place they had spent happy hours together.

Every morning and evening, she would kneel at the sanctuary, talking tearfully to Mac's gravestone, telling him she was sorry she couldn't protect him, that she missed him every night and needed him back. Young Mac had belonged, in every sense of the word, heart and soul to Joannie, who had nurtured him since puppyhood through her own turmoil and isolation.

Jake had believed his daughter would eventually recover, but two months after little Mac's death, she began to sink further into a frightening isolation, not eating or talking to her father, crying easily, skipping school to visit Mac's shrine.

The father didn't know how to console his daughter. He tried skipping his nightly drinks to read from her favorite book, to talk about her dog's short but happy life, but nothing separated the girl from her grief.

He knew she needed another dog, a good dog and believed this would be the only thing that would restore her happiness. He could find a shelter rescue, but he didn't have the money. That, and shelters required background checks, and Jake kept a low profile, nearly an invisible one. His drunken outbursts and petty theft had pulled him down further into his self-imposed isolation.

One night, Jake sat on his porch staring into the dark woods, drinking one beer after another, wondering how he would do it.

By morning, his decision had been made. It shouldn't be difficult. He had seen stray dogs running around towns he visited. But he wouldn't take just any dog. His daughter deserved a good dog, a dog worthy of her love and attention.

That morning, after Joannie got off to school, he loaded a new rope, a blanket, and Mac's old treats into his truck, and drove off into the unknown.

He had no plan. He had never taken a dog. He wasn't even sure he could steal one. But still, he drove his old green truck out to Farnsworth, then farther out, to Orford. Then another town up the road. No stray dogs about.

In Woodfield, there was a small dog picking around garbage cans at the local diner, but it was street smart and quickly disappeared behind a building when he stopped.

Jake drove out to Riverdale, a more upscale community. But as he drove through town, he grew increasingly aware that he looked out of place in his old dented pickup truck.

He had wanted to fit in, and this morning, had worn his better trousers and a new white short-sleeved shirt. He had even taken a bath and trimmed his beard but thought it absurd he had gone to all this fuss just to take a dog and, as he drove through the streets, he began to reconsider.

Perhaps he shouldn't go through with this. But he pictured his daughter just the night before, rocking anxiously on the floor of her bedroom, Mac's leash in her hand. He would do anything to bring her back, anything to see her smile and hear her laugh again.

He turned onto the next street. Nothing. Then he remembered the Riverdale Recreation Park at the edge of town. They allowed dogs.

Jake pulled onto Riverdale Road and followed it to the edge of the park. One side road curved off to his right toward the Recreation Center. Perhaps dogs would be in the park, but taking one there would be too risky. This was probably the wrong place and he should leave.

He accelerated along the exit road toward the recreation building to find an exit. His window was down. He heard something off to his left. A bark.

He slowed the truck.

A dog appeared from around the building. It was a larger dog, a beautiful golden dog. *Joannie would love this dog*, he thought. He pulled off to the side, cut the engine and climbed out, leaving his door open. He grabbed the rope and reached into his trousers for the treats. His heart pounded in his large chest as he approached.

The dog had its head down, sniffing the building's edge, a tennis ball in her mouth. He crept toward it.

Chauncey looked up and dropped the ball. Her gaze fixed on the man.

Unsure of his next move, Jake stopped and crouched down. He didn't want to hurt the dog.

He looked around. In the distance, he saw two boys walking near the park's edge, not appearing to pay attention to him, but nothing else.

"Here doggie," he whispered.

Chauncey stared at Jake. Her sturdy body and noble head unnerved him. He knew she must be someone's pet. Maybe something more.

She stared at him and barked. She lowered her head and backed away. Could he go through with this?

"Here, doggie, come over here."

She stood her ground and barked again. A warning bark, Jake thought.

He crouched in submission and held out the treats.

The smell of liver wafted to her. In her short life, Chauncey had been trained to trust. This was just a nice man with treats. Her favorite. She tentatively moved toward him, her tail between her legs.

"That's it, come here. Have some nice treats."

Chauncey lowered her head and ate the treats from his hand. Jake grabbed her collar and yanked her toward him.

He looped the rope around her neck. She pulled back, the rope jerking hard against her face.

She let out a sharp bark and a sharp cry. Jake knew the dog was panicked.

From the other side of the recreation building at some distance, he heard a man yelling.

Chauncey's head snapped around. She smelled Dirck's fear and fiercely pulled against Jake's rope.

He yanked her back, but the dog was stronger than he had anticipated and she nearly broke free.

He dove in and picked her up. She squirmed frantically but couldn't find the leverage to push away. He threw her into his truck but she lost her balance and slid across the smooth leather seat and onto the passenger floor.

He jumped in, turned the key, and raced to the park's exit, veering on and off the grassy edges, nearly ditching to the side.

In his rear-view mirror, he saw a man was running from the other side of the building, his hands at his mouth, yelling something. He looked down at the cowering dog.

Jake couldn't do it. He pulled off to the side and leaned over to open the passenger door to set her free. His sobbing daughter appeared before him, her pleading eyes at his. He kept moving.

Only thirty seconds had passed since he had seen the dog.

Jake turned onto the main highway and sped away, the Riverdale Recreation Park in his rearview mirror. His cabin sat twenty-five miles north in Woodsdale.

Chauncey had climbed onto the seat opposite him, the rope still draped around her neck. She was staring at the man, her eyes wide, barking at him, moving nervously about on the seat.

Never in her life had she been treated like this. She knew this wasn't training. This was real. Her life was in peril. Her barking intensified.

He reached over to comfort her but realized he couldn't risk anyone seeing her and pushed her back down onto the floorboards. She continually struggled to get back onto the seat.

Escalating panic and dread filled both dog and man during the long ride to Jake's cabin. She had stopped barking and was now on the floorboards, shaking.

Thirty minutes later, Jake pulled onto his long dirt driveway and opened the door. He climbed out. Chauncey bolted from the open door, dragging the rope from her neck. Jake slammed his boot onto it, flipping her backwards. She yelped. She moved around in erratic circles, her eyes blinking oddly. He thought he had broken neck and knelt to her.

She lifted her head and erupted in threatening barks. He removed the rope and picked her up. It was after four in the afternoon and the autumn light was fading behind Hilltop Mountain. Joannie would be home soon.

Jake awkwardly opened the unlocked door and let Chauncey loose. She raced around the cabin and through the open door to the girl's bedroom, sheltering under her bed. Jake found Mac's old kibble and poured it into a bowl and put it at the edge of the bed, but the dog remained tucked in the far corner beneath the bed.

Chauncey stared out at her captor. She tried to comprehend the meaning of this sudden disruption in her life. She had never experienced such an unknown turn in her short life. But she knew this was real.

And Jake knew he had stolen someone's valuable dog, but it had been done and there was no turning back.

He tried tempting her with treats but she only crawled farther from him. He finally returned to his kitchen, out of sight. She crawled out from under the bed and raced through the cabin, desperately searching for an open door or window. From the kitchen, Jake watched the dog move about. Her gait was light and coordinated. She was a fine dog.

He knelt and held out the liver treats but she cowered in a corner, staring at him. He carried her back into his daughter's room and closed the door.

At 5:30 p.m., his daughter came home. The dull expressionless face that had met Jake every afternoon suddenly brightened. There was whining and scratching from the other side of her bedroom door.

"What's…that?" she said. "What's in my room?"

"I got you a nice doggie, honey. Do you want to see her?"

Her face lit up. "Yes…*yes.*"

She ran to her door and opened it. A large dog bounded out, knocking her to the floor. Chauncey headed for the open front door but Jake jumped forward and grabbed her hindquarters, jerking her back. She cried out. He slammed the door.

His daughter's face soured.

"Daddy, don't hurt her, don't…please," she pleaded.

She walked to the dog who cowered by the door. Her hind legs were shaking and she panted in fear.

"She's a little excited, honey…she'll calm down soon," he said but was again troubled at his daughter's reactions. The happy face was gone.

Joannie hugged Chauncey, but the dog pulled her head through the girl's arm and ran back under the bed. Joannie crawled next to the shaking dog.

By that evening, everyone was exhausted, especially Chauncey, who by this time would have eaten her dinner and been lying with Dirck on the couch before bed.

Instead she lay on the cold floor in the dark austerity of the cabin, staring at the strange girl kneeling before her.

"Why won't she come to us or eat, daddy? Is she sick? Is she okay?" Joannie asked again, confused by her new dog's reactions.

Jake sat in his rocking chair, watching his tearful daughter. Joannie was again looking anxious and unhappy and he now hated himself for stealing this dog.

He should just tell her the truth but knew it would bring more distrust along with more confusion and heartache. And now, he wouldn't even know where to return the dog.

"Just give her a couple of days, honey. She'll calm down, I promise." But Jake's continuing reassurances rang hollow.

That night and all throughout the next day, despite increasing urges from the young girl, her new dog remained under the bed, staring at the wall, refusing food, cowering at the comings and goings of the big man and the little girl.

And sometimes, in the night, as she lay exhausted in half-sleep, upon hearing the bedroom door rattle open and believing Dirck would appear, the joyful bark that trembled in her throat was twisted back down into another mournful cry.

8

The park's field lights had illuminated over an hour ago. It was 8 p.m. and Dirck had been in the Riverdale Recreation Park for over six hours.

He had run the park's perimeter and through the surrounding woods a dozen times, driven the back-connecting road again and again to incomprehensible exhaustion.

Each time, in the distance, he could just make out her familiar silhouette in the distance.

He called the Riverdale Police on his cellphone, explaining that his service dog had vanished and that he needed them to help him search. Twenty minutes later, a patrol car pulled into the parking lot. The officer was a young man, probably no more than twenty-five. Just out of the academy.

"You say your dog was a service animal? And she ran free in the park?" the officer said, his tone almost accusing. He stared at Dirck.

"It was a minute. Not even. She was…she was having her recreation time, running with other dogs…just..." He couldn't speak.

"Take a breath sir," the officer said. "Dogs run away or are stolen all the time. You'll find her."

The word *stolen* reverberated in him.

The officer knew the longer the man's dog had been missing, the less likely she would be found, but he didn't say anything. Dirck asked the officer to help him search, but after another hour with flashlights in the woods and around the park's far perimeter, no further signs were found, and the young officer was called back to the station to take care of other urgent business.

"I'm sure she'll show up," the officer said blankly as he left.

That October night, it had grown cold and Dirck sat in his car with the heater running.

He slumped over the wheel, staring out at the bright, empty field set against the dark hills. It looked like a dream, some unearthly vision of the park. He sat there for another hour, waiting for something, just something.

he still believed she had gotten trapped or lost and he had to alert her. He removed his shirt and hung it outside of the window for his smell and emptied the liver treats into her drinking cup and set them outside his car door.

He sat in the running car, the door ajar and fell asleep.

At four in the morning, Chauncey appeared, her face inches away, her soft eyes staring at him. He woke to the darkness. The field lights were now off and it was pitch-dark around him.

He turned on his flashlight and pushed opened the car door. The treats were gone. Probably squirrels. No signs she had been there. He waited for another hour in the darkness, the only sound his idling car.

Dirck had been at the park fourteen hours now.

At some point, not knowing whether or not it was the right time, he put his car into drive and drove away. He felt as if he were abandoning one of his own, a soldier lost and alone on the battlefield. A soldier never leaves a man behind. It was his code, the code of the military, and against everything he was taught, that he believed.

And Chauncey had been his most valuable companion and partner. This was worse than the battlefield, worse than the war.

As he drove through the back of the Riverdale Park, he began to think she had been stolen. He tried to imagine what she was doing now, so many hours later. Was she locked up and struggling? Perhaps she was injured somewhere. Maybe her trauma was over now and she was licking the face of her captor. The thought made him sick.

He drove home, twenty or thirty miles from Riverdale, he wasn't sure how far it was, each dark mile farther more excruciating than the last. Several times, he stopped and turned back.

He walked into his dark house. There was no sound except for the ticking of the mantel clock in the front room.

He slumped onto his couch, his jacket still on, and pressed his aching head into his hands. Around him were Chauncey's bed, toys, pictures on the refrigerator, all silent reminders of her.

He reached down and picked up the towel that he had used to dry her off only yesterday. It was still moist. He pressed his face into the fabric and breathed in slowly, deeply, hoping for the faintest smell of her, the sweet fishy stink of Chauncey, but there was none, only the memory of her. Nothing was left but what he held in his hands.

Fear rose in him. But this time, it was worse, like death itself. He fell onto the floor, enveloped in panic. He tried to calm himself but the constant realization his dog was gone tightened around him like that familiar, relentless vice of death.

He sobbed until he couldn't breathe and scrambled through the house, desperately searching for tranquilizers, and found one forgotten bottle of Xanax in his bathroom. He took several pills and passed out.

At 6:30 a.m., barking woke him.

He stumbled toward the sound. Hoppie and Chester were at his kitchen door, wanting their morning outing with Chauncey. He opened the door and the lumbering Bernese and athletic Weimaraner bounded into the house, circling him, climbing on him, whining. He lay on the floor, hugging the dogs, trying to draw some measure of strength from them but could not. It only intensified his grief.

And as quickly as they had appeared, they disappeared without their companion. It was a terrible way to wake up.

He staggered through the house, searching for his phone. He called Dru. They had talked only last week, like the many weeks before that, the conversations upbeat, always about Chauncey, how his life had been transformed, how happy they were together.

"Chauncey is gone, Dru…gone! Missing. Stolen, I don't know, but she's gone…she's gone, Dru!"

He sobbed between words. Dru had never heard him like this.

"What? How? What happened?" she said. Her voice wavered as she tried to comprehend what she had just heard.

He recounted the story in detail but there were few specifics. She had simply vanished from the park.

He felt mildly better, knowing that he was talking to Chauncey's trainer, the woman who knew and loved his dog.

"Dirck, she might have been taken by someone. You saw no sign of foul play? She simply disappeared from the park? Did she have her vest on? A leash? We need to get her back now," she said.

Dru was moving through the possible options as quickly as they occurred to her.

"We have to get her picture out there. I'll call the producer at Vermont WCAB. They'll want to get you on the air and tell your story…someone must have seen her by now.

I'll even get NBC or another big network to air this, get the CAS trainers and get ahold of other vets with our dogs."

That morning, Dirck went to the local post office to print posters and flyers. The poster had a color photograph of Chauncey in her red vest and another taken with him.

He was in his Army uniform with his dog sitting by his side staring at the camera, the photograph that Dave Ballard had taken on the day he had brought Chauncey home from CAS.

The large poster read:

STOLEN SERVICE DOG—FEMALE GOLDEN RETRIEVER THREE YEARS OLD. ANSWERS TO "CHAUNCEY."

THIS IS A VALUABLE SERVICE DOG BELONGING TO A WAR VETERAN. THERE IS A $6,000 REWARD FOR HER SAFE RETURN. NO QUESTIONS ASKED.

CONTACT DIRCK HANSEN AT 802-444-3393 IN GLENRIVER OR DRURY VAUGHAN OF CAS AT 380-880-2209.

CAS had donated two thousand and Dirck had put in four thousand of his own. He thought it should have been more.

The local Glenriver Bank had gone out of business some years ago, and he had a steel-cased safe installed in his home, where he kept one hundred twenty thousand dollars in cash. It was all the money he had. Dirck owned his home and lived frugally.

He placed posters in the local humane society, stores throughout Riverdale, local veterinarian offices and grooming places, feed stores, post offices, markets, even the town bulletin boards.

That night, Dirck appeared on the Vermont news, telling his story over photographs of Chauncey. The story quickly drew attention. Within minutes, the WCAB switchboard had lit up with tips.

The next few days, things moved quickly. National news organizations grabbed the story. They wanted Dirck to tell the country, the world, about his service dog. Someone had to know where she was. Someone must have seen her.

Chauncey had been taken on a Saturday. By Tuesday, Dirck had appeared on four local news stations, and tips poured in. Most were false sightings.

Then on Thursday, an NBC News producer called CAS and spoke to Dru. They asked them to appear via satellite from CAS.

The well-known veteran newsman, Matthew Palmer, stared somberly into the large studio camera in New York.

"Good evening, I'm Matt Palmer. Tonight, we bring you an important story from Vermont, where retired Army Captain, Dirck Hansen, is without his service dog, Chauncey. Captain Hansen had owned his dog for only a year before she disappeared. He and the dog's trainer, Drury Vaughan, of Canines Assisting Soldiers join us now from Upstate New York. Good evening Dirck and Dru."

The two sat at an empty table in a CAS training room, one of the rooms where he had first seen Chauncey. They looked exhausted from several heavy days. On the right side of their split screen, photographs of Chauncey appeared.

"Good evening, Mr. Palmer," Dru said. Dirck stared down at the table.

"Tell us about your story, Captain Hansen, about your service dog, Chauncey."

Dru put her hand on Dirck's shoulder. He looked up into the camera. His eyes were somber and dark. He hadn't slept in days.

"Chauncey is my three-year-old Golden Retriever service dog. She keeps me from having panic attacks…she…she has been a lifesaver for me. She has a microchip implanted in her. To identify her." He paused. Through stinging tears, he looked directly into the large camera feet away.

"Please…please help bring my dog Chauncey home to me."

He looked like a young boy pleading for his lost dog.

The producers and directors were visibly shaken as they watched from the broadcast booth. The NBC producer who owned three dogs sobbed at the controls.

Dirck recounted the many details of Chauncey's last sighting. Dru filled in where she could. The story was told over photographs and videos of Chauncey taken during training. It ended with the screen showing the handsome picture of her in her red service vest sitting smartly next to Dirck.

The story went "viral" on social media. It was immediately shared by tens of thousands on Facebook, Twitter, Google.

By the next morning, all the major networks had picked up the story. The story of Dirck and Chauncey spread throughout the country and overseas to millions of viewers who expressed outrage at the theft of the veteran's service dog.

Immediate help arrived from service families who began mobilizing groups near Riverdale and other communities in Vermont. Veterans, many who didn't know Dirck, brought posters to every store in the towns around Riverdale and vets in local communities near Riverdale began mobilizing search parties.

It had been only five days since his dog had disappeared but hundreds of people were now searching for Chauncey and the entire world now knew about Dirck Hansen and his lost dog.

The Riverdale police station received hundreds of calls, mostly false leads and many angry callers telling them "to do their goddamned job and get out and find the dog."

Then, on the following Tuesday, several days after Chauncey's disappearance, one call caught the attention of Riverdale Chief Gerald Markle.

"This is Chief Markle. You say you have information about the stolen service dog?"

"Yes, sir. My name is Alan Zuker and my twelve-year-old son told us about this last night. We didn't know about it until we saw the newscast about the missing service dog. My boy Paul said he was hiking with one of his schoolmates this past Saturday afternoon near the woods in the Riverdale Recreation Park. They noticed a man trying to get a dog into his truck. Said the dog was struggling and the man picked it up and threw it inside his truck and drove off. Took off fast like. Didn't look right to the boys. Said there was another man running across the field, yelling. It happened fast, like I said. My boy said the truck was dark green, older model, maybe a Chevy or Ford…he knows the cars."

Markle took notes in his log.

"Paul noticed the truck was sort of banged up—dents on the fender. Had the green Vermont plates but he didn't catch the number," Zuker said.

"You say both boys saw this? Did they get a description of the man? What sort of dog did they see?"

"Paul said he was a bigger man, think he had a beard. Wore trousers and a white shirt, maybe had dark hair," the man said.

"Oh, yeah…said it was a blonde dog, a bigger dog…looked like that dog on the lost-dog poster my boy saw at his school."

"Can I get your address so we can send someone out to talk to your son Mr. Zuker? Maybe he'll remember more."

But when an officer visited the boy the next day, he couldn't recall any further details.

That afternoon, Markle faxed an urgent request to the Vermont Department of Motor Vehicles to search their database for green, older model trucks in the Riverdale area.

Especially after his theft, Jake Tollinger stayed put, and warned his daughter not to mention the dog to anyone and only to take her out near the cabin.

Chauncey remained invisible to the world.

9

Chauncey's life in the Tollinger cabin moved from one waking torment to the next. She had been ripped from her work, her home, her master, and thrown into an uncertain ugly existence. She barely slept or ate.

The big man would come at her with the rope to lead her outside but she cowered from him, always hiding under the girl's bed. And despite the young girl's continued calls for her, she remained as far from her as she could. Several times, she tried to escape, but each attempt was squelched by Jake and his rope.

After several days, mostly from necessity, she began eating and drinking and going out for poddy breaks.

But Jake and his daughter could see that the dog was withdrawn, keeping her distance from them both. The dog seemed to be longing, continually searching for something far beyond the walls of the small cabin and the forests surrounding it.

The girl had named her new dog "Kady," a favorite character from the book *Kady and Kathy* that her mother often had read to her. Every night, Joannie brought Kady to her bedroom, sitting with her on the floor, petting her, whispering to her about her little dog Mac, what school was like, how pretty Kady was, how much she loved her, where they would go the very next day. The girl's soft voice relaxed Kady. She sensed the girl was unhappy and needed her close, and, as time passed, she increasingly trusted Joannie.

Although the girl seemed happier, as the weeks went by, his daughter's brightened mood was largely unbalanced by Jake's mounting guilt, and increasingly, he dulled his discomfort with more alcohol.

By winter, two months after Jake's theft, the fear and sorrow that had enveloped the dog's heart had begun to relax. Her disciplined training at CAS helped her to adapt to a new life and, by Christmas, Kady had settled into more normal routines. She woke to the girl's hand on her back, spent hours walking the nearby woods with her, and enjoyed novel treats of pumpkin and sweet potato chips that the girl had learned to bake.

And despite her father's insistence not to mention the dog or otherwise draw attention to it, at her school, Joannie knitted Kady a blue macramé collar.

"That's a pretty macramé piece, dear," her teacher said. "Is it for you?"

"No, it's for my dog, Kady. She needs a new collar. The old one was dirty," the girl said.

"Oh, you got a new dog, Joannie? What kind of dog?"

"A Golden Retriever dog. She's so pretty, not very big, but very sweet and…"

Joannie stopped, remembering what her father had told her. "Uh, well, she's just visiting us right now," she added.

Chauncey's reward poster had been pinned on the Woodsdale School bulletin board. Joannie had seen it but hadn't paid it much attention. Until now.

The teacher asked whether she had seen the poster. The dog looked like Kady but Joannie was afraid of her father, worried he would get angry and take her dog away.

A trusted neighbor who had once been a veterinarian came to Jake's cabin to care for the dog's needs.

A family friend, Janie, also came to their cabin once a month to bathe and groom Kady. But on one visit, an older teenage girl showed up instead of Janie.

"Hello, Mr. Tollinger. I'm Denise…Janie's sick this week and she asked if I could come and do the grooming today," the girl said.

"How do you know Janie?"

"I used to tutor her in school…our families are friends."

Jake stared at her through the half-opened door.

"When will Janie be better and back to work?"

"She's got a bad flu and went into local care here…gone for a while, I think."

Jake considered the girl. He didn't know whether he should risk this new person seeing the dog, but Janie already knew about the dog anyway.

"Okay, come on in. Dog's in the back."

But it wasn't Jake's trusted neighbor or Denise or Janie who would eventually tie Jake Tollinger to the stolen dog.

A week after Denise had groomed Kady, Chief Markle received the report from the Vermont Department of Motor Vehicles. The one-page facsimile read:

Motor vehicles matching the description of DARK GREEN OLDER MODEL TRUCK within the Riverdale, Vermont area (5 total):

-1959 Green Chevrolet 3100: James Tilliston, 3208 Route 4A, Jameston

-1962 Green Ford F100: Jake Tollinger, 39 Hill Top Road, Woodsdale

-1966 Green Ford F150: Mike & Joan Blunt, 140 Academy Road, North Riverdale

-1960 Green Chevrolet 3300: Mary Francisco, Rural Route 39, East Riverdale

-1968 Green GMC: Bob Thorton, 199 East Drive, Riverdale

Each entry had a color photograph of the truck and the license number.

One dark-green Ford truck had distinct dents on the right front and left rear fenders.

That afternoon, Chief Markle and a deputy showed up at Jake Tollinger's cabin at 39 Hill Top Road.

Jake's heart jumped when he saw two uniformed policemen on his porch. He stepped out to greet them. It was only ten degrees outside.

Markle stepped forward.

"Are you Mr. Tollinger? Jake Tollinger?

"Yes. What can I help you with?"

"Do you own a 1962 dark green Ford F100 truck, plate number EGT428?" Markle said.

The deputy was craning his neck around the cabin to look for a truck.

"Uh, yes, I own the truck. Did I do something wrong or…" Jake broke off.

"We received a report of a dog being taken from Riverdale Park weeks ago—a Golden Retriever—and there is evidence the dog was put into your truck."

Jake's heart jumped.

"A dog? In my truck? Oh, no, sir, I don't know anything about any dog. You're welcome to look at my truck if you wish."

Markle was looking beyond the man through the half-opened door.

"Can we come inside out of this cold, Mr. Tollinger?"

"Oh, uh, yea, come in. But it's not tidy in here."

As was her custom this time of day before their walk, Joannie had taken Kady into her bedroom and closed the door.

The policemen walked inside and Jake closed the door. Behind them on the door hung Kady's new leash. Jake led them into the kitchen, away from his daughter's room.

"Is there something you need from me, officers?" He was fidgeting with a pen he had picked up. "Can I give you my phone number or something like that?"

"No sir, we have that already. Can you tell us where you were Saturday, this past October fifteenth?"

The sergeant pulled out a notebook and began writing something. The deputy was looking around the kitchen. He noticed a half-empty bowl of water on the floor.

"October fifteenth? I don't know…probably here with my daughter. She's not well and I have to give her medicine every day, you know."

"What's your daughter's name? How old is she?"

Jake was inching farther into the kitchen away from his daughter's bedroom. If the dog barked it would be over.

"Well, she's eleven and a half and her name's Joannie." His face sagged. "What's my daughter have to do with this?"

"We received reports from a teacher at the Riverdale School about a young girl who mentioned her new dog, a dog that matched the description of the stolen Golden Retriever."

Jake's jaw was set in a way that conveyed he wouldn't be saying much more. He stepped back.

"Sir, like I told you before. I don't have a dog and my daughter wouldn't have said anything like that. She doesn't have a dog either. She's not well and I am looking after her. And if you're going to continue standing in my house asking me questions, well, unless you have a search warrant or something, you need to leave."

He stepped forward to usher the policemen to the cabin door but suddenly realized Kady's leash was hanging in plain sight and walked ahead of them, standing with his back to the door. He opened it oddly behind him.

They walked out and Jake slammed the door. The dog barked.

Jake locked the door and ran to his daughter's room.

"Keep her quiet, honey." He was out of breath.

"Kady got scared when the door slammed, Daddy…who's here?"

"Just keep her down for a while. I'll tell you why later, okay?"

The two policemen stood on Tollinger's front porch staring at each other.

"Did you hear a dog bark?" Markle said.

"Not sure. But I thought I saw a leash swinging on the back of the door and there was a bowl of water on the kitchen floor," his deputy said.

They walked to the back of Jake's cabin. His truck was parked in an open garage.

It fit the description the boys had given Markle. The back was filled with lumber and the cab was empty. There were no obvious signs a dog had been in there. They considered going back to the house but didn't have a search warrant and left.

As Markle and his deputy walked back to their cruiser, Kady ran out of the girl's bedroom and jumped to the window to watch them.

Chief Markle knew Tollinger had taken the dog. There may have been a leash on the door and the water bowl was a giveaway. And the boys' accounts were just too accurate to ignore.

But it had been Jake Tollinger's defensive attitude that had raised enough suspicion for Markle to put forth a warrant, highlighting the national search for Dirck Hansen's service dog.

The following week, a Riverdale County Judge issued a formal search warrant for the Tollinger cabin.

A week later, Markle and two deputies returned unannounced to 39 Hill Top Road.

Samuel Terry, one of Markle's most trusted men, himself a veteran, had followed the story of Dirck Hansen and his stolen service dog and especially wanted to find the veteran's dog.

At 2:30 p.m., two cruisers pulled around opposite sides of the cabin. Markle and his two men stood outside, listening for a dog bark. Nothing. They walked to the front door.

Outside in the back of his cabin, Jake was on his knees, scooping Kady's poop into a container with a trowel. He heard men talking and peered around the edge of his cabin and spotted a police cruiser.

"Check the back of the front door for a leash," the Chief said to Terry. "Clap your hands and call for her. Maybe she's being hidden."

The search warrant was under a "knock and announce" restriction. Markle banged on the heavy wooden door.

"Jake Tollinger, this is the Riverdale Police. We have a warrant to search your premises."

Silence from the other side of the door. Markle banged harder.

"Jake Tollinger, this is the police. Open your door!" Another minute passed with no response.

Markle and Terry walked to the back of the cabin to look for Jake's truck, leaving a deputy at the door.

The green truck was parked in the same spot as their previous visit. They opened the doors but again, there was no signs a dog had recently been inside. They walked to the back of the cabin.

Jake had climbed down the hill out of view, taking the trowel and container filled with dog poop. He crouched behind a large maple tree. The policemen stood at the back of the cabin, looking out to the woods.

"Jake Tollinger, we know you're out here. We have a warrant to search your property," Markle said, his big voice echoing through the forest.

It was a Saturday and earlier that afternoon, Joannie had taken Kady into the woods for her walk. She had been gone for almost an hour and would likely be home soon.

Jake didn't want her to walk into this trap. He yelled back.

"I'm here…pruning trees down here." But it was early winter, not pruning time. He emerged from behind a stand of trees, empty-handed.

"Mr. Tollinger, we have an order to search your cabin," Markle repeated.

Jake looked at the warrant but his mind was elsewhere. He had to get the policemen in and out of the cabin quickly.

Why were the police making such a fuss over someone's pet dog? Jake thought.

"Let's go in the back way here," Jake said.

Joannie would be taking her usual route through the woods along the hilltop facing the cabin and would return to the front door.

As had been their recent custom, Kady was off her leash, staying close to Joannie with treats. And Jake knew if the dog spotted the men, she would run down the hill to greet them.

Inside, Samuel Terry checked the back of the door but the hook was empty. He turned and clapped.

"Here Chauncey," he yelled. "Chauncey!"

There was no response.

"What are you looking for?" Jake said. "I told you before, I don't have a dog here."

"Mr. Tollinger, you need to stay out of our way while we conduct our search," Markle said.

"Yes, but you'll not find any dog here."

The deputies searched separate rooms. Markle went into the kitchen and began opening cupboards and cabinets. In one, he saw an opened bag of dog food.

"Mr. Tollinger, please come in here."

He held out a half-empty bag that read "Nature's Ingredient Diet." On the linoleum floor sat the bowl of water. The floor was wet next to it. Jake clenched his jaw.

"That food belonged to the dog we had before, our Cocker Spaniel, Mac. He was hit by a car a while ago. Never got rid of it…my daughter has been pretty beat up about her dog…likes to keep reminders of it around the house."

He could not think of an excuse for the water bowl. It had been over a year since Mac had died.

The third deputy was searching inside Jake's bedroom, but found no evidence of a dog.

Samuel Terry was in the daughter's bedroom on his hands and knees. Under her bed, he noticed large wisps of blonde fur floating among the thick dust. On the bedside table sat a dirty pink dog collar and a dog brush filled with twisted blonde hair.

"Chief, you'll want to see this," Terry said. "Take a look under the bed and at this pink dog collar and brush."

"I told you before, those belonged to my daughter's dog, Mac," Jake said. "She was a blonde Cocker and that's her hair and collar. She just feels better having the reminders of the dog, like I said before. We don't clean much in here."

Mac had been a black-and-white Spaniel.

"We're going to have to take a look in your shed and truck, Mr. Tollinger," Markle said.

That was fine with Jake. At least they hadn't found the other leash in his bedroom drawer. Maybe this would end the search.

The men had been there almost a half hour. Joannie should have been back by now. He knew his ruse would be over if she came home with the dog.

The deputies walked to Jake's shed. On one shelf sat bags of dog treats. They were hard and old.

"Yeah, like I said, those belonged to our dog Mac...my daughter couldn't throw them out."

He was right about that. He thought this would end the search.

Markle reached up for a rope hanging from a hook. It was new and was configured into a lasso. The knot was filled with tufts of blonde hair.

"Did you use this on your Cocker Spaniel too?" Markle asked.

"Yes, we didn't have a leash when we brought her home and used it to keep her close."

His explanations were becoming increasingly transparent.

The Chief knew a dog had struggled in that lasso. He pulled out a clump of blonde hair from the knot and dropped it into a plastic bag.

"We'll have to take this along with the dog brush and collar and water bowl for evidence," Markle said to him. "The missing dog's DNA is in a database and we'll compare it to these items."

Markle was hoping for a quick confession.

Jake watched him write something on the plastic bag. He couldn't understand why someone's pet dog would have DNA in some file.

The police chief didn't look ready to leave.

"Mr. Tollinger, where's your daughter now?" Jake didn't anticipate the question.

"Now? Well, she's at her school." But then, remembering it was Saturday, he quickly added, "Today, they have a mid-winter creative arts program all the kids attend."

Markle knew the Riverdale School—his boy had gone there. The school wouldn't hold such an activity in winter. Their weekend programs took place only in summer.

"You mentioned she was sick and needed medication."

"Yes, well she takes her inhaler and meds with her. She has bad asthma."

"When do you expect her back?"

"What's my daughter have to do with this?"

Jake began fidgeting with some string he had picked up. His jaw clenched. Markle thought stretching out the search would produce something.

"When will she be home?" he asked again.

Jake looked at his watch. "Probably in a couple of hours or so."

It was 3:45 p.m. His daughter should have been home by now.

Markle and Terry were pulling open drawers and cabinets, ignoring Jake. The amount of junk in the shed looked endless.

Jake stepped outside and looked back toward the woods where his daughter would have taken Kady.

Ten minutes passed. Then twenty. Joannie had been gone almost two hours and the winter light was beginning to fade behind Hilltop Mountain. Perhaps she was lost. Or hurt.

Now Jake thought he should end this charade and tell the police what they wanted. They could at least search for his daughter. That's all that mattered now. He'd go ahead and tell them he had stolen the dog for her. After all, it was just someone's pet. How serious could it be?

From the top of the hill above them, a dog barked.

Joannie was running through the woods, Kady chasing her. They were late and she knew her father would be worried. She had taken a wrong turn somewhere off their normal path and had gotten lost. But Kady knew how to find her way home and led the girl back toward the cabin.

When they reached the edge of the woods overlooking the cabin, Joannie saw the two police cars.

Police had been out before. Last year, her father had been in trouble with one of his neighbors but she didn't know why. And one night this past December, her father had been outside shooting his rifle in a drunken outburst. Each time, the police came to the cabin, each time with more warnings for Jake. Joannie didn't want any more trouble.

Does this have something to do with Kady? she thought.

Kady caught up with Joannie and they both crouched behind a tree. She knew she had to get out of there. She latched Kady's leash and led her dog back into the woods.

Markle's head snapped around. He ran to the front of the cabin and looked up the hill where they had heard the bark.

Terry scanned the hillside with his binoculars but it was getting dark and he couldn't see much. Markle clapped.

"Chauncey," he yelled. No response. "Chauncey!"

Jake now knew that the dog he had stolen was named Chauncey. And he knew that had been her bark. If the dog didn't come down from the hill, his daughter was likely okay. He waited.

Markle and his deputies stood outside for another minute. No more barks. There was nothing else they could do.

On the way back to his cruiser, Markle smelled dog poop on his shoe. He turned to Jake.

"Mr. Tollinger, we know you have the dog. We are taking the hair samples and water bowl. We will be in touch."

Marke knew Tollinger wasn't going to tell him where Chauncey was. And the police had no way of matching the evidence to her. Without the dog, their search would grow stale.

Thirty seconds after the police had turned off Hill Top Road, Joannie and Kady walked out of the woods.

10

In the months that came and went, despite the continued suspicions of the Riverdale Police and the unspoken uneasiness within the rural cabin, Jake Tollinger grew accustomed to the silent lies and deceit that maintained his daughter's happiness.

Each day, Joannie would lavish her attention on her dog Kady. Without regard for the cold and now, the thickening mud from spring rains, they set out at the same time each morning before school and late afternoon when Joannie returned, venturing into the surrounding woods and fields for hours of discoveries and new vistas.

Every day, it was "Kady, look, see this." And "Kady, look what I found for you," as the girl held out another stick she thought her dog would like. Each evening, Joannie and Kady came home exhausted from hours of walking and playing.

Neither Jake nor his daughter thought the dog wanted to run away anymore and she roamed without a leash. After all, she had only ever been someone's pet, and Kady belonged to them now.

Every night before sleep, the girl enacted ceremonies of her own making, always beginning with an elaborate lighting of sandalwood and pine candles, followed by a reading from some new schoolbook and a recitation from a poem she had written to the dog. She ended her ritual by singing to Kady, who would tilt her head at the girl's soft, high-pitched voice.

Sensing the girl was happier, Kady, too, felt more reassured and looked forward to the evening ceremonies. But it had now been seven months since she had seen Dirck and sometimes at night, after long walks and dinner and ceremonies, she would lie on the girl's bed lost in thought a moment before sleep and summon him. His smell and touch remained strong and she longed to find him.

Jake's mood, too, lifted as he watched his squealing and laughing daughter race through the cabin as she chased her dog.

"She's ours now, Daddy. She knows where home is, our home."

"That's right, honey. She sure is yours now, your own dog. A good dog."

Jake had found new ways to cast off the lingering doubts and strengthen their bond.

One early spring morning, he surprised them with an unplanned outing to a secluded spring meadow the locals enjoyed.

"Joannie, bring Kady and we'll go to your favorite meadow, out to Woodsdale Corners. She'll love the spring smells."

The girl's eyes lit up. She yelled for Kady, who bounded into the large room, her tail swishing at the prospect of a new adventure.

"Kady. Want to go somewhere? A new place with grass and flowers?"

Kady approved the outing with short bark.

A half-hour later, Jake had parked his truck at the dead-end of the Woodsdale Corners meadow and let them out.

The large meadow was bright and dewy. Kady raced into the tall grass dotted with fresh yellow dandelions and white buttercups.

She stopped and looked around—it reminded her of the meadow at her Glenriver home, the place she used to run with Chester and Hoppie. And with Dirck. As she swished through the high grass, she pictured him walking alongside her.

Jake sat at the meadow's grassy edge, watching his daughter chase her dog in wide circles, wherever the dog led her. As he dozed in the morning sun, he could hear her distant laughter and Kady's bright barks. They began to fade.

He sat up. Kady was at the far end of the field, running out toward the forest's edge, his daughter well behind her, trying to keep up. Something seemed different in the way the dog was running and barking. Probably it was his imagination.

He dozed off.

A minute passed, maybe less. He was bolted awake by distant high-pitched screams.

"*Kady...Kady!*" The girl's woeful cries echoed across the meadow.

Jake stood. At the far end of the four-acre field, his daughter was running erratically in and out of the woods. He couldn't see the dog. He lumbered across the field.

"Daddy, help…Kady…she's gone!"

The girl knelt at the forest's edge, sobbing in short spasms. He ran past her into the dense woods.

"Kady…Kady!" he yelled and clapped.

He ran in farther, calling for the dog. He looked at the still pines and maples for what seemed like several minutes, each time hoping to catch sight of the dog bounding through the woods toward him.

Several minutes passed. He returned to the meadow. Joannie was still crouched in the tall grass, crying in fits.

He returned to the woods, yelling for the dog, clapping, waiting. Another thirty minutes passed. The dog didn't appear.

After two hours of frantic searching and trying to console his hysterical daughter, he gave up. He was barely able to coax her back to his truck.

He sat in the cab looking out to the path of bent flowers and grass where they had just been running. He thought of the Riverdale Recreation Park, the place he had first seen the dog, the place he had stolen her. Jake would forever remember that field and now, the meadow before him.

After driving twenty agonizing minutes with his hysterical daughter, he pulled into Winger's Market to buy her a favorite ice cream, thinking vaguely it might help. But Joannie remained slumped in her seat, crying in short fits as she held onto Kady's leash. Her dog had just been sitting next to her.

At the counter with two ice creams, Jake noticed a large poster on the store's bulletin board. He didn't often read the posts but this one caught his eye—it had large color photographs of a dog. He walked to it.

STOLEN SERVICE DOG—FEMALE GOLDEN RETRIEVER THREE YEARS OLD. ANSWERS TO "CHAUNCEY."

THIS IS A VALUABLE SERVICE DOG BELONGING TO A WAR VETERAN. THERE IS A $6,000 REWARD FOR HER SAFE RETURN. NO QUESTIONS ASKED.

CONTACT DIRCK HANSEN AT 802-444-3393 IN GLENRIVER OR DRURY VAUGHAN OF CAS AT 380-880-2209.

Below the message were images of Dirck and Chauncey and a close-up of the dog's head.

Handwritten at the bottom was "Thief may have driven an older dark-green truck with dented fenders."

Mabel, the store's owner, had written the note when chief Markle called her. He knew Tollinger had stolen the dog.

Jake stared at the poster in disbelief. The dog in the photograph was Kady! The dog he had stolen—a veteran's service animal—a fellow soldier's valuable service dog. Now he knew why the police had been after him.

And Jake's truck had been identified on the poster. He looked over at Mabel.

"Mabel, let me use your phone."

He walked around the counter and dialed 9-1-1.

"9-1-1, what's your emergency?" a woman said.

"I have information about that stolen service dog, the one belonging to the war vet."

"Let me connect you with the Vermont State Police," the operator said. A few seconds passed.

"Sir, you have information about the stolen service dog? What is your name?" the officer said.

"Never mind that," Jake said. "I saw the dog less than an hour ago in the woods outside of Woodsdale, right near the Woodsdale Corners Road, out in the big field there, out there near Baker's Ferry, out in those woods there. She was running in the meadow by herself. I know it was her."

His explanation sounded weak. He felt dizzy.

"How would you know this, sir? What is your name?" the officer asked again.

"I'm telling you. I *know* it's the dog. That dog named Chauncey who was taken from that veteran last year. The sooner you get out there, the faster you will find her. I can tell you, it's her…I saw her up close. Please hurry."

Jake nearly admitted to stealing Chauncey but instead hung up. He was angry. And ashamed.

Mabel shook her head at Jake.

He dumped the ice cream bars and ran outside to his truck. On his way home, he passed three Vermont State Police cruisers, their lights flashing.

Please let them find her, he thought as they sped past. He pictured the man running across that park in Riverdale last fall. Dirck Hansen, desperate to find his dog. He couldn't imagine the veteran's misery these past long months. It eclipsed his own feelings of guilt and now, his daughter would learn the truth, and he'd lose her forever.

Joannie remained slumped in her seat, sobbing.

Ten minutes later, the police called Winger's.

"Winger's," Mabel said.

"This is the Vermont State Police. Is your manager or owner there?"

"I'm the owner. What's the problem?" She knew what this was about.

"We received a call from someone at your number about the missing service dog. Do you know who made the call?"

Mabel knew Jake Tollinger well, and in this part of the world, people stayed close and protected one other.

"I don't know who used my phone."

"Can you give me a description of the man who made the call? We believe he might have been involved in the dog's disappearance."

"Not much to say. Average lookin' fella, smaller build, younger, clean-cut, blonde hair I think. Drove off in a red mustang, maybe a convertible…New Hampshire plate."

"Okay ma'am, thank you for your information."

Jake drove on, wishing to God he had returned Dirck Hansen's dog those many months ago.

But by now, nobody knew where Chauncey was.

11

News traveled quickly. Dru and Dirck were at CAS when Dave Ballard burst into their conference room. Dave had been Chauncey's lead trainer.

"The Vermont State Police just called! Chauncey was spotted outside Woodsdale," he said. "Reported anonymously…someone at a local market there. They're in the woods searching for her now."

It was two in the afternoon and although the light might be good for maybe four more hours, Woodsdale was three hours away.

Dirck loaded his wagon with supplies and he and Dru were gone in minutes. They reached Woodsdale Corners Road near dusk.

"My name's Dirck Hansen, Captain Dirck Hansen. Chauncey is my service dog. Have you spotted her? Have you seen her?" he said. He was looking beyond the man toward the woods.

"No sir, not yet. Tip came from a caller at the local market. We have several police and volunteers searching in coordinated areas out here. Even got some veterans looking. You can search in this area here," he said pointing to a map section.

Dirck and Dru set out into the designated area. It stretched hundreds of miles into the state forest.

"We can track ourselves with my phone and the map," she said.

"Chauncey will smell me and the treats," he said. He was out of breath.

It was dusk when they entered the forest. They stayed within viewing distance of each other, yelling for her. In the distance, they heard others calling her name. *We will find her…find her tonight*, he thought.

After two hours searching with flashlights in the dark, they had covered several sections of the map without luck. They turned back.

Dirck remembered this feeling, the same, sinking feeling seven months ago at the Riverdale Recreation Park.

"She's got to be out here within earshot," he said. They prayed the tip was true.

After several hours of running from fear of again being captured, Chauncey found herself in a heavily wooded area fifty miles farther from Riverdale, an area not being searched.

She was lost without a scent to guide her. It was dark and on a spring night like this one, temperatures would grow cold. She circled a bed of leaves and lay down.

Her CAS training had given her many skills but surviving in the wilds was not one of them.

She thought about her hunting companions Chester and Hoppie who had once taught her how to track through the wilds by smell and sight but back then, it had been folly and she had a home. The memory made her think of her life before it had been so abruptly ripped away. She pictured herself lazing in the sunshine with Dirck, her stomach full, her heart light. It seemed so long ago.

Now, here in this wild and unknown place, there was nobody to help her and she had no moment's peace. Throughout the long, nervous night, she lay awake at unsettling rustling about her, the disquieting faint sounds of the many night hunters slipping in and out through the silent shadows about her. She did not yet know the dangers of this wild place, home to many great predators. It was an unforgiving place for a lone dog.

Dirk and Dru spent the night at the Woodsdale Motor Hotel, close to the search area.

"Dirck, I think Chauncey would have run in the opposite direction from her captors," she said as she pointed at their map.

"She'd be farther away from the search area, out here toward the town of Clover. She's a smart girl. She wouldn't have doubled back, knowing her captor was there—we should get over to Clover, where she might be headed."

The next morning, they drove the twenty miles north to Clover, reaching the small village by six. Nothing was yet open.

An old man in dirty overalls walked slowly down the sidewalk. He was a local farmer and had lived here since birth and spoke in a familiar Vermont drawl. They stopped and asked him for help.

"Ah-yep, I'm Lester Lincoln," he said.

His wrinkled face made him look older than his fifty-eight years but his eyes were direct and kind.

They explained their search for Chauncey. The old farmer smoothed the worn map on the car hood, studying it closely.

"The town of Woodsdale is over theyah…and we're hereah," he said, pointing to spots on the map. "Reckon tha' dog could be headed out hereah." He pointed to a large forbidding empty area.

"All woods theyah. Go down the main road and left at the light for 'bout half mile and the edge of them woods—go straight on in theyah," he said, pointing farther down the map.

Lester was smart about his world beyond the map. This was his home, and he knew well these towns and the woods that surrounded them.

Lester Lincoln's brow furrowed.

"But tell you what. Wouldn't give tha' pup a good chance over days in them woods…coy-otes might be a danga' to a dog," he said.

Dirck's heart sank. He knew Lester was right.

"But it bein' spring and all, maybe them wild dogs are busy with their young-uns now," he said but it didn't reassure Dirck.

They drove in the direction Lester had given them and came to a dead end, the woods in sight.

They ran into the forest yelling for Chauncey. It was 6:30 a.m., and the sun had just peeked over the near hills. Dirck hoped it would warm his girl. He couldn't imagine her alone in this vast wilderness.

He didn't even know where she had been these past many months.

The dappled sunlight through leafing maples woke Chauncey. The morning warmth was welcome after the cold night. Her nose caught something nearby. Food. In the town of Clover, cooks were preparing breakfast at the local diner. She had not eaten in over a day and broke into a full run toward the smell.

She reached a glen and stopped—the aroma of food was suddenly overpowered by another smell, something unfamiliar. She froze, nostrils quivering in the morning air. Before her something rustled in a large bush.

From around the thicket, coyotes appeared. Four of them, two to her right, two to her left. They appeared strange—their triangular ears and long narrow muzzles weren't like a dog's. And their eyes—those unblinking bright yellow eyes—were foreign, angry, like a large bird. And they were directed at her.

They approached slowly, their heads low. One of them pointed her nose to the air and let out a long, mournful howl, a sound unlike any Chauncey had ever heard. Yet the call sounded familiar, something that resonated deep within her. Other coyotes joined in, the wailing howls echoing through the forest.

The howls then mixed with yipping from the thicket before her. She had stumbled upon a pack of coyote mothers and pups. She was an unknown threat that had entered their den.

Chauncey lowered her head in deference and backed away. She knew she was no match for them. They converged on her.

But she was trained and knew her way around a threat. She ran straight at the coyotes, leaping over two of them at the last second. The coyotes were stunned, jumping and yipping about in confusion.

They turned back after her. She gained some ground but the coyotes were faster and more adept in their forest home and they would reach her within seconds.

A loud metal snap stopped everything. A high-pitched animal screech filled the air. Chauncey stopped and turned.

One of the mothers had stepped into a large bear trap, her hind leg devoured inside its massive steel teeth. The coyotes yipped and barked in panic around their stricken mother.

Dirck and Dru stopped. The animal screams were just in front of them.

"Oh God…that could be Chauncey," he said. They were less than a quarter mile away.

Chauncey watched as the other coyotes circled the stricken female, trying somehow to help her. She knew the animal was in grave danger, but did not approach it. The cries grew increasingly desperate.

The three coyote mothers turned back toward Chauncey. The strange animal had hurt one of them and they came after her with renewed anger. She was too close to outrun them.

Down in a bog close to the growing commotion, the hunter Miles Cornthwaite sat on a stump smoking a cigarette. At the ridge in front of him, desperate animal cries were mixed with the growling and yelping of fighting animals.

He shouldered his deer rifle and looked through the scope. Two coyotes were pulling at a dog's tail and another was moving in toward her neck. In the blur of brown and gold fur, he aimed and fired, the first bullet grazing the coyote at the dog's neck. It spun away. He shot near the other two at her tail. They flipped back away and retreated into the forest.

The dog before him was stunned. Miles crouched down and held out his hand. He reached into a pocket and pulled out the walnuts he used to lure deer.

The frightened dog approached him. Her tail was buried between her shaking legs. She could tell the man was kind and ate the nuts.

"What you doin' out here in these deep woods, friend? You ought not be out here," he said.

He stroked her back and she relaxed into his lap. Miles emptied his bag of nuts for her. It wasn't food she had tasted, but it was good. Miles had a dog of his own. This was no place for a dog. He'd take her back to his farm to safety. He pulled out a rope.

"Come on pup," he said, holding it toward her.

Chauncey turned and ran. Cornthwaite watched in bewilderment as the dog disappeared over the ridge.

Dirck and Dru had been running toward the animal's cries, which had now faded. But they heard the gunfire.

They came upon the injured coyote. The wounded animal reared its head in terror as it screamed and snapped at them.

Dru held the coyote, trying to calm it. Dirck examined the trap—in the military, he had trained to use non-explosive traps and knew this one.

He pulled the release, and the huge trap sprang open as if nothing had happened. But the freed coyote couldn't move. She pressed the leg with a rag.

They didn't notice Miles Cornthwaite approach.

"Hullo…hullo. I'm Miles," the man said, warning them of his presence.

"Poor coyote was injured in this trap," Dirck said to him.

"Yep. Heard it yelping a-ways off. I can help make a tourniquet and splint," Miles said.

The hunter pulled out the rope and splints, part of an emergency kit. He knelt by the stricken animal.

"Leg looks broken. Artery's severed but looks like it's not bleeding much anymore. She'll make it," Miles said as he leaned over the struggling animal.

"Damnedest thing, though. I saw some coyotes chasing a dog through these woods. Shot at them. Poor dog would have been a goner. Fed her my walnuts but she wouldn't come with me to safety…ran off."

Dirck bolted up. "You saw a dog? Was it a Golden Retriever with a thick coat? A female about sixty pounds?"

"Yep. That was the dog alright. Pretty pup. But dirty and tired—may have been in these woods awhile. She looked smart. You know her? She was hungry. But ran off," Miles said, pointing off to his left.

"How long ago? Where exactly did she run?" Without an answer, he turned in the general direction Miles had pointed and began yelling for her.

Dru yelled after him.

"Go find her. I'll help Miles here with the animal. Meet me in the Clover hotel. If you have reception, I will call you later."

He ran into the woods, calling her name, hoping his smell would alert her, drive her to him. But he had no idea where she was and it had grown dark.

By now, Chauncey had run two miles west of Dirck but faced a stiff headwind and she couldn't smell him. And she was just out of earshot of his calls.

She stopped, her uncertain nose to the air. A smell came to her—the familiar rank odor of coyotes filled her nose.

Long plaintive howls rose into the forest about her. Several large males had examined the empty bear trap—the smell of an injured mother was mixed with Chauncey's smell. They took off in her direction.

Behind Chauncey, twigs snapped. In the moonlight within the shadows of the dense woods, she several saw dark shapes running toward her.

They would surely reach her, but not before she put up a fight they could never have imagined.

12

Gregory Swathe stared lazily out into the darkening expanse of his eight-acre cornfield at the edge of his dairy farm in Hortonia. As was his after-dinner custom, he warmed himself by a bonfire and smoked his last cigarette.

The Vermont spring moon shone brightly across the field and tonight, the coyotes were active. More active than usual. They had been howling out in the distant woods earlier but now, they sounded closer, louder, yipping and growling right out there at the far end of his field near the woods. He leaned forward.

The usual pattern of bright snow-filled furrows alternating with rows of dark corn stubbles were flickering in the distance like an old, silent movie. Then the sounds reached him.

Several growling animals were snaking across the far end but he couldn't quite make them out. One of them zigzagged toward him in a full-out sprint. It was a smaller animal being chased by larger creatures.

Large male coyotes, each at least eighty pounds, the size of wolves, scrambled furiously around the smaller animal. *Coyotes wouldn't be fighting one another in an open field*, he thought. This looked serious.

Swathe ran back to his house and grabbed his shotgun and searchlight. He scrambled back to the field and flicked on the lamp.

Blinding white light flooded the field like the runway for an approaching aircraft. In front of him, large coyotes twisted about the smaller animal. It was a dog with blonde fur.

The dog broke free and ran directly into his light, pulled in as if by some divine intervention. Its snout and fur were smeared with blood. One big coyote had grabbed ahold of one of the dog's hind legs, but the dog pivoted and came viciously at the large animal. The coyote yelped and retreated. But others had reached the dog's front.

The farmer shouldered his loaded shotgun and fired. The huge blast stopped the coyotes.

They stood close together, transfixed by the sudden explosion, their whispery breaths steaming thickly above them. The injured dog limped toward Gregory and collapsed behind him.

But the animals were not giving up. Their heads lowered as they crept forward.

Gregory wasn't having any of this. He stepped forward, blocking their access to the dog.

They were no more than twenty yards in front of him, their gold eyes glowing like devils as they deliberately inched toward him. Again, the shotgun exploded, sending a massive concussion of dirt and buckshot in front of them. One defeated coyote yelped and scampered back into the woods.

Gregory opened the smoking barrel and slid in more shells. He fired again, this time closer to the animals. Another coyote cried and ran off.

One large male remained, undeterred. It leaned forward and broke into a full run, closing the short distance in seconds.

An enormous blast flipped the creature backward like a limp rag doll. It screamed and righted itself, slinking back to its woodland home like a frightened dog.

Gregory kept the hot smoking muzzle aimed toward the dark figures scattering through the distant field. The yelping stopped. The fight was over.

Farmer Swathe knelt to the shaking dog and placed his warm steady hands on her. She looked up at him, great fear radiating from her blinking eyes. Her muzzle had been punctured and her fur was matted with blood.

He carried the limp dog back to his farmhouse and banged on the kitchen door with his boot.

"Grace!"

An older woman ran to the door.

"Dog here was in a bad fight with them coyotes out there in tha' field but I let them know about it."

He laid Chauncey onto the rug next to his warm wood stove. She was whimpering, licking his hands in submission. He had never seen a dog in such fear.

"What n' the hell was tha' dog doin' out in them woods, Greg?" She looked at the shaking dog. "It's a female. Looks thin. Let's get her some food."

"No, not yet, Grace. We have to get her wounds fixed on up. Go get me my vet bag in the barn side room."

Gregory Swathe had inherited the farm from his father. It sat just outside Hortonia surrounded by one hundred beautiful acres of rolling Vermont hills.

They had fifteen cattle for dairy, two riding horses, chickens for eggs, goats for cheese, and stray cats. Early on, the local veterinarian had trained Gregory's father and he had inherited his skills before he passed away.

That was over fifteen years ago. Gregory and his wife had both turned sixty this year and he was now quite skilled in treating his farm animals for most any condition. But an injured dog was another matter.

Grace brought in two black suitcase-sized bags filled with instruments, antiseptics, syringes, antibiotics.

"Get me a pan of hot water. And them hotdogs we had for lunch," Gregory said.

He ripped the hotdogs and fed Chauncey a small piece at a time. He tried to get her to stand to take water, but she couldn't move. Her back legs had been bitten. It was obvious she had survived through her own fierce determination and strength.

"Grace, this girl must have put up a damned tough battle with them big male cy-otes…she's a fighter. And smart. Most dogs would be finished by now for sure."

He shaved Chauncey's fur to assess the damage. Her tail and back legs were punctured in spots. He wiped her wounds with antiseptic and injected antibiotics with steroids. And tetanus. He bandaged her lacerated wounds. Her muzzle had been opened in two places, which had to be taken care of, too.

Chauncey watched the man while he dressed her wounds. Tending to her took two hours. She looked at him with an expression he couldn't quite define. Relief, perhaps, but something else, a look of gratitude, almost trust. Her body was damaged but her eyes were steady.

"We let them big dogs have it, didn't we girl?" he whispered to her as he smoothed his hand across her back. "We let them know about it."

Chauncey's tail wiggled weakly. She knew this man was kind and would help her.

As he moved his hand across her head, Gregory considered the dog more closely.

She had beaten back large, vicious coyotes. Her strength and fierceness were remarkable but the dog before him was gentle, her eyes beaming deep warmth and affection. Her mouth curled slightly into a smile.

She wore a handmade blue macramé collar, probably someone's pet. *But this dog is special…more than just someone's pet*, he thought.

By evening, half of Chauncey's body had been shaved and her wounds dressed. The steroid contained a mild narcotic and she lay next to the warm stove and closed her anxious eyes. She slept for over eight hours.

Powerful smells of bacon and eggs woke her. It was nearly five in the morning and the farmers were up, ready for another day of farm work.

It would take them ten hours to milk the cows and herd them to the field for grazing and back for the afternoon milking. Then, the horses had to be groomed and fed, hens' eggs collected, and the four goats milked for cheese making. There were the barn repairs. And this past March, sugar maples had produced plentiful sap and there were hours of syrup-making in the sugar shack.

Chauncey had not moved from her spot. Her head raised to Gregory as he checked her bandages. She felt better.

"Hey good girl, how about some breakfast for ya'?" he said.

She was hungry. Chauncey's bushy tail thumped. *Good progress* he thought.

He cooked three fresh eggs and threw in the maple-cured bacon from the neighboring Malcolm farm. He filled a bowl with raw cow milk.

Chauncey had never seen anything like this. Hunger overpowered her discomfort and she got to her shaky feet, gobbling the food and lapping the sweet milk. It was exquisite.

Chauncey's mind was still fuzzy and her wounds stung but this was the first time in months she had felt safe. She collapsed back by the wood stove and closed her eyes. Her belly was full and she was protected.

Grace put down one of her thick quilts for a bed. Chauncey crawled onto it.

Chauncey slept while the farmers tended their early-morning chores. But an hour later, she woke to a powerful, familiar smell. It was Dirck—she smelled his fear!

She limped to the kitchen door and looked through the glass window toward the large field and woods beyond. His smell came from that direction. She barked and scratched at the door but nobody could hear her and her limbs were not cooperating.

It had been so many months since she had last seen him yet she could picture his face clearly. He was yelling for her.

She limped about the room, crying, barking, desperate to escape. But great exhaustion overtook her and she collapsed next to the door. She had to alert him. Somehow.

At that moment, Dirck Hansen lay in his bed at the Clover Hotel, embroiled in another battlefield nightmare. He had woken with a vision of Chauncey.

He jumped to the window, his heart pounding, anxiously looking out to the woodland ridge toward Hortonia.

His girl was less than three miles away.

13

Dirck and Dru had lost track of how many days they had been searching.

As they trekked deeper along lush glade-green paths and dense brush, he began noticing scattered leaves, broken twigs, flattened grass in the otherwise undisturbed forest floor.

He spotted newly sprouted leaves splattered with red. He sampled it. It was blood, fresh and thick. He noticed tufts of blonde fur embedded in bramble bush. He pulled it away and moved his fingers over the fur.

"Dru, here…animal blood, fur. Do you think it's the coyote's or…?" He stopped, not saying his dog's name.

There had been fierce fighting here. He remembered Lester Lincoln talking about the coyotes.

He tried to picture Chauncey in a fight with a coyote. He knew her strength and speed: for a sixty-pound dog, she was deceptive.

He thought back to when he had first brought her home. They had been hiking in the woods and his dog had run ahead of him. A black weasel—a large fisher cat—jumped from a tree immediately in front of her. Dirck knew the vicious animal could rip a dog apart. She had blocked the weasel's path and it was ready to fight, its tail whipping about as it hissed through tiny razor teeth.

The fisher lunged. But it hadn't anticipated its opponent's speed. She spun to the weasel's left, grabbing its neck, snapping it instantly.

She could easily fight off smaller coyotes he thought but then realized these animals had not been small and there had been several of them. As they walked in farther, the blood trails and disturbances disappeared.

They had been searching six hours and the light was fading. They considered if they should keep moving.

At that moment, they were standing just off the edge of the eight-acre field of Gregory Swathe's farm. Just beyond, Chauncey was at the farmhouse kitchen door, frantically barking and crying.

Dirck grabbed Dru's arm. He tilted his head.

"Wait …did you hear that? Sounded like yelping or barking," he said and pointed to the edge of the woods. "Listen!"

The wind had kicked up and the trees were rubbing against each other, creaking and groaning. Maybe that's what he had heard.

They waited for another minute, but the sound wasn't there anymore. They turned back.

They were exhausted from days of searching and that night decided to have a drink at the local Clover Barntable Restaurant. But it upset Dirck to be sitting in the comfort of a warm fire drinking a beer while his dog was alone and lost somewhere in the woods.

Why couldn't he find her? They seemed so close. He stared blankly out the dark window.

"Dirck, try not to worry. We need to stay strong for our girl. She's alive, I know it. I can feel it. We need to take fliers to the other townships."

There was Barton Township, Eden Haven, and Hortonia, the next town over. They planned to visit stores in every town within fifty miles of Clover.

They were certain Chauncey couldn't have traveled more than fifty or sixty miles based on the timeline they had established. But she could be headed in any direction.

"Stay strong, Dirck. We're close," Dru said but her words weren't delivered with any new reassurance.

Their thoughts were interrupted by a tickling bell at the restaurant door. An old man walked in.

"Dru, there's the farmer we saw our first day in Clover. Lester Lincoln. The farmer who told us where to look for Chauncey.

As the man walked in their direction and Dirck stood to greet him. Lester's craggy face was in shadow and looked unwelcome. He reached for the farmer's hand.

"Sir, you talked to me and my friend days ago about our lost dog. Helped us with the map," he said.

The man's face brightened and he smiled. His crooked teeth were yellowed from years of smoking, but his smile was direct and honest. He pulled off his gloves and grabbed Dirck's hand.

"Ah yea'. Rememba' now. Find your dog yet?"

"No sir, not yet. Would you sit with us? Perhaps give us ideas? I'll buy you something to drink."

Lester liked that idea. They recounted details of the past days—what they had seen in the woods, the coyotes, the hunter, the animal fur and blood. All of it.

"Chauncey is a trained service animal, my service dog. I'm an Iraq War veteran and I need her back. I have war trauma."

He pulled out a folded paper with two of Chauncey's photographs, one headshot and another full-length shot. Lester held the paper close to his face. It shook as he examined the pictures. He looked back at Dirck.

"Tha' a damned shame, tha' is." He took another swallow of beer and considered the man. "Ah yeah...don' think she's headed much for Clova' town now. She'd be over near Hortonia way by now, I reckon. She'd smell them farms around these parts...they have food tha' smell good to a hungry dog. Let me see tha' map again."

Lester and Dirck sat at the edge of their chairs and leaned over the crumpled map with its many markings.

"You say you were hereah today when you spotted tha' blood?" Dirck nodded. "She might have headed over to Hortonia or Craftsbury Township now. Many farms out in them parts. Let's see now...there's the Fairfax Farm, Ira Lowell's place, Lyndon Township Farm with John Malcolm, and Greg Swathe's farm place out theyah," Lester said pointing to blank spots on the map.

"You are just out of smell shot of that dog here in Clova'. You need to get ova' to this area, right hereah."

He circled his finger around the town of Hortonia.

He looked at Dirck.

"You be in the war then? You fought for us?" he said. "I have a farm just south of Clova', dairy mostly. You're welcome to my place sometime."

It was uncommon for a local Vermont farmer to make such an invitation to a stranger. He reached out and shook his hand, holding it longer this time.

"Thank you, Lester. Thank you. This is Dru, Dru Vaughan, she's Chauncey's trainer, also a veteran. She knows the dog, but we don't know how Chauncey would react to being alone in the woods with the dangers, the animals, no food," he said hoping for more ideas from Lester.

"Coyote dogs are danga', yep. And in these parts, them gray wolves are around this time of year. They are wicked smart, more than them smaller prairie dogs."

Silence surrounded the table as they pictured his dog encountering coyotes and wolves.

"But I can tell your dog is a smart one, and she protect herself good." Lester's furrowed brow told them he wasn't certain.

He took Dirck's hand. "I hope you find your dog soon, sir."

The strategy had now changed and they had new hope. But there were new fears that she'd been attacked. The thought of her injured, alone, or even dead in the forest overwhelmed Dirck.

In the Swathe's kitchen, Dirck's smell had disappeared and Chauncey had fallen asleep, weak and uneasy. At 4 p.m., she was jarred awake by stomping boots.

She was glad to see the farmers again. Gregory looked her over. Her wounds were healing well. He gave her another shot of antibiotics and steroids and smoothed her bites with fresh ointment. Chauncey loved the farmer's attention.

For dinner, Gregory cooked a hunk of beef brought over by his neighbors at the Lowell farm. He dropped in yams, cabbage, carrots into a skillet. She was at his side, watching her meal being cooked. It was better than anything she had ever tasted. She devoured two helpings.

"Greg, she's a real beaut. Where'd you think she come from?" Grace said. "A dog like tha' wouldn't be loose about. Wonder what her name is?"

"Yep, she's a special girl. Somethin' right keen 'bout her," Gregory said.

He had noticed the way she would sit quickly at attention, her alertness when he walked toward her, her smooth, purposeful gait, her steady, strong eyes.

Chauncey lay on her back with her legs open to Gregory.

"Yep, she's a special one, she is," he said as he stroked her belly.

Chauncey looked up at him trying to understand. She knew the kind man would help her. Help her find Dirck.

As Gregory stroked her, she closed her eyes and dreamed of Dirck. She could feel his strong hand on her, his low and soothing voice talking to her. He seemed so near. She slept through that night, dreaming she was lying next to him in their bed.

At five the next morning, Gregory and Grace were back up for another day. Chauncey stood. Her hind legs were improving.

This morning, maple sausage, cabbage, and eggs were on the menu for everyone. She was at the stove again, now a favorite place. She ate ravenously. The food was gone before Gregory could even look back.

"Look, Grace. She's eatin' good and standin' good, too. Looks like she's on the mend for sure," he said. "Let's take her out to see the other animals. She'll like that. Help her to walk."

The spring sun had just peeked over Blair Mountain, casting warming fingers across the farm.

A mix of powerful new smells welcomed Chauncey as she followed Gregory toward the dairy barn.

He opened the large paddock. An overwhelming stench of cow dung filled her nose. Several cows were standing behind steel bars. One saw the dog and let out a long moo, its breath steaming into the cool morning air. The cow pushed its muzzle through the bars and stuck out his thick pink tongue at her. She crouched onto her front paws with her rear end in the air, her tail swinging freely. She barked.

Gregory and Grace laughed at her as they worked the milking machines. Chauncey particularly enjoyed the horse paddock where Gregory groomed and walked the big animals she had never seen.

One young mare bent its long neck over the fence to her. She loved the Swathe farm.

After the morning's outing, she collapsed back to her spot by the kitchen stove. Gregory laid his hand on her back as she slept. He was beginning to love this dog.

He would keep her if they couldn't find her owner.

14

Dru and Dirck were back at the map. Lester Lincoln had been right: they should start searching in Hortonia Township.

They'd start at the Fairfax Farm, then over to Ira Lowell's place, the Lyndon Township Farm, and finally drive out to the Swathe place.

The farms were all rural and sat within the vast state forest that ran back through Riverdale where they had started their search. It had been five days since the Vermont State Police had alerted them and two days since the hunter Cornthwaite had seen Chauncey. Someone, somewhere must have seen her or heard something.

At the Lyndon Township farm, John Malcolm told them about coyotes the other night.

"Yep. Out in tha' direction, there was a bunch of them coyotes howlin' and yelpin' in the fields. A real ruckus tha' was. Them males were fightin' each other, but tha' not normal," Malcolm said.

"What's in that direction?" Dirck said as he pointed out to the woods beyond the Malcolm Farm.

"Farmer Giles's place, but he's not here, mother's been sick and he's away for a time," Malcolm said. "Then, there's the neighbor 'bout one or two mile down from here—Greg and Grace

Swathe's farm." He was pointing in another direction at the woods. "'Bout three or four miles ova' in Hortonia way theyah."

Hortonia was a small village with one small post office, town hall, and diner. They stopped for sandwiches at the diner and asked for directions to the Swathe farm. It was one mile south on old Route 10A, along a dirt road.

Gregory Swathe had finished his morning milking and returned to the kitchen.

"Gracie, can you finish my chores in the horse barn this afternoon? Have to go ova' to Craftsbury for feed. Think I'll take the dog with me, give her companionship. She seems to be doin' good now," he said. Grace agreed.

Gregory drove the five miles to Waterman's Feed and Seed in Craftsbury. Through the half-open truck window, Chauncey's nose filled with the early summer smells of Vermont. They reminded her of her first ride home with Dirck over two years ago. As they approached Craftsbury, Dirck was on her mind.

Inside his feed store, Paul Waterman saw Gregory lead in a dog.

"Get a new dog, Greg?" Waterman asked. "She's a beaut."

"Yep. Dog was hurt in my field few nights ago…coyotes after her. Let them know who's boss. She's a good companion. Reckon I'll keep her 'till we find the owner," Gregory said.

The dog looked vaguely familiar to Waterman. Several days earlier his clerk had put up the poster of a missing service dog. But by now, the board had now been covered with local notices and flyers from people looking for work and he didn't connect the poster to Gregory's dog.

Greg walked Chauncey to the back of the large store. An older woman came upon them. She knelt to Chauncey.

"Hey, sweet girl. How 'ya doin'?" Chauncey sat at attention, staring at the woman. "Look at that…she's well trained. She didn't even try to jump on me," she said.

"Yeah, we saw tha' too. She's trained real good. A smart girl," Gregory said.

He was proud of his companion.

Gregory poured himself a coffee and sat on one of the old stools, stretching out his legs. He was tired from the four hours he had already worked that morning.

He unlatched Chauncey's leash, which he had fashioned from a horse strap. She lay next to him, her head up, taking in the new sights and smells. The feed store was quiet.

Five minutes passed. Gregory dozed off.

A customer came through the front door. A rushing wind delivered smells down the aisle. Chauncey sprang to her feet, her head pointed toward the door.

She bolted down the aisle and out the door. In the street, she stopped, pointed her nose to her left, and ran out the main road toward the woods beyond.

By the time Gregory had woken and run into the street, she was gone. Paul Waterman and two clerks were out there, yelling for the dog.

Thirty minutes passed, then an hour. She was gone. Gregory Swathe returned to his farm, thinking she might be headed there.

Dirck's scent was now distinct. Chauncey sensed it had come from the farmer's house, but she'd have to re-enter the woods to reach it. It was midday. Coyotes would not be out and it was warm this early summer day.

The pain from her wounds was blunted by the drive to find him. And he was close. The Swathe farm was a straight-line east, two miles away. She entered the edge of the woods at the Craftsbury-Hortonia Township line.

Grace Swathe was on her way out to the grain silo to check its levels but turned back when she saw the car approach.

Dirck stepped out of his car and extended his hand.

"Hello. I'm Dirck Hansen. This is Dru Vaughan. Have you seen a dog here? She was lost and alone in the woods, and we're…"

Grace cut him off.

"Yes! Yes…we found a dog…a beautiful blonde girl, about fifty pounds or so. My husband Greg rescued her from them coyotes a week or so ago. He went ova' to Craftsbury Common Township couple hours ago for seed. Took the dog with him."

He stared at Dru, his eyes wide. He couldn't believe the stroke of luck. He pulled out the poster.

"Was she a Golden Retriever that looked like this?"

"Yep. That's the dog all right."

"That's wonderful, ma'am…she's my service dog and I need her."

"Just knew somethin' special 'bout tha' dog when I seen her," Grace said. "She was injured but Greg fixed her up good and she's betta' now. Took her ova' to Waterman Feed and Seed in Craftsbury. Off route 4A in Craftsbury Township," Grace said as she pointed to a spot on the map.

They thanked her again and raced to Waterman's Feed and Seed. Dirck had his dog back!

Chauncey stopped and pulled in the warm air. Dirck's scent had suddenly vanished.

It took Dirck and Dru less than fifteen minutes to reach Craftsbury. They spotted Waterman's Feed and Seed and ran into the store expecting to see his dog. A young woman approached them.

"I'm Dirck and this is Dru…we are looking for a dog that was here with the farmer Swathe," he said.

"Oh, yeah, Greg Swathe. He was here with a dog earlier, but it took off after something," she said. The dog ran out and down the road and into those woods out there, I think. Greg lit out after it but he hasn't come back. That was a time ago, over an hour."

He stared at the woman in disbelief. They ran outside.

The familiar cry was again heard. "*Chauncey!*" Dirck yelled toward the woods. But again, no response. They ran toward the woods. Their initial hope had again given way to the familiar desperation.

From his cellphone, Dirck called the Swathe farm but there was no answer.

"Chauncey must have smelled me when we were at the Swathe farm. It's all that makes sense. We need to get back there," Dirck said.

They raced back to the Swathe farm.

For the past hour, Chauncey had been zigzagging through the woods, trying to locate Dirck's scent.

She was growing weak and was now famished. There were the familiar smells of the forest—chipmunks coming out of hibernation, fresh sprouts of mushrooms, juniper and pine. Then a new powerful scent wafted past her. Fresh meat, off to her left. Maybe that was the farmer's house and Dirck might be there. She ran in the direction of the meat smell.

It was a path that took her farther from the Swathe farm, towards Hortonia town.

At the Grafton Farmtable Restaurant in Hortonia, cooks were preparing the evening meal service. Alongside the restaurant, a truck had pulled up for the week's meat delivery.

Chauncey walked out of the woods and spotted the truck.

The back doors were open. Two men were carrying large sides of beef and boxes of sweet sausages through the back door of the restaurant. The truck sat empty for a moment.

By the time Dirck and Dru arrived back at the Swathe farm, Gregory had returned.

"Mr. Swathe—my name's Dirck Hansen and this is Dru Vaughan," he said but didn't offer his hand. "We understand you had my dog Chauncey. What happened to her? Where is she?"

Dirck was trying to remain calm but was furious that his dog had escaped while in the man's care. Gregory recounted the story beginning from the night he rescued the dog until she ran from the feed store.

"We reckoned she might have smelled you and lit off after your scent up here. That was ova' three hours ago now," Gregory said. "Don't rightly know where she headed except back here, I reckon. Tha' dog is special. I could see how it behaved."

"She's my service animal. I'm an Iraq War vet with PTSD and I need my dog with me!" he said and at that moment, realized how much he needed her back.

Dirck took one of his t-shirts he had brought and put it out in the Swathe's back yard along with a chicken Gregory had cooked for her. She would surely catch the smells. They sat in the Swathe's living room and waited. Several times, he thought he heard his dog barking in the distance. But after several anxious hours of drinking stale coffee, Chauncey didn't return and they left in darkness.

Dirck couldn't imagine what lay ahead for his dog.

15

Frustrated by the continued close calls with Chauncey, Dru hired a tracking dog from FINDFIDO, the best in the business, that had located hundreds of lost pets.

Before she started FINDFIDO, Jan Hill had lost her own ten-year-old Labrador Retriever and hired a tracking Bloodhound to find him. Her Lab had been missing for three weeks but it had taken the Bloodhound only thirty minutes to locate the lost dog over fifteen miles away deep in the woods.

Dru wished finding Chauncey would be that easy. She had been missing for a year. She called Jan Hill.

"Jan, this is Dru Vaughan from CAS. I need your help. You remember the dog Chauncey? She's one of my special service animals, the young Golden Retriever that we think had been stolen. The dog had been spotted recently up here in Vermont. But now we've lost track of her again. It's super important. Chauncey belongs to one of our vets, Dirck Hansen. He needs her back."

"Dru, good to hear from you. Yes, I've followed the story on the news. Where did you last lose track of her?"

"The dog was last seen in Vermont, over in Craftsbury, headed toward a farm in the next town over, Hortonia. She must have smelled Dirck, and we thought she was headed there. But we can't locate her now. This all happened just yesterday afternoon."

"Okay, let me get ahold of my team and we'll get something moving for you, pronto."

That afternoon, Jan called back.

"Dru, I'm sending over two of my best trackers. A brother-sister team. They're super good. And you're in luck—our hound Rufus just finished a job," Jan said. "He'll be on the case, too."

Rufus was the famous Bloodhound that had tracked three notorious criminals in high-profile cases in North Carolina and Tennessee before coming to Jan Hill's company in New York. At FINDFIDO, the young Hound had found over fifty lost dogs, some missing for nearly a year.

"If any dog can find Chauncey, Rufus can. He's amazingly sensitive…he can distinguish one smell in a trillion," Jan said. "And he's super smart about lost dogs…he'll find your girl, I'm certain of that."

The following afternoon, two dog trackers, Billy and Lizzy, arrived at the Clover Hotel.

The Bloodhound lumbered out of the van and began sniffing the ground. Dirck knelt to the dog. Rufus's long floppy ears and saggy face made him look sad but he could tell the dog was eager to work.

Rufus looked at him and let out a loud blubbery *ruff*. He cupped the dog's head in his hands and stared into his droopy eyes.

"You'll find my girl, Rufus. I know you will," he said.

"Hi Dirck and Dru, I'm Lizzy Norse and this is my tracking partner, Billy. He's my twin brother," Lizzy said.

The pair were not young, maybe in their mid-fifties, but they were energetic and fit. They looked official with matching fatigues, heavy boots, and red vests embroidered with **FF TRACKER**.

"Thank you, thank you for coming so soon," Dirck said.

Lizzy looked at Dirck. His eyes told her everything. Dark circles rimmed his sunken eyes. The man beamed a profound sadness. She'd seen the face before but never this bad.

"This is how we're going to work," Lizzy said. "First, we need some recent material Chauncey had come in contact with for Rufus to get her scent. A blanket, towel, anything recent."

"I'll get ahold of Farmer Swathe in Hortonia where she'd been for a few days," he said.

He dialed the Swathe's number.

"Greg, this is Dirck Hansen. We have a tracking dog here in Clover who's going to try and find Chauncey. We need anything she had been in contact with. A blanket, clothing, anything you have. Bloodhound needs her scent."

"Yep. Got a quilt and small towel she was on. Tha' has good smell on it…I'll drive them over now.

That evening, Chauncey's search strategy was launched. They all sat in the small Clover Hotel lobby hunched over a crumpled map marked with many dots with different colors and notes.

They told the trackers they had no idea where Chauncey had been the previous seven months before pinpointing her last known sightings. She considered the timeline when Chauncey escaped last May from the meadow in Woodsdale to recent sightings. Dirck went through the sequence.

"Most recently, she was last seen with a farmer named Gregory Swathe over here in Craftsbury at Waterman's Feed and Seed," he said and pinpointed a spot on the map. "Then, she ran out of the store down this road here and into the woods toward Hortonia, right here."

Dirck drew another mark on the map. He was animated.

"I went to the Swathe farm to search for her. She would have picked up my scent and headed for it, but we then drove to Craftsbury, not knowing she had headed back to the farm. She would have crossed paths with us. My scent must have disappeared when I was in the car. She's got to be out here, somewhere still looking for me…she's just got to." He stared down at the map, almost seeing Chauncey running across it.

Lizzy and Billy compared the map with government topographical maps to get a sense of distance and elevation and the size of the surrounding forest.

They considered the terrain, the temperature of the last days, and the dog herself. They knew Chauncey was one of Dru's dogs, that she was smart and loyal. They thought about the other wildlife that the dog might encounter in the wilderness.

They spent that evening forming a detailed search plan, taking in every aspect of the search world. As the known sightings seemed close to their search area, and given that it was summer—the best time to track. Lizzy was hopeful that Rufus would find Chauncey by the next day.

The search might finally be over.

"Let's let Rufus settle in and get a sense of the area. We'll set out at first light," Lizzy said. They checked into the Clover Hotel, Rufus in tow.

At five the next morning, Dirck and Dru waited in the lobby. Dirck had slept only three hours but it was from excitement of the search.

Lizzy and Billy came down dressed in bright orange fatigues and backpacks. Rufus lumbered down the stairs behind them wearing a yellow halter with large black letters reading **TRACKING DOG**. The Bloodhound looked clumsy and haphazard but they knew he was a steadfast tracker.

They met at Waterman's Feed and Seed in Craftsbury Township. It was now 6:15 a.m. and Paul Waterman was opening his store for the local farmers. Inside, Dirck looked around, almost expecting to see Chauncey walk around the corner. He approached Paul.

"I'm Dirck Hansen. You remember me. It was my dog that was with Gregory Swathe and that ran from the store. We've brought a tracking team to find her."

"Yep, I was there tha' day, I rememba' the dog," he said. "Greg was sittin' ova' theyah on tha' stool with the dog lyin' next to him easy like. But she bolted out through the front door. Went out to the street and down tha' road and toward those woods. Don't think it had a leash."

Lizzy and Billy stood in the middle of the road, talking between themselves, looking at the map, pointing in one direction, then another, checking the woods with their binoculars. Rufus sat at their feet. They knelt to him. He knew it was time to work.

"Let me have that quilt," Lizzy said.

Lizzy brought the fabric up to Rufus. The dog took on a serious look and pushed his wide wrinkled snout into the quilt and back out, back in. He bellowed a throaty *ruff*.

"Rufus…find. *Find*," Lizzy commanded.

It was up to Rufus now. The hound jerked off to his left into the store, his long ears and sagging skin flapping as he jerked his head about, his nose aimed to the ground.

"*Find*, Rufus," Lizzy repeated.

Rufus lumbered through the store, back to the street, paused mid-road, and lurched left down the road toward the town's line.

He had found the scent. Lizzy and Billy followed. The dog trotted onto a field, climbed through a fence, and ran to the edge of the woods. He paused and sniffed the air and let out a knowing howl.

Dru and Dirck were behind them. Lizzy turned back to them. "You need to stay behind and let us work on the track. We'll call your cellphone when we have a direction."

Dirck wanted to follow them. Chauncey could be in those woods and she would smell him but they drove back to the Clover Hotel and waited.

It was 2 p.m. when his phone finally rang.

"Rufus found Chauncey's scent over here in Hortonia—pinpointed it at the Grafton Farmtable Restaurant. We're not sure where it goes from there. You need to get out here," Lizzy said.

They sped to the restaurant and spotted the team next to the building in a small driveway. What had Chauncey been doing here?

"Rufus tracked her to this spot, but he wasn't able to regain the scent from here," Lizzy said. "I took him back into the woods but he kept returning to the same spot, right here, in this driveway. He's never wrong. Chauncey was here. But we're not certain how long ago or where she went from this point."

Dirck went to the restaurant and tried the door but it was locked. He banged on it. A girl appeared.

"We're closed until five, sorry," she said.

He waved his arms. "Open the door. *Please.*"

The girl unlocked the door and he explained their situation and asked her to let them bring the Bloodhound inside.

Rufus wandered through the restaurant sniffing the tables and walls but sat back and looked up at Lizzy.

It was clear Chauncey's scent was not in here.

At this hour, the restaurant's manager was home. Dirck called him and put the phone on speaker.

"Sir, this is Captain Dirck Hansen. You may have heard about my missing service dog, Chauncey. We recently hired a professional tracking hound that just picked up her scent outside your restaurant. We believe she might have been here a day or two ago. Did you or your folks see anything? A dog?" he asked.

"Yes, I heard about your dog, Captain. But we didn't notice anything. We are a small place and I would have noticed a dog about. You say it might have been outside our restaurant?" the manager said.

"Yes. Our hound tracked her to a spot just outside your place, to the left of the back door in your small driveway there. Don't think anyone would have taken her," he said.

"No, not likely. Folks in these parts know about you and your dog. Was on the local news. Thought Greg Swathe had her."

"Yes, but she got away and we tracked her here next to your restaurant," he repeated.

"Well, let me think. You say by the back entrance? In the driveway? Well, we do get food deliveries there and we had a meat delivery a couple days ago, but I don't know how a dog would…"

Dirck interrupted him. "A meat delivery?" He looked at Dru.

"Yes, they come here every week or two to deliver our beef and chicken and sausages. Company out of Boston. But not sure how that might help."

"Thank you for this. We'll be in touch." He clicked off the call.

"Could she have gotten on a truck and taken off?"

"That doesn't seem likely," Dru said. "She wouldn't go somewhere that wasn't safe. Seems impossible that someone didn't spot her."

Lizzy shook her head.

"Get the name of that meat company. You need to track them down."

Dirck called back the manager and got their name and contact—Rowland-Boylton Meat Company in South Boston. He dialed the number given him.

"Rowland-Boyton," a man said.

"My name's Captain Dirck Hansen. We received your name from the manager of the Grafton Farmtable Restaurant in Hortonia, Vermont, where you made a delivery a few days ago. We need to talk to whoever was delivering that day. It's possible they may have driven off with my valuable service dog inside the truck's cab," he said.

The story sounded preposterous to the man.

"Yes sir, let me check the roster. Let's see…two of my men, Wayne and Jeremy, were on the Farmtable job couple days ago. Let me page them and I'll call you back," the man said.

They waited outside the restaurant. Rufus was slumped on the ground, his big head on his paws. He looked sad that his track had gone cold.

Dirck's phone rang.

"This is the manager at Roland-Boylton. You just talked to our dispatcher. I spoke to the two men who delivered our meat at the Grafton Farmtable up in Vermont. They didn't see a dog the day when they delivered. I even called the meat warehouse in Boston where they unload. Spoke to Petey, our man unloading the truck that day. He didn't see any dog when they opened the truck's doors. I'm sorry. I have two dogs myself. I hope you find her."

He clicked off his phone.

"I can't understand this. We were so close," he said.

Lizzy and Bill and Rufus had no other recourse but to pack up and return to FINDFIDO in New York.

Dru and Dirck stayed behind in Clover, but they found no further leads.

16

Chauncey's mouth was watering. The sides of beef and links of sweet sausages were irresistible. She had made it undetected into the truck's open cab. Links cascaded from a half-open box of sausages and she reached up for one. As she was working on a second sausage, she heard were voices from outside the cab. She hid behind a large crate.

"Okay, Jack, see you next week. We'll bring those chickens for you then," a man said.

A rattling metal chain and a loud bang startled her. The daylight at the back of the truck disappeared. She barked but nothing could be heard from inside the heavily insulated truck.

It lurched forward.

Wayne and Jeremy set the truck's GPS for their destination: Rowland-Boylton dispatching butcher in South Boston. As usual, the trip would take about four hours from their Vermont location, and this serene, warmish summer night, it would be a leisurely journey—the sunroof open, job done, no worries.

But the dog trapped in the back was in trouble. Inside the refrigerated cab, the temperature had dropped to twelve degrees, and Chauncey's fur had been partly shaved. She struggled to stay warm. Then, she began to feel sick and vomited. The open box of sausages had spoiled and she had already eaten two. Again and again, the truck slowed and stopped then lurched forward as it traveled the long miserable miles inside the dark freezing cab.

When the truck finally stopped, Chauncey had been trapped sick and shivering in the freezing cab for over four and a half hours.

A loud metallic clanking filled the cab and bright light flooded inside. Two men pulled down a large ramp and walked off. She crept to the ramp, looked both ways and bolted down the gangway. She was inside a large warehouse with a large open bay door. She ran undetected out the building and into a street.

But where was she? It was night, but everything around her was bright and noisy with cars and buses and trucks speeding down a busy road. She sniffed the air, but the scents were foreign. The familiar smells of the Swathe farm and the Vermont forests were gone.

Another sudden wave of nausea hit her and she vomited onto the sidewalk. She had never felt so miserable in her life.

People walking by avoided the pathetic-looking lost dog. She collapsed at the edge of a building and tried to sleep.

In the middle of the anxious night, she felt a gentle hand on her back.

"Hey, good dog. You alright?"

The voice was raspy and deep. Chauncey woke to a man sitting next to her. He was tall with a scraggly beard and looked old.

"Are you okay, pretty dog?"

He removed his knapsack and pulled out plastic cup and a bottle of water. She drank three cups.

"Drink the water, good pup," the man said as he stroked her back. "It'll make you better."

The water calmed her. She curled in next to him and slept. The man stayed awake through the night, watching over her. He knew these streets and their people and would protect her.

The morning's sun woke her. Light shot down the streets in strange angles about her. The man was still there, his hand on her back. He looked down at her.

"Hey sweet dog…good morning. You feel better now? You slept good."

He looked her over more closely in the light. Some fur on her legs and back was missing, and in places, bandages hung from her. He could tell she was not feeling well. The man poured her more water. He struggled to his feet and slung his knapsack over his shoulder.

"Okay, friend. You and I are going to my place down the street. You'll be safe there. It's where I'll take care of you," he said, and raised his hand. Chauncey followed him.

The man hobbled down the sidewalk, stopping frequently to rest. Years earlier, he had lost his leg in a car accident and wore a poorly fitted plastic prosthesis.

It was slow going down the busy boulevard and people took a wide path around the old man and his sick dog. She again felt nauseous and retched but not much came out. The man poured more water.

It took them over an hour to walk the six long blocks before reaching a narrow side street. This was Boyton Street, the man's home, a quiet place with no crowds. Along the sidewalk, Chauncey saw dirty blankets, old sleeping bags, ripped pillows, all part of the man's place. He sat down on one blanket, and Chauncey plopped down next to him. A few feet away, an older woman sleeping on a crumpled blanket woke.

"Where'd you get that nice doggie?" she said.

"Found her down the street. She was sick, needed my help," he said.

He looked down at his new companion.

"I can see you're a girl, a sweet one, too. You have some old wounds here. Let me help you out."

He told his street companion to watch the dog and limped away. Chauncey sat at attention on her blanket, waiting for the man to return. The older woman looked over at the dog.

"Hey good dog…you'll be taken good care of by my friend here. He's on the street but he has a heart of gold. He won't let you down."

The man—Jim (Jimmy) Bartles—was just fifty years old, but looked closer to seventy. Jimmy was a gentle man, but time and place had torn him apart. He stood six feet and, although once fit and muscular, was now overweight and bloated. His deep-set brown eyes were worn and sad, eyes that had once been bright and full of promise. Jimmy Bartles had lived in a small Boston apartment with his dog and kept a job with the local butcher but his drinking had escalated and his job and funds ran out. Then his dog had died.

That was over five years ago. Now, almost inexplicably, for the past two years, he had found himself on the streets with little hope left in life. And as life on the streets became more intolerable, alcohol became his only escape, the only thing that relieved his increasing anxiety and pain. But alcohol also compounded Jimmy's debilitating panic attacks and declining health.

It was more misery and heartache than life could throw at any one man.

Thirty minutes later, Jimmy returned with a large bag jammed inside his dirty backpack.

"Tommy in the store let me have this stuff for free. He looks out for me," he said.

He removed a sack of dog food, water, rubbing alcohol and a tube of antibiotic ointment. He immediately went to work on his new dog, removing the dirty loose bandages, smoothing her wounds with ointment. He could see his new dog was hungry and poured kibble into a plastic bowl and filled a glass with water.

"Okay, girl, you have what you need now."

Chauncey devoured the strange food. It wasn't anything she had tasted before but she was famished and finished a large helping of the kibble.

"Guess I need to get my new message out," Jimmy said.

His cardboard sign read:

PLEASE HELP ME, I'M HOMELESS

He turned it over and wrote:

**HOMELESS MAN AND HIS DOG.
ALL ACTS OF KINDNESS GREATLY
APPRECIATED. GOD BLESS YOU**

He propped the sign against the building next to them. Chauncey moved in toward him on her makeshift blanket bed. She was strangely drawn to this kind man, Jimmy Bartles—he was like Dirck and she sensed he needed help.

Later that morning, a tall man with slicked-back white hair came upon them. He wore black trousers and a green army jacket adorned with several medals. He leaned into his cane.

"I'm sorry you are out here on the streets, friend. I was on the streets for a time, just like you."

He pulled out his wallet, and thumbed through several twenty-dollar bills. He folded a stack and handed it to Jimmy. It was two hundred dollars. He looked down at the dog.

"Looks like your dog could use help, too, sir. She's a good-lookin' pooch," he said and produced more bills. Another hundred dollars.

"Protect her. Take good care of her."

Jimmy stumbled to his feet and shook the man's hand.

"God bless you, sir. Thank you, thank you for helping us. My dog and I greatly appreciate it. I'll make sure she eats good."

The man limped away on his cane.

"Guess having a dog doesn't hurt," Jimmy said to his homeless companion.

But Jimmy Bartles knew the dog had lost its home and didn't deserve to be here on the streets. But he just couldn't just let her go hungry or become a stray.

With the cash bonanza Jimmy bought sandwiches to share with his friend and different bags of dog food, the better kind. This time, he also purchased three quarts of Jack Daniels, not an afterthought. But not until he had purchased his new dog more kibble.

The fresh food and whiskey brought Jimmy some relief from his dull days and nights, and besides, it was a nice summer day, and he'd take his new dog for a walk.

He removed Chauncey's dirty macramé collar, washed it in drinking water, and hooked on a new leash he had just purchased. Every afternoon, Jimmy walked her up and down the block, staying close to his spot. He enjoyed his new responsibilities and felt like a good citizen when he deposited her poop in the Boyton Street dog containers but Chauncey didn't understand the small fences around the trees where she otherwise might find privacy.

Here, there were no woods, no big trees, no fields or meadows. Only concrete and buildings. And many people. The strange noises and smells of the streets were unpleasant. But with her new companion, she wasn't in danger anymore and she enjoyed the attention he gave.

On Tuesday nights, Jimmy took his new dog to the local homeless shelter for their free dinner. Dogs were allowed. It was Jimmy's one hot meal of the week, and he shared it with her. They looked forward to Tuesdays, when Chauncey would get extra helpings of beef stew and bread.

One evening, Jimmy purchased a large pizza for everyone. He broke off pieces for Chauncey, who loved the new taste. By the end of their little party, Jimmy had downed an entire quart of Jack Daniels and passed out. Chauncey was alarmed by the man's foul odor, one she had never experienced, at least not from a man.

She could tell something was wrong with her companion and sometime after 2 p.m., she was woken by the familiar cries.

"No," Jimmy screamed. "Stop, no."

Jimmy was in the middle of an alcohol-laced nightmare. He thrashed about on the sidewalk, crying, yelling.

Chauncey recognized the familiar cues and crawled on top of him, licking and nudging his face. He slowly regained consciousness and opened his eyes to his dog. He didn't comprehend what had happened. These attacks would usually leave him anxious for hours, but with this dog, an odd calm had come over him.

She let out a low, soft moan. Jimmy didn't know what it meant or what she had done.

"What did you…how did you know what to do?" he whispered to her.

Chauncey had halted one of Jimmy's panic attacks. It was miraculous to him, something inexplicable even to his homeless companion, who by now had fallen back into her own drunken stupor. He stared into the dog's warm eyes.

She was his dog now and needed a proper name. He would call her "Sati," a name he remembered from a book his mother had read to him long ago—Sati, the Hindu goddess, meant truth and protection.

Chauncey had the right name. And a new home and mission.

17

By early October, Jimmy Bartle's street companion had found space in a local homeless shelter and Jimmy and Sati had the street all to themselves.

The locals who lived on Boyton Street often talked about the man and his dog at their neighborhood parties or afternoon gatherings.

"Every day he's out there, always in the same place, now by himself. And despite his desperate situation, he's always smiling, always saying 'hello to you' or 'have a nice day' or 'thank you for petting my dog' even if you didn't donate money. That dog is really sweet and protects him so."

The locals would often donate money, new blankets and pillows, sacks of dog food, or dinners they had made for the man and his dog.

One late October morning, a young woman came upon them and noticed the dog.

"Sir, my name is Aiko Akari. You have a nice dog…she's beautiful," she said and ran her hand through Sati's fur. It was matted and dirty. "But she needs attention. I was once a dog groomer and I hope you'll let me take care of your dog for you."

Jimmy struggled to his feet and looked at the young woman. Her dark round eyes were direct and honest, her voice soft and kind. Aiko saw the despair in Jimmy's face and a dog in need of care. Jimmy nodded yes.

Aiko Akari became their protector, both for Mr. Jim—as she preferred to call him—and Sati. That day in her nearby small efficiency apartment, Aiko bathed and groomed the dog for over three hours. Sati enjoyed the warm bath and attention. And Jimmy enjoyed the hot meal Aiko prepared for him.

"My father was on the streets for a time. I helped him get back on his feet before he died last year. I worked with the Salvation Army for a couple of years. I'd like to keep helping you and your sweet dog, Sati, Mr. Jim," Aiko said.

She allowed the man to take a shower and she laundered his clothes. It was an extraordinary act of kindness from a stranger.

"I will come by each month to your spot on Boyton and take care of Sati and you, if you let me, Mr. Jim," she said. "You don't deserve to be out there. You don't have to repay me."

Aiko even paid to have Sati checked by a local veterinarian. The dog's hair had evened up and her wounds had healed but after months living on the streets, her health had declined from little exercise and an uneven diet of shelter food, pizza, and cheap kibble. The veterinarian gave them high-grade food and antibiotic pills, but the supplies only lasted two weeks.

Aiko or Jimmy's friends at the shelter or the veterinarian connected the dog to the missing service dog pictured on hundreds of posters throughout the city. They all knew Sati as Jimmy's dog.

That October afternoon, they were both clean and relaxed after visiting their new friend Aiko. Jimmy leaned back against the warm brick building and Sati climbed onto his lap, put her head on his chest and closed her eyes.

Passers-by were drawn to the remarkable scene: a man, alone in the world, living on the street in desperation with his dog, protecting him, giving him a reason to live. The dog didn't distinguish class or race or have want for anything. She only wanted to save the man, give him a reason to live in an otherwise hopeless existence. Sati had given Jimmy more love than anyone had in his entire life.

By late autumn, the nights had grown cold and this winter promised to be unusually bitter. Jimmy was on the shelter waiting list and the week before Thanksgiving, two men approached him.

"Mr. Bartles, James Bartles?" a man said.

"Yes, I'm Jimmy Bartles," he replied.

"We're from the Boston Homeless Shelter Coalition. We have approval for you to receive shelter this winter at the Lutheran Church annex," the other man said.

"That would be most welcome for me and my companion here." Sati was asleep on his lap.

"Well, sir, we don't allow dogs or any pets at the shelter. I'm sorry."

"This is my dog, Sati. Wherever I go, she goes. Give my spot to someone else." Jimmy said and wrapped his arms around his dog.

The two men looked at each other. Why would anyone remain on the streets for just a dog? They thanked him and left.

"I don't go anywhere without you, friend, you know that."

Sati looked up at him with half-open eyes.

Jimmy now worried how he would keep her warm this winter. And by early December, Aiko Akari had taken a new job in New York and was forced to leave Boston. It broke her heart to leave Mr. Jim and Sati on the streets without help.

As Christmas approached, Boyton Street was festive. The white street lamps had turned red and green, strings of lights zigzagged from the small walk-up porches, wreaths hung on doors along the narrow block, and people were gay.

But for Jimmy and his dog, the season wasn't cheery.

For the past several weeks, Sati had lost more sleep trying to help Jimmy stave off his increasing nightmares. And in the past weeks, the infection in Jimmy's leg had spread and he drank more to stop his mounting pain.

On Christmas Eve, without warning, the infection in Jimmy Bartles's leg silently reached his brain, and sometime in the middle of the night, he slipped into a coma. Sati tried to wake him but he didn't respond. The foul odor that rose from him wasn't his fear.

At 2 a.m. on Christmas Day, Jimmy Bartles took his last breath.

In her walkup apartment in front of their Boyton Street spot, Beverly Magee woke to a barking dog. She looked out the window. A dog was pacing around a man lying on the sidewalk. She knew about the man and his dog and would often leave them a few dollars, but she didn't know their names.

She ran outside and knelt to the man. He had no pulse and his face was cold. He had been dead for an hour. The dog paced anxiously about the dead man, whining and barking. She looked at Beverly as if to ask for help.

"Oh, honey, you can't be out here," she said. "Come on, come inside with me to get out of this cold."

She pulled at the dog's collar but it wouldn't move. She ran inside and called 9-1-1. It was 3:30 a.m.

"I don't know the man's name, but I think he's passed away—he's lying in front of my apartment at 949 Boyton Street," Beverly told the dispatcher. "Please hurry. His dog is also on the street alone and it's only five degrees out there."

The flashing ambulance lights had wakened most of the residents along Boyton Street, many of whom gathered in robes across from the gruesome scene.

Medics examined Jimmy Bartles and declared him dead. They laid him on a stretcher and covered him with a sheet.

As they wheeled him into the ambulance, the dog put her paws up onto the bumper and tried to jump inside. Beverly grabbed her collar and led her back to the sidewalk. A paramedic told Beverly to call the Bingham Animal Shelter.

Beverly sat with the panting dog on the cold sidewalk, trying to console her, to warm her, but as the ambulance pulled from the curb, Chauncey broke loose and chased the speeding vehicle down Boyton Street. Beverly ran into the street yelling for her, but the dog could not be stopped.

The ambulance turned off onto the busy parkway.

Beverly called the Bingham shelter and left a message. Not much later, they called back.

"This is the Bingham Shelter. You reported a dog with a homeless man but it ran off? Do you know in which direction from your location on Boyton Street?" a woman said.

"She ran north toward the parkway, chasing the ambulance that took away the dead man. She needed to stay with him, I guess. Happened so fast...I couldn't catch her. She's out here in East Boston somewhere. She couldn't have kept up with that ambulance—I am worried about the poor dog—she's already been living on the streets for months now and is in bad shape. And it's very cold. I hope you can find her."

"We'll send someone out to look. Thank you for reporting it," the woman said.

But after four hours searching the East Boston streets, the Bingham Rescue squad couldn't find the lost dog.

18

By the time the ambulance had disappeared down the four-lane Boston Greenwood Parkway, Chauncey had chased it over a half mile, as far as her remaining strength could afford her. She anxiously watched the ambulance disappear around a curve.

Now she was alone, just one of many homeless dogs roaming the streets of Boston. And the city streets were an unforgiving place for a dog in winter. Temperatures had barely reached five degrees and there were few places for a dog to shelter or find food.

Early morning Boston commuters sped down the wide Greenwood Parkway, swerving around the disoriented dog as it jumped erratically about in the traffic. A woman spotted the dog and pulled over to stop cars in her path. She guided Chauncey to the side of the freeway and tried to comfort her. The woman could see it wasn't well and ran to her car to call for help, but as she turned back, the confused dog ran onto a side street and by the time the police arrived two minutes later, the dog had disappeared.

Chauncey found herself alone in a deserted area of East Boston along rows of old, seemingly empty warehouses. She had not eaten in two days and dire hunger drove her to overturned garbage cans in an alleyway. One had dumped a discarded half-eaten pizza and a stale sandwich. They tasted foul. She curled between two garbage cans to gather some warmth. A voice alerted her.

"Open that door," a man yelled. Large metal doors clanked open.

The warehouse foreman, Tony, jumped off the platform and walked between the two buildings. To his right, something moved. In the shadows of the alleyway, he noticed a dog lying between garbage cans. Stray dogs didn't usually come around here looking for food. He crouched to her and held out his hand. She crept toward him.

"Hey good pup, are you okay? You need some water?" he said. He went to the warehouse and filled a large container.

Tony sat by Chauncey as she drank. He had owned a dog like this one, a dog his family loved, but he had to put it down earlier this year.

"You're a good dog. Why are you out here?" he said as he stroked her back.

Her head hung down but her eyes rose slowly up at him, a look that broke his heart.

Tony could see she was not well. Beneath her twisted fur, he felt ribs and her face looked emaciated. And she was cold. He wrapped his arms around the shivering dog.

Tony thought he would take her home. His wife and young son would love another dog, especially one like this. But his landlord didn't allow dogs. And he wanted her to have a chance, a home.

He called a local East Boston animal shelter.

"East Side," a man said.

"I found a stray dog out here on Chelsea Street, at the Meridian Company warehouses. She is lost and cold, not well. Can you come out here and get her? She needs attention. I'll stay with her until you arrive. It's 201 Chelsea, on the east end along the tracks."

"We'll send out a truck." The man sounded annoyed. It was barely 6 a.m.

Tony knelt to Chauncey. She wore a dirty blue knitted collar but had no identification. She looked like someone's lost pet, a good dog someone had once cared for, but now she was alone and sick. Even in the cold morning air, she was panting heavily and Tony knew she was frightened, maybe in pain. She curled up next to him.

"You're a good dog," Tony said. "We'll get you better and they'll find your owner. I'll help you as much as I can."

Chauncey sensed the man wanted to help her, but fifteen minutes later, a white unmarked van pulled up and two men got out. One held a long pole with a plastic loop. Tony rose to meet them.

"Are you from East Side Shelter?" he asked.

The men didn't answer. They spotted Chauncey. She backed away.

"Yes, we're here to get the animal you called about…is this it?" one man said.

The other man inched toward Chauncey, his pole out. Tony stepped in front of him.

"Hey, that's not necessary. She's gentle. She won't hurt anyone," Tony said.

"We can't let it run off again. Just a precaution," one man said, but the other had already lassoed Chauncey, who jerked violently against the plastic strap.

"Listen, fellas, don't hurt her…she's a gentle dog. She's just lost. Please don't hurt her," Tony said.

The two men pinned the sick dog to the pavement, loosened the noose, and carried her into the van. They slammed the door.

"Please take care of her. She deserves to be treated well," Tony pleaded as they walked away in silence. He watched as the van drive away.

Chauncey slid around the metal floor as the van swerved through the streets. It was dark but at least warm. She couldn't make sense of what had happened. Maybe they were taking her to be with Jimmy. Her mind was growing increasingly confused and her body was beginning to shut down. She was having trouble catching her breath.

East Side was one of several small, low-level nonprofit shelters that took in strays and abandoned animals. Dogs and cats were housed for short periods and euthanized if they were not adopted or if their owners couldn't be found. The facility had six enclosures, but they were nearly full.

The shelter's manager, Roscoe, was on duty when Chauncey was led in by a choke chain. She was shaking and panting heavily. Roscoe wasn't an animal tech but he could see the dog was in bad shape. He weighed her. She was barely forty pounds.

He called for his lead technician, Wanda Wheeler who was in the back examining another dog. Wanda was on loan to other shelters and was one of the area's best animal techs, having trained at the Bingham Animal Shelter, a well-known, high-end animal facility.

She took good care of her animals at East Side but didn't enjoy the facility because of the incompetent leadership and lack of response much of the time.

Wanda carried the sick dog to an exam room. She was having trouble breathing and her heart was racing. Her body temperature was dropping and she had a weak pulse. They gave her a shot of prednisone and antibiotics and let her drink water.

"Dog's pretty sick, but the steroid and antibiotics will help her," Wanda said to Roscoe. "I'll keep a close eye on her."

They put her in a pen and fed her high-protein kibble. She ate some of the food and slept, but by 4 p.m., she had vomited and emptied her bowels.

Wanda found Chauncey lying on the floor, shaking in own feces and vomit. She called in Dr. Abby Kraft, the shelter's lead veterinarian.

"This dog's in shock and her body temp is dropping," Kraft said. "Start her on an IV and push fluids and prednisone. *Stat.*"

Wanda inserted the IV and covered the shivering dog with warm blankets and began massaging her. By later that afternoon, Chauncey had slowly improved and by the next morning, Chauncey had started drinking and eating solid food again. Dr. Kraft cancelled her other shelter appointments that day to care for the sick dog.

"She's maybe about five years old but she's obviously been through an awful lot," the veterinarian told Wanda. "She's probably been on the streets for months now and hasn't been fed well. She has infections and her blood electrolytes are way off. Despite her troubles, she's strong and I can tell she wants to pull through. She has a good spirit. She'll be better by tomorrow when I return. Keep her hydrated and warm tonight."

Over the next two days, more dogs were brought into East Side but the shelter was full and they had to be sent to other area shelters, which were also near capacity. Wanda kept Chauncey on a dog bed in the front office, but it wasn't a safe place for her.

East Side's director, John Pense, oversaw five other nonprofit shelters and ran a tight ship. In the past year, contributions had fallen and staff cutbacks had squeezed services, East Side being no exception.

That week, Pense visited East Side. The shelter was overcrowded and losing money. They risked getting shut down by the state if animals were housed inhumanely. Roscoe showed him East Side's roster.

"When was this dog brought in, this sick one?" Pense asked.

"Couple days ago. They found her on the street in Chelsea," Roscoe said. "She's been pretty sick. Needs treatment but Dr. Kraft's been with her every morning since she came in."

Dr. Kraft normally visited East Side only once or twice a week.

"Well, we can't have that. She's the only veterinarian we have right now. Kraft's services have to be spread out. Have you found the dog's owner?"

"No, our only microchip scanner broke and we don't have funds for a new one right now. The dog is doing better but she's still weak and needs attention."

"Well, in her condition, nobody will adopt her. We have a review coming up in a week—we have to find a way to reduce the population and get things back into the black."

Roscoe knew what Pense was telling him.

"Let me know how it looks when I come back next week," Pense said blankly and left.

Roscoe considered the grim task before him. He re-read the roster.

They had seven dogs including Chauncey. Four had been identified by their owners and would leave East Side that week. Lucy, the small Shetland, had just been adopted by a local couple. An older black Lab had just been transferred to East Side but one of the techs wanted to adopt her.

Then, there was the sick Golden Retriever with no name or owner. She would have to be put down first.

It was too bad. Roscoe liked the young dog—she had spirit and wanted to please. But his job depended on this.

He would take her first thing in the morning.

19

"Wanda! Haven't talked to you for so long," Teri said. "How are you holding up with your shelter rotations these days? We miss you out here."

It was early evening and Wanda had called Teri at home. Teri Pierce was the owner of Bingham Animal Shelter, a high-end facility where Wanda had trained and worked as their head technician. Wanda had left Bingham to take on supervisory duties at the nonprofit shelters in the area.

"Teri, good to hear your voice again. Listen, wanted to ask you about a dog we brought into East Side a couple days ago—she was found out on the streets. A Golden Retriever. Came in pretty sick and Dr. Kraft is taking care of her. I seem to remember one of your techs mentioning a call into your shelter about some dog living on the streets several days ago. Apparently, it ran off and they found her over in Chelsea. Something about the dog seems familiar to me, but can't think of why. Do you know anything about a lost Golden Retriever?"

"Yes, Wanda. I remember that call. Came early Christmas morning. From someone on Boyton. Let me look at the log here. Yes, Beverly Magee called. The dog was with a homeless man who died on her street. Said the dog ran off after the ambulance. What was it about her that seemed familiar?"

"I don't know. She was in bad shape, underweight, malnourished, had infections. She was in shock and nearly didn't make it. Dr. Kraft stabilized her. There's just something about her, something I can't quite explain. She's quite affectionate for a dog that had been on the streets. I don't think she was a street dog at all. She came into us scared and sick, but didn't react aggressively with any of the techs. Didn't act like the other dogs we've seen in such poor condition. It was almost like she was asking us for help…she looked so lost. I suspect she's someone's pet or maybe something more."

"Wanda, wait a minute, hold on, I need to check something." A minute later, Teri returned. "Can you describe the dog?"

"She's a smaller girl, medium gold hair, short snout, shorter legs, probably about fifty-five pounds at normal weight. Pretty face. Despite her condition, a beautiful dog."

"Oh Wanda, could she be the dog that was lost or stolen over a year ago? We have a poster here describing a similar Golden, a service dog belonging to a war hero, Dirck Hansen. About the same stature and size. Her name is Chauncey. She's about four or maybe five years, I think."

"Maybe that's why I remember her—from those posters. They're all over Boston. I didn't connect it until you mentioned it just now. Not sure it would be her."

"Okay, but the main thing is she's safe in your shelter. When's your next shift?"

"Well, Roscoe told me not to come in until tomorrow afternoon. I'll snap a picture of her then and send it to you."

That night, Marie was on duty at East Side. She couldn't face having to euthanize the pretty young Golden Retriever. She walked by Chauncey's pen. She was asleep but raised her head as the woman approached.

"It's okay, girl, just checking on you," she said.

Chauncey continued staring at Marie. She had felt better that day, but tonight, she was filled with deep sadness.

Over the past days, her mind had been clearer and Dirck again appeared in her dreams. How had she come to this awful place so far from the life she had once known, the supremely happy life she had shared with him? She closed her eyes and tried to summon his smell, his touch and voice. But tonight, it was all too far away. Instead, something else loomed in front of her. Something dark and dreadful that she couldn't understand.

At 6:45 a.m., Roscoe walked into East Side. He hadn't slept much. This wasn't going to be a good day. As he donned his overalls and booties, Marie walked in.

"How's everything in the back? Quiet?"

"Yes. The dog is quiet but she feels the tension."

"Well, we need to get this over with. Do you have everything ready?"

"Yes, we're all set up in Room 2."

Roscoe went through his checklist. He was anxious. It had been well over a year since he had to euthanize a dog. But he had to get this over with.

When Marie approached the pen, Chauncey stood and backed away. She opened the gate and knelt, holding out her arms. She relaxed and buried her head into the woman's chest. She felt safe in Marie's warm arms and, for a few seconds, thought she would be okay. But when Marie latched her leash, Chauncey sensed something bad was about to happen and yanked away.

Marie picked her up and carried her to Room 2.

The room's fluorescent lights cast a clinical glare on everything. The blinds were drawn. Marie laid her onto the metal exam table. Chauncey began shaking. She looked at Marie and began to whine.

Roscoe looked at the dog before him. He was about to put to death this young and beautiful Golden Retriever, a dog he imagined once had been vibrant and loved by someone. Now she was alone and filled with fear.

She struggled to get off the table but a sudden sharp stab in her hip made her jump. The injected pentobarbital quickly pulled her away into an unknown blank world.

In her stupor, she couldn't summon any images and she began to panic when couldn't move. Marie inserted the IV line into her front paw. Chauncey could hear faint voices, but they were distant and echoed as if inside a long, dark tunnel.

"Do you have the syringe ready?" Roscoe replied.

"Yes, but let's give her a minute to relax," Marie said.

She didn't want the dog to die, but she had no choice, no way out now. Marie wanted to give the young dog a moment of peace. She bent over Chauncey and whispered a prayer into her ear.

When Wanda woke that morning at 6:30 a.m., she felt anxious about the sick dog at East Side. She got dressed.

At 7:15 a.m., she walked into the facility. It was quiet. Too quiet—something was wrong. She ran back to Chauncey's pen. Gone!

"Roscoe, Roscoe!" Wanda yelled as she ran through the facility. She could hear the muffled voices from Room 2.

She burst in.

Before her on the metal table lay the Golden Retriever under the bright light, her eyes closed. Roscoe was leaning over the dog's IV line with a large syringe filled with an ugly green liquid. He looked up.

"What the hell are you doing here, Wanda? You need to leave. We're performing a euthanizing procedure. Get out."

"*Stop!* Put that syringe down *now*," she yelled. "We know this dog—she's a valuable service animal."

She stepped toward him.

"You don't know that, Wanda. I'm under orders to euthanize these dogs to keep this facility running. Orders from Pense himself. Get out!"

He glared at Wanda, his mouth pursed, and lowered the syringe toward the IV line. Marie stepped back from the table.

Wanda was a large woman, well known for lifting even two-hundred-pound animals off the floor with ease. She came at Roscoe, slamming him against the concrete wall. The syringe flew out and shattered onto the floor.

"You don't get to decide which dog lives or dies," she said, staring down at the man crumpled on the floor.

She turned to Marie.

"Push pentobarbital antidote into the dog's IV line. *Now*!" she commanded.

Marie injected the clear fluid. Within seconds, the dog's legs began to twitch.

Roscoe looked up at Wanda.

"I am going to report this and you to Pense—you'll never work here again."

Roscoe was out of breath.

Wanda ignored him as she continued helping the disoriented dog. Now, Marie was now taking orders from Wanda. The two women were pulling for the dog.

Wanda leaned over to the limp dog.

"You're doing fine, good girl, you'll be okay," she said. "I promise, Chauncey."

Chauncey had not heard her name in over a year. She lifted her head to Wanda in recognition. Her tail thumped the table slightly. Wanda knew she had Chauncey.

Wanda continued barking out orders to Marie. Roscoe stood in the corner of the room, not moving. He knew the woman would stop at nothing.

Marie removed Chauncey's IV and readied her for transport.

"Don't worry, Roscoe. I'm taking the dog off your hands. But your careless disregard will be noted to the review board. First of all, you're not even licensed to euthanize any animal and worse, you were using the wrong drug cocktail for this procedure: you were about to pump enough chemicals into this poor dog to kill a cow, you idiot!"

He stared at the floor.

Wanda lifted the limp dog off the table and carried her to her pen. She locked the door from the inside and sat in the pen, holding the dog in her lap. Chauncey shook as the pentobarbital wore off.

She pulled out her cellphone and called Teri Pierce.

"Teri? Wanda. I've got her! She was in the middle of being euthanized by Roscoe…caught them in the middle of it," she said. "I'll stay with her this morning. We need one of your vans out here with medical equipment. Right away. Alert Dr. Kumari. I'll get her what she needs for now."

"Oh, Wanda, thank you for saving her! I can't wait to see her."

Wanda then called the local animal-care advocacy group and notified them of that morning's events, knowing East Side would lose their license. She was glad it would be shut down. She was sick of the incompetence.

The rest of that morning, Chauncey slept in Wanda's arms. Wanda was her savior now. She was in a good place, a safe place.

At noon, the Bingham animal ambulance arrived.

Dr. Latika Kumari, the lead Bingham veterinarian, examined the dog who appeared disoriented. She was still underweight and weak, but Dr. Kumari could see her spirit was unspoiled.

The dog wiggled her tail as the veterinarian moved her hands across her body to examine her.

"Wanda, let's get her bathed and clipped. I need to examine her skin more closely," Dr. Kumari said.

Wanda and another technician bathed and clipped her. The remaining infections and wounds were treated. Chauncey was fed a raw diet and vitamins. That night, she slept over twelve hours in her spacious warm pen. She had been malnourished and exhausted for months.

Early the next morning, Teri Pierce arrived at Bingham.

"We examined the Golden Retriever brought in yesterday. She's just over five years old based on her teeth and bone structure," Dr. Kumari said as she looked through the dog's chart.

"She had been living for months on the streets with a homeless man and was found wandering around East Boston. The morning they picked her up, it was nearly zero degrees. She was in shock and came close to dying. She was malnourished but we're taking care of that. She's strong and will come back," the veterinarian said. "She's an impressive dog. And well trained. When we finished her bath, she grabbed one of our hair brushes and handed it to the tech. I've never seen a dog do that."

"Yes, we think she could be the service dog missing for well over a year now," Teri said, and handed Dr. Kumari the poster.

"Well, the dog they brought in was thinner and her hair was matted, but that could be her," she said. "Hard to say right now."

They walked back to the facility. Chauncey lay curled in her bed. She didn't wake.

"She's been out for hours. As soon as she's had more rest, we'll scan her for a microchip," Dr. Kumari said.

Chauncey slept that day and into the next morning. Her vital signs stabilized. Dr. Kumari spent the next day treating her with antibiotics and steroids. With the high-grade raw diet, Chauncey's weight climbed to fifty pounds.

"She looks so much better," Dr. Kumari said. "I really like the way she's walking and actively reacting. Let's get her scanned."

They lifted Chauncey onto an exam table. She looked curiously around, her tail wagging. This was a happy room, a place she felt safe. She licked the technician's hand as the woman moved the small scanner across her shoulders then back down to her loin. Nothing. She aimed the scanner along the back of Chauncey's neck.

There was high-pitched beep and a bright red light. A hit. Chauncey looked back to see what all the excitement was about. The reader displayed *ID2432-2225-43* and the phone number of the registry. The chip was registered in New York. Teri called the number.

"New York State microchip registry," a woman answered. "May I help you?"

"This is Teri Pierce at the Bingham Animal Shelter in Massachusetts. A dog was brought to us with one of your chips. Could you please reference it for me? It's 2432-2225-43. A female Golden Retriever, about five years of age. Super important."

"Just a moment. I'll check our registry database," the woman said. The phone was silent for almost five minutes before she returned.

"Yes, Ms. Pierce, we found the ID match. The dog is named Chauncey and registered to Dirck Hansen of Glenriver, Vermont. Mr. Hansen is a veteran and the dog is a registered service animal from Canines Assisting Soldiers in New York. We have an alert in the file that's been active for several months. This dog has been reported missing since October of last year. There's a substantial reward for her return."

Teri was stunned. They had found Chauncey! And she was a service animal from CAS, a place Teri knew as one of the top training facilities in the country. She reread the poster.

STOLEN SERVICE DOG—FEMALE GOLDEN RETRIEVER THREE YEARS OLD. ANSWERS TO "CHAUNCEY."

THIS IS A VALUABLE SERVICE DOG BELONGING TO A WAR VETERAN. THERE IS A $6,000 REWARD FOR HER SAFE RETURN. NO QUESTIONS ASKED.

CONTACT DIRCK HANSEN AT 802-444-3393 IN GLENRIVER OR DRURY VAUGHAN OF CAS AT 380-880-2209.

There was a close up of the dog's head. She could see it was Chauncey. The six-thousand-dollar figure had been crossed out and overwritten with eight thousand dollars and a signature by one of her staff members. Several months ago, at Dirck's insistence, they had increased the reward.

Teri ran back to Chauncey's pen and opened the door. She looked at the dog's face. It was fuller now. The same as in the photographs. She backed up, turned around, and clapped. Chauncey stood.

"Chauncey! Come, girl," Teri called as she held out her arms.

Chauncey's ears perked forward and pranced to Teri, happy to hear her name again. Over the past year, Teri had seen the TV spots and read the news articles about the decorated war veteran, and his service animal. She was elated she had his dog safe in her facility.

Teri spent the day with Dr. Kumari going through the dog's medical plan. In another day or two with medications, Chauncey could go home.

Her hands shook as she punched in Dirck Hansen's phone number.

20

After Chauncey's trail had last gone cold at the Grafton Farmtable Restaurant in Hortonia, Dirck had driven the four hours down to the Boyton-Rowland Meat Company in Boston. He showed up in his officer's uniform. They weren't expecting him.

"I'm Captain Dirck Hansen," he said to the man at the desk. "I want to speak with a man named Petey."

"Yes, sir. He's in the back. I'll get him," the dispatcher said.

A young slender man wearing a bloody apron walked out of a side room. When he saw the uniformed soldier, he froze.

He walked up to the young man.

"Petey, I'm Captain Dirck Hansen. I understand you unloaded the truck that arrived from The Grafton Farmtable last June."

Petey remembered being questioned about the service dog. He had told his dispatchers and manager he hadn't seen anything. He didn't want to get fired but he knew a dog had been in that truck.

He could see the stress in the man's eyes but also his resolve.

"Oh yes sir. Yes, I was one of two men unloading that day. I did see half-eaten sausages and blonde dog hair in the back of our truck. I cleaned up back there—didn't want to get in any trouble."

"Did you see a dog run out? Anything you could tell me about where she might have gone?"

"No sir. I didn't see the dog but it had been in there for sure—those sausages were chewed up pretty good and looked like a dog had made its bed on one of the tarps in the back of the truck…may have run out to the street out there," he said and pointed at the large bay door. "I wish I could help you find your dog. I know how much you must need her."

Petey had a dog himself, a pet that he loved. He had seen photographs of Chauncey from the poster in the front office and it bothered him that the dog had been caught inside his truck. But he couldn't offer the man anything more.

Dirck now knew his dog was somewhere in Boston. The next day, he returned to Vermont, packed some clothes and posters and rented a small apartment near the meat company.

He stayed throughout the summer and into the early fall, searching the streets, putting up posters about the city, talking to anyone who might have seen a Golden Retriever.

But after three months questioning people on the streets, contacting police and businesses, and hanging over three hundred posters throughout Boston, no leads surfaced. He had even questioned some of the homeless people in the area, but they were suspicious of anyone asking questions for fear of being arrested or their makeshift homes being disrupted, and they stayed silent.

He never went to Boyton Street.

In November, Dirck returned to Vermont, again without his dog. But now, he had reached a dangerous tipping point and was drinking more and taking more narcotics. His mind grew more chaotic.

He felt like his first drill instructor, Kelly Bradford, a man who later in life had taken a job at the World Trade Center Building One. When the first plane hit on September 11, intense fire forced Bradford out his office window and he fell one hundred agonizing stories to his death. Dirck was now at that point, on the edge of living or dying, only one way out.

In a narcotic- and alcohol-soaked stupor, he would often call Dru in the middle of the night, shaking with fear and rage, afraid to sleep.

"Chauncey is the only reason I haven't killed myself yet…I don't want my dog to end up with someone else. She's all I got. Fuck this PTSD!"

The erratic phone calls became more frequent with talk of suicide. Dru knew he was desperate. She called Robert Telly who returned with his dog Tippy, the German Shepherd he had first met. But the dog only reminded Dirck of Chauncey and worsened his mood, and, as winter approached, he refused to continue their visits. And Dirck grew increasingly angry with Dru's continued suggestions that she bring him another dog.

At night, he lay awake for hours thinking about Chauncey. Was she happy somewhere? Was someone mistreating or helping her? Maybe she had been attacked by wolves or other predators and was dead. He began to doubt whether he would ever find her again and began thinking how he might memorialize her. A burial in the backyard with her toys? Planting a tree in remembrance of her?

At Christmas, Dirck spent a week at CAS with Dru and Dave Ballard, Chauncey's main trainer. Being where Chauncey had trained and once lived lifted his spirit a bit. She introduced him to a young female black Labrador Retriever, Sparks. But the dog sensed the man's profound sadness and didn't want to go near him. And he didn't even want to touch Sparks. Being around the dog worsened his mood. He felt like a lost dog himself. He returned home alone.

Dirck's nightmares of battle horror had become more violent. One night, he woke in his dark room, but the bedroom itself had become the battlefield spread out endlessly before him.

At some point early that morning, he stumbled downstairs and poured himself coffee with some whiskey. It was still dark. He sipped the warm liquid, staring out his kitchen window into the black void. He began thinking about his gun.

His cellphone buzzed. UNIDENTIFIED NUMBER showed on the screen. Only to shift his attention, he answered the call.

"Yeah?" he mumbled.

"Hello? Is this Mr. Dirck Hansen?" a woman said.

He hesitated. "Yes. I'm Captain Hansen," he said, wanting to ward off any advertisers with his title.

"Captain, my name is Teri Pierce and I'm the Director of the Bingham Animal Shelter in Bingham, Massachusetts. We have located your dog, Chauncey," she said straight out.

He dropped his mug.

"You what? You have…Chauncey? How do you know it's her?" he said, doubting any of what he had just heard. "Who is this again?"

"Captain, I am Teri Pierce. I'm the Director of the Bingham Shelter near Boston. We are certain we have your dog. She was identified from her implanted microchip. It's definitely your service animal, Chauncey. She's fine, a lovely girl."

He looked out his kitchen window. It was pitch-black and freezing but beautiful.

"Oh dear God…you found her? I've spent over a year looking for her!"

He brought his hand up to his face.

"She's being well cared for and is safe in my secured facility. She's lost some weight and has had infections but she's strong and coming back quickly. She'll be healthy enough for you to take her home within the next day or so."

"Yes, *yes*! I can come tomorrow morning. Would that be okay? If she needs a bit more attention, I'll stay down there and visit her."

"Yes, Captain, that's just fine. Chauncey will be so happy to see you. I've followed your story over these many months. We all look forward to meeting you. Bingham is just three hours south of you in Glenriver. It's right off Route 2. I'll text you our location."

The rest of the conversation was taken up with details of when and how they had found his dog, how she looked, how she acted, what treatments she had received. But all Dirck heard was: *We found your dog!*

He almost didn't want to end the call, knowing Chauncey was on the other end with the woman.

He took another drink: straight whiskey this time, a toast to Chauncey and raised his mug into the air.

"I'm coming for you girl," he said and took a long, warm swallow.

21

Jackson Stoney—"Jax" as his few friends called him—arrived at Bingham Animal Shelter to start his assigned night shift. He was filling in for Amanda, the regular night tech who was away for a month's training.

It wasn't a job he had wanted or even liked, but he had taken it after being out of work for over eight months. Being unemployed pissed him off because Jackson considered himself smart, even clever. This job was just another means to one of his money-making schemes. Tonight, though, he'd have to get through another boring night shift.

At 6 p.m., Jackson met with Dr. Kumari and Teri to go over the instructions for the six dogs in her facility.

"The Golden Retriever in Pen 8 is a valuable dog. I need you to pay particular attention to her and check on her throughout the night. She's under treatment and must be given the utmost care," Teri said.

Jackson nodded at her. There were detailed instructions for Chauncey in his log. Steroid ointments and antibiotic capsules every six hours, water bowl filled, no food after 9 p.m.

They walked through the facility and came upon Chauncey. She was asleep.

"Under no circumstances should you move her unless it's an emergency. And then, you call me on my cell. My number's in the log."

He listened as he blankly flipped through the log.

"Yes, ma'am. I'll make sure she gets good treatment," Jackson said.

They left and by 7:30 p.m., he was alone. As was his custom, he sat in Terri's front office on one of his many long breaks throughout the night. Just another monthly paycheck. He didn't particularly care about the animals at Bingham, let alone the special dog.

He lazily swung about in Teri's swivel chair, his feet up, drinking coffee and smoking. He leaned over to snuff out his last cigarette and noticed the large poster on her desk. It was for a lost dog and it had photographs of a Golden Retriever. He looked more closely.

"This is the dog we have here. Six thousand…no, wait, *eight* thousand dollars!" he said under his breath.

He wasn't sure he had read it right. He stood up and read it again.

"My God! Eight thousand dollars!" he said out loud. "We have this dog in the back!"

This would be more than enough to clear his mounting debt and back rent. Maybe even buy a new pickup truck.

And this might bring him a particularly large windfall. For the past two years, Jackson Stoney had been stealing dogs to breed in an illicit puppy mill scheme.

Right now, he had one dog in his outdoor pens, a young female black Labrador he had stolen several weeks ago from his neighbor, a local farmer. But with this new dog, the Golden, he had hit the jackpot. He'd receive a hefty reward, plus she'd make babies for a good price. But maybe the dog was spayed. It didn't matter, really. He'd still get the eight grand.

But he'd likely need help to somehow pull this off. He called Ryker Falls.

Ryker Falls was a thirty-something, down-and-out tradesman who had been on his own for most of his life. He had never known his mother, and his drunken father had abused the boy, who from an early age had bounced between foster homes, detention houses, and shelters before running away the year he had turned thirteen. He was a broken, angry kid. Even as a young man, he had racked up a nasty police record, mostly misdemeanors: heroin possession, petty theft, assault, and vandalism. But later, burglary and armed robbery landed him in prison for ten years.

The year after his release, Falls had met Jackson at a local bar and ended up partnering with him on his nefarious jobs, most of which had failed. Even as an uneven young man himself, Jackson had been unnerved by many of Ryker's disturbing behaviors, particularly his cruelty toward animals. Last year, they had been caught stealing puppies from a breeder in Pomponoosic in northern New York, and when the authorities had found several small mixed-breed pups in Ryker's house, they discovered two had been burned with hot pokers. Ryker Falls later characterized his punishment as "putting them in line" when the animals didn't behave the way he wanted them to. Jackson owned a dog, a mutt named Buller, and couldn't comprehend anyone mistreating a dog.

"Hey Ryk. Jax. Listen. We can get some easy money. I have a special dog here that's worth a bundle."

"Jax, hell yeah, man. Whatcha got?"

"I'm at the Bingham now. There's a valuable dog here in the facility. Eight-grand valuable. They're willing to shell out the money for her return. The director and vet are gone now, coming back in the morning. I can get the dog out to my cabin sometime after midnight but need your help. Can you meet me there in a couple hours?"

Ryker was irritated by having to cut his drinking short, but money was involved and he agreed to meet.

"I'll be there. Got any beer out there?"

It was 9 p.m. and Jackson was ready for his rounds. As usual, it was quiet in the back, especially this time of night. He spent an hour checking the animals, making notes in his log. Just for show.

At the end of a long row of enclosures, he came upon Pen 8. Chauncey was asleep in the back but heard Jackson and raised her head.

In the dim light, Jackson could see the dog in profile. Her head was noble looking, almost regal. And despite her uneven fur, she was impressive. She stared at the man outside her pen. He looked unsteady.

"I see why they want you, doggie. You're a fine lookin' pooch," he said. "You'll make pretty babies for me."

He pulled out his cellphone and took a picture of her. For the reward.

But Jackson was uncertain how he was going to get her out without trouble. He knew they kept treats in the facility. Those might lure her, he thought.

But that was the extent of his scheme. How would this all play out? He worked at the shelter and was about to take a valuable dog for a reward. They knew his number and where he lived.

He completed his chores and returned to the front office. He needed more time to think through the scheme, but after another hour of more coffee and cigarettes, he was still uncertain.

It was midnight when he finally decided on a plan.

He grabbed a harness and leash and liver treats from the storage shed. He reached Pen 8. His presence again alerted Chauncey. She sensed uneasiness in the way the man was moving.

Jackson unlatched the door and pulled it open. He knelt before the dog and held out his hand with the dried liver.

"Come on, girl, you want some nice liver treats?"

Chauncey loved liver treats. But her mind was on the man before her.

"Let's have some treats, come on," he urged, his voice wavering.

He put the treats on the floor and backed up. Chauncey stared unblinkingly at him, not moving.

"Come on, doggie, come." He then remembered her name from the poster. "Chauncey, come."

After a year of mistreatment and abrupt, uncertain turns in her life, Chauncey had developed a distrust of people, something unnatural for her and her training. She sensed a clear threat before her and backed away. Jackson moved to her right along the next chain-link enclosure.

Other dogs sensed the uneasiness in Pen 8, particularly Arko, the large male Rottweiler in Pen 9. Arko wasn't having any of this. He crept up behind Jackson and erupted with deafening barks. Jackson jumped away and landed on the floor.

Barking exploded from the facility.

Jackson backed out of the pen and ran to the front office, his heart pounding. He tried to calm himself from the unexpected turn.

He had to find some way to get this dog out without alerting anyone. After an hour, the barking had subsided and he went back.

Jackson opened Chauncey's pen and walked toward her more certainly holding a harness and leash. The pen was large, twelve by six feet. She backed up. He stepped in, unsure of how close he should get. Barking again erupted from the other pens.

"Chauncey, come. Just going for a little walk." The barking intensified.

He stepped in closer. Chauncey's head lowered and her muzzle wrinkled. She let out a deep chesty growl. He knew the dog was serious. He'd have to find another way. He went to the storage room and picked up a small crate and a blanket.

For a third time, he opened Chauncey's pen, dragging the crate behind him. This time, Chauncey came toward him, her eyes wide, ears flat. Jackson backed away but tripped on the blanket and fell back, grabbing onto the chain link fence. Arko was there, waiting. The Rottweiler ripped deeply into his hand as he violently shook his powerful head from side to side. He twisted about, his hand inside the dog's powerful churning mouth.

Arko released him but not before inflicting serious damage.

"God *damn* it!" He screamed, clutching his hand and rolling on the floor.

In the desperate seconds that followed, acting purely on adrenaline and desperation, Jackson got to his feet and cast the blanket onto Chauncey, catching her head and part of her body. He lunged at her, but miscalculated the dog's speed. She pivoted and pounced on him, forcing him onto his back, her powerful barks blowing onto his face. For a smaller dog, she was strong and commanding. He knew she would immobilize him and remained still. From the next pen, Arko watched him, wanting another shot at the man.

Jackson brought his boot up underneath Chauncey's stomach and pushed back hard. She catapulted away and slammed into the pen's fence, stunning her. It afforded him a second to sling the rope around her neck and he pulled back, jerking her sideways. She let out a sharp yelp. He grabbed the edge of the small crate and jammed her head-first inside.

He closed and locked the gate. Any reserve strength Chauncey had was gone and she stopped moving.

The furious barking had reached a deafening crescendo in the enclosed facility. Jackson knew this would alert the Bingham neighbors and especially the police. Bingham was known to be quiet. He had to get the dog out. Now.

He picked up the heavy crate, dropping it at the back door and ran to his truck. His right hand exploded in pain. *I'll have to get shots for this goddamed bite*, he thought as he backed the truck to the door. He hoisted the crate over the bed and drove off, leaving the other animals behind and taking Chauncey without her medications.

It was 1:30 a.m., and Ryker Falls had already been at Jackson's cabin for over forty minutes. His cellphone rang.

"Ryk…ran into trouble. One of those fuckin' dogs bit me bad. But got the valuable one in the truck. Be there soon."

He dropped the phone and floored it.

The drive took twenty minutes. The air had dropped to ten degrees but in the back bed, the wind chill was five below zero. Chauncey came to consciousness and found herself jammed painfully inside the crate in the numbing night air. Her crate jostled about as the truck sped through the turns.

By the time Jackson reached his cabin, Ryker was outside pacing, angry as usual, yelling at him. Jackson jumped out and into the cab bed. They lifted the crate out and carried it behind the cabin.

The entire area lit up from motion-detection floodlights. Jackson's six chain-linked pens sat empty except for the far one where a black dog was curled up with a blanket.

They opened the first pen nearest the house and dragged the crate inside. Ryker unlatched the door and pulled Chauncey out. She was awake but stunned. She backed away and stared up at the men. In the bright white light around them, their black eyes and pale skin looked sinister. Ryker stepped forward and kicked her flank.

"Take that, you goddamned dog," Ryker said as he grimaced.

Chauncey yelped.

Jackson grabbed the man's throat.

"Ryker, if you hurt that dog, we're not gonna' get that eight grand. Damn...don't be so stupid, you bastard," he said through his teeth and pushed the man against the pen.

He stared at Ryker's sullen face. It was incredulous to him that any man could be cruel to any dog. Especially this one. Despite his nasty bite and the considerable trouble he was now in, Jackson felt remorse about stealing and mistreating the Golden Retriever, and at one point during the night, he wasn't sure when, even considered returning her to the Bingham shelter.

"She's already injured, asshole," he said.

Ryker stared at him. He knew Jackson could hurt him. He had in the past. But this all only intensified his already considerable anger.

Ryker had already injured the black dog, who knew not to make a sound, especially when she heard the man's high-pitched voice. The dog lay still in her pen, awake, her eyes tracking the man's every move in and out of the far pen.

Jackson knew the night was headed toward zero, too cold for the dogs to be outside in their pens, and moved two smaller, insulated doghouses into the pens, loading them with more blankets.

"That should help," he said as he considered the two dogs. "Don't want you girls to get too cold tonight."

Inside the cabin, Ryker was already drinking beer, reading the copy of the reward poster Jackson had brought.

"You need to take the poster to your place and do the calling from there and arrange for the reward. Put the Bingham number on your phone," he said. "I'll send you my snapshot of the dog. Once they know we have her, we can collect the money and give them what they want."

But beyond these few sketchy ideas, the plan was unclear.

Ryker went home for the night. Jackson returned to the pens to check on the dogs before heading back to Bingham. Both of them had climbed inside their smaller crates, burying inside the blankets. He looked at Chauncey.

"Keep warm pup. We'll be back to get you, and you'll be home to your owner soon. You'll be okay," he said.

Chauncey peered out at him from her crate. The man's voice sounded calm but deceptive.

As Jackson sped his truck back to Bingham, he kept thinking about Ryker kicking the dog.

He began to regret bringing him in on this caper. Somehow, he knew the whole thing would go south on him and then he'd be in a far worse place than just plain broke. He slowed the truck as he considered calling him back, telling him the dog had escaped. He'd just take the dog back with him. Start from scratch.

But eight thousand dollars was difficult to argue against. After all, how hard could this all be to pull off?

He kept going.

By 3 a.m., the dogs at the facility had calmed down. In the facility's back treatment room, Jackson rummaged through veterinarian's supplies, trying to find a way to ease the angry bite on his hand. The Rottweiler had hit bone. His entire hand was badly swollen with bright red halos around punctures that were oozing fluid. He poured alcohol over the bite and smoothed ointment on it but he knew he would need treatment. Likely a tetanus shot. What about rabies? Another goddamned thing to worry about.

But mostly, Jackson dreaded facing Teri Pierce in just a few hours. He didn't yet know what he would tell her.

As the night wore on, he began fabricating stories as he tried to calm his fear.

Chauncey was lost. In the eerie silence of her icy prison, she tried to orient her compass, but this latest twist had thrown her into a dark and faraway place. She lay buried beneath blankets and stared out into the endless shower of brilliant, tiny stars spread across the clear night sky. They reminded her of home, of Dirck.

Another dog's soft cries alerted her.

22

Teri Pierce arrived at Bingham earlier than usual. It was 6:30 a.m. The temperatures had barely climbed above zero degrees. She couldn't remember a more bitter morning.

But as she approached the facility, she knew the day would be warm and joyful. Dirck Hansen would be reunited with his beloved service dog Chauncey after her disappearance over a year ago. Teri couldn't wait to witness the reunion.

But as she stepped inside, her facility was strangely quiet. Her office was in disarray. On her desk, the poster was gone and some papers had drops of blood on them. As she took off her coat, she spotted Jackson Stoney walking toward her from the facility back. He stopped. He hadn't expected her this early.

"Mornin', Jackson. How's it all going?"

There was some alarm in her voice.

He was looking down and his hair fell onto his face. He smoothed it back and looked up at her. His eyes widened.

"Ma'am, um, something happened last night," he began. "Can't quite understand or explain how it happened, I mean, I wasn't sure how…" He trailed off. He had rehearsed this story for hours but it wasn't coming out right. Not at all.

She dropped her coat. She *knew* it had something to do with Chauncey.

"*What?*" she blurted out.

"That dog, that gold one, Chauncey I think is her name. Well, she escaped."

His words hung in the air between them.

"*What the hell…*" she said and stepped toward him.

Jackson didn't look at her.

"Um, well, she was whining and crying and I just took her outside for a short break, just to calm her down and let her relieve herself and all. And, well, she pulled the leash away from me. Took off after something."

He cringed as heard himself recount the preposterous lie. But he hadn't thought of a better one. It was all that he had.

"You took her *outside*? What in the *hell* possessed you to do that? I told you to leave her in her pen, Jackson!" Her voice was shrill and wavering.

"Ma'am, I'm sorry. I just thought…"

He stopped, not sure of what he thought.

Teri slammed her fist down onto the desk. She was shaking.

"You thought *what*? Good God, man! That dog is extremely valuable and her owner is a decorated war veteran and he's on his way here now. I told you to leave her in her pen, *goddamn it!*"

Teri shoved him aside and ran to the back of the facility.

Pen 8 was closed and other than the lone blanket lying on the concrete floor, it looked as if no dog had even been inside. She stared at the empty pen in disbelief.

In Pen 9, Arko, the Rottweiler looked up at her and barked.

She knew something had happened in here. She ran to the exit and opened the door and yelled back to Jackson.

"Get the hell out here and show me where she went."

Jackson walked out and pointed to the woods off to his right.

"It was dark but I saw her run out right about there," he said as he pointed vaguely to the edge of the woods about one hundred yards out across the long snowy field.

"When did this happen? What time was it when she got away?" she said. She was near tears.

"I guess it was around four or so this morning. Don't remember. I didn't look at my watch," he said nonchalantly and shrugged.

His eyes projected remorse. But something darker.

"Why didn't you call me when this happened?

He had no answer. His senseless lie was expanding rapidly. Without an answer, she ran out into the freezing morning air toward the woods, in the direction that Jackson had pointed. She yelled back at him.

"Did she have a leash on her?"

"Yes, she would have," he said, knowing she did not. He hadn't thought about that either.

"You should have called me *immediately*. Now we are unlikely to find her!"

She stood in the snowy field, rapidly running through her options to make some sense of the situation. Dirck would arrive soon and she would have no reasonable explanation for him.

She ran inside to phone the police. It was a small town and the Bingham Chief, Johnathan Perry, was a good friend. She asked him to get some of his men out to search for the dog. Perry had served in Vietnam and had come out of retirement to serve as the town's police chief. He knew about Dirck Hansen and wanted to help find the now-famous service dog.

It was barely 7:30 a.m. when Dirck Hansen pulled into the parking lot. This morning, he had worn his Army dress uniform and service visor cap. His dark-green jacket was decorated with gold bars signifying his Captain rank. Pinned in the center was his Purple Heart, the medal Chauncey had worn on her service vest.

The trousers were starched and crisp. He looked impressive. He sat in his car, giddy as a child.

He walked into the facility carrying a limp lamb toy. His heart raced.

Teri Pearce waited in the front office to meet him. She stepped forward and held out her hand.

"Captain Hansen. I'm Teri, Teri Pierce. I was the one who called you about your dog, Chauncey and…"

She stopped, her lip trembling. He took his hand back.

"Is everything okay? Is she okay?" Dirck said almost knowing what might come next.

"Captain, we had a mishap last night. My night tech took Chauncey outside for a break and she apparently pulled her leash away from him and ran into the woods," she blurted out, not wanting to sugarcoat any of it.

It sounded preposterous. And underneath it all, somehow, Dirck knew he would lose his dog again. And now it was true—she was gone. Again. He dropped the toy lamb and stepped toward her. His eyes narrowed.

"How in the *hell* did she get out? Where is she now?" he said. "Christ, Teri, how did you let this happen?" He wanted to grab the woman's neck.

She stepped back.

"I have two police officers searching the woods now. It's not certain why she would have just run off like that. Chauncey knew she was safe here. It doesn't make any sense," she said but knew none of this was helping. They went to the back of the shelter.

"Perhaps if she can smell you, she'll come back—let's go out where she ran off, out here."

She was trying to appease him but nothing could lessen the man's growing heartache.

On their way through the facility, Jackson stepped out from a side room and stopped.

"This is Jackson Stoney. He was the tech on duty last night," Teri said.

Dirck didn't extend his hand. Jackson was staring at the ground, his hands buried in his pockets. The body language was unmistakable.

"Jackson told me Chauncey just ran off when he took her out for a break, pulling the lead away from him," Terri said to him, as if Jackson wasn't even there.

Dirck glared at him. Despite his clean white jumpsuit, the man looked uneven. His brown eyes were soft but sat in shadows of deceit. He stepped toward Jackson, backing him against the wall. Teri was afraid he would grab him.

"I…I'm sorry, sir, I know the dog meant a lot to you. I never meant to let her out of my sight," he said softly.

Deception beamed from him. But he meant what he had just said—he regretted taking the veteran's service dog.

Jackson's hair fell back onto his forehead and he reached up to smooth it away, exposing his right hand. It was badly swollen with deep puncture wounds that oozed fluid. Dirck had seen bite marks on prisoners from the K9 service dogs in his unit. This one was fresh.

"How'd you get that nasty bite, son?" he said.

Jackson grabbed his hand. *Fuck!* he silently cursed to himself. He hated himself for this mindless act—stealing and mistreating the man's service dog, locking it perilously into an outdoor pen in freezing weather—and now, unable to explain the obvious dog bite, he knew he would pay for his ill-conceived scheme, somehow.

As the army captain stared at him waiting for answers, he should just tell him what he had done, where his dog could be found, even take him there himself. He looked down.

"Uh, oh, that's a nip I got from my dog. He, I mean, I had to separate him from another dog who came into my yard," he said holding onto his hand.

"That's a lot more than a nip. You're gonna need shots for that bite," Dirck said as if to extract the man's confession.

Teri broke in.

"Let's go to the back of the facility."

They walked outside. Teri indicated the direction Jackson had pointed. She looked at him.

"Do you believe his story? Teri asked.

Dirck didn't acknowledge her. He was facing away from her like a statue, staring into the still woods. He knew this feeling well, the despair of staring into an empty landscape where his dog had just been. The feeling was just as strong as that day over a year ago when she vanished in Riverdale Recreation Park.

He didn't know if he could stand any more grief.

She didn't know how to console him. There probably was no way to.

Then his expression changed. He turned to her.

"This man, Jackson Stoney. How long has he worked for you?"

The question surprised Teri. She hesitated but wanted to help him.

"Mr. Stoney. I hired him as a temp. One of our best techs was out training for a month and I needed someone right away. I checked one of his references, which was fine. He was hired for the night shift, when there's not much to do. But I obviously made a mistake."

The reference Jackson had given Teri was Ryker Falls who claimed he managed a facility in Virginia and had hired him as an animal technician and that the man's work was fine. But Teri never verified any of this—another careless mistake. This one could ruin her career.

"Do you know where he lives? When is he off duty? Can we get his contact information? Just in case we need it."

"He has a place in Stanton ten miles from here. I have the address. A rural route. He goes off duty in an hour but I'm going to let him go now."

Teri knew she shouldn't release anyone's personnel information but it was all she had to give Dirck and, at this point, she didn't care about possible consequences. She wrote down Jackson Stoney's address and cell phone number.

"I can call you when we get some word about Chauncey. The police hired a couple of trackers to search for her. At least it's sunny this morning," she added vaguely.

Without a word, Dirck held out his hand as if he had never met the woman. His eyes were awash with grief but his face was hard and determined, a look that frightened her.

He turned, almost in a military about face, and walked out the facility door to his car. He turned the key and slumped over the wheel.

Minutes later, Teri told Jackson to leave and not return. That was fine with him. He had to get back to his dogs. He sped his pickup truck out of the parking lot, the tires spinning on the ice.

He didn't notice the car following him.

23

It had fallen below zero in the night. Chauncey remained balled up beneath blankets inside her small crate but couldn't sleep. Since her arrival at this new place, she had heard the quiet cries of another dog, the dog that knew not to arouse attention.

Over the past month since coming to this place, the young dog had been beaten, and she knew to keep silent when anyone was there, especially the man with the distinctive high-pitched voice.

Chauncey climbed out of her crate to the edge of her large pen and let out a sharp bark. The other dog came out of her crate. They were both less than twenty yards from one another. In the bright moonlight, they could clearly see each other through the chain-link fences.

The dog was black, somewhat larger than she. Chauncey barked again. The two dogs came as close as they could to the edge of their pens, staring at each other. Chauncey wagged her tail—she had a new purpose, an important mission.

The black dog was a four-year-old female Labrador Retriever named Callie. She had once been a strong young dog with all the heritage of her sturdy working forebears—a powerful build, a broad noble head, and a deep, gentle mouth. But she had been locked in this prison for many weeks now with little food and exercise and appeared gaunt, a shadow of the dog she had once been.

Jackson Stoney had stolen Callie over a month ago from one of his neighbors, a farmer who worked a night job. In the middle of the night, he had lured the man's pet dog away with treats. This time, he hoped to breed the black Lab with his own dog, Buller, a large mutt who lived with him. He thought puppies might fetch one hundred fifty dollars each, if that. But he didn't have the proper facilities to breed dogs or much knowledge of how to care for newborn pups.

Chauncey paced around her pen, examining the metal struts and wire mesh. She focused on her pen's front door. It had a horizontal latch held in place by a vertical bar next to it. There was no padlock.

Chauncey had seen this latch before at CAS and most recently, at the Bingham facility. Dave Ballard, her trainer at CAS, had shown her how to open this type of latch. And just a few hours before, she had seen Jackson Stoney lock the gate.

She jumped onto the pen's chain-link door, nudged her nose under the metal hinge, and pushed it upward. The hinge lifted and the door swung open. Chauncey dropped to the ground.

A triumphant bark echoed out across the yard. She ran to Callie, who was at her pen door, inches away, her tail swinging wildly at the prospect of freedom.

But her door was latched with an unlocked heavy padlock. This would be harder to open. Chauncey jumped onto the door and pushed her nose around the large lock but it was too heavy to nudge away from her end. Callie watched her new friend move the heavy lock and jumped up onto the opposite side, copying her. Their noses touched one other as they maneuvered the lock from opposite sides of the pen door.

They inched the large padlock up and out. It thumped to the ground. Chauncey pushed the latch up and the door swung open.

The two freed dogs danced about each other like triumphant woodland wolves in the night.

In the cold hour before dawn, a deep orange glow broke through the frozen blue sky. Chauncey barked brightly at her new companion and they both ran with abandon into the woods.

In front of them lay a vast wilderness with unknown dangers.

24

Jackson was worried. He had aroused enough suspicion at Bingham and now his swollen hand was beginning to hurt like hell. That, and the dogs had been out in below-zero temperatures all the night before.

As he turned onto the dirt road leading to his house, he looked into his rearview mirror. Nobody was behind him.

Dirck was just out of view. This would be a search-and-rescue mission, a stealth operation. He knew the man had his dog. There could be casualties. Unlike Jackson, Dirck was prepared for the unknown. The unknown drove him.

Jackson sped his truck down the driveway to his cabin, which sat nearly one hundred yards off the road, but he hadn't noticed the car behind the trees at the driveway's edge.

Dirck watched him from the camouflage. At the far end was a cabin, but he couldn't see much else. From his glove compartment, he pulled out his binoculars and his eight-inch MK3 Navy Knife, a weapon he had used in close combat. Since leaving Iraq, he had carried these items, especially this past year when he believed he was under attack from an enemy here at home.

He raised the binoculars. Jackson was running around, waving his arms, disturbed about something. Dirck waited.

He knew being in the open would carry his smell to Chauncey and she might start barking. He looked again. Now, he couldn't see the man. Maybe he was in the cabin. His dog might be in there. He had to get to her. Now.

Dirck pulled out slowly and into the man's driveway. He floored the pedal. His V8 Subaru accelerated down the driveway, reaching the cabin in five seconds. He cut the engine and coasted away from the entrance.

He dropped out the car door and rolled onto the ground, crawling toward Jackson's cabin, his knife in hand.

He heard a bark but it was high-pitched from a dog he didn't recognize. He couldn't hear Chauncey. She would bark if she smelled him. Maybe his girl was hurt down in the man's basement and anger rose in his chest. But he had to remain calm. He crawled to the cabin's edge and pressed against it. He'd take the man by surprise.

Inside, he could hear Jackson yelling. He peered up to the edge of the window. The man was pacing the floor, cellphone to his ear.

"Shit, Ryk…did you come and get the dogs? They're *both* gone. Pens are wide open…they escaped!"

Dirck knew someone else, someone not there, was involved in this scheme.

Jackson threw his phone at the wall. He looked out the kitchen window and saw a car parked near his cabin. He dropped to the ground and crept upstairs for his loaded hunting rifle and then inched down into his basement.

Balancing his rifle in one hand, Jackson lifted one side of the cellar door to peer outside. But he miscalculated its weight and the huge steel door slammed down.

Dirck dropped. He was by the man's front door, but the loud bang came from his left around the other side of the house. He recognized the sound of a storm door.

He crawled toward it, but Jackson had already walked away from the house into the adjacent woods. He circled around to the other side. The two men were walking in opposite directions around the cabin toward the same point.

Then they saw each other. They were thirty feet apart.

Jackson shouldered his rifle and fired. Bullets spit on the frozen ground around Dirck, who swung around and ran to the other side of the cabin. He had to be within ten feet of his opponent.

Unprepared for the other man's moves, Jackson twisted about erratically while Dirck ran diagonally to his left into the woods, disappearing under the cover of his green-and-black uniform.

He dropped and crawled toward the house, his eyes trained on Jackson who was now frantically running in the back yard, shooting into the woods where he thought the man was hiding.

Dirck picked up a branch and hurled it to his right. Jackson turned toward the sound, his gun at his shoulders. He looked as if he were stalking an animal, unaware of the danger immediately in front of him. Dirck remained invisible, half-crouched.

"Come out, asshole…I know you're there," Jackson shouted. "I can see you." Another shot rang out.

Dirck moved in closer. Jackson looked around nervously, his rifle up. Where was the man?

From the hidden shadows of a tree, Dirck sprung and slammed Jackson to the frozen ground. The stunned man rolled and righted himself. The veteran stood in front of him, crouched, the knife pointed out.

Jackson Stoney had faced danger before. While hunting just a month ago, a large, angry mother black bear crossed his path. The animal had been ten feet from him on her hind legs, arms out, her sharp teeth bared in a menacing growl. Jackson had calmly backed away and walked off, leaving the bear behind.

But now, before him was a combat soldier with a large knife. The man looked stark and inhuman, his piercing eyes focused like an angry animal coming in for a fatal strike. He raised his rifle.

But it wasn't nearly fast enough. Dirck sprang low at Jackson's legs, plunging his knife's blade deeply into the man's right upper thigh, the place he knew would inflict the most damage. The sudden intense pain overwhelmed Jackson and he fell, dropping his rifle. His hands clutched the edge of the knife handle. The man's screams echoed through the still forests around them.

Dirck planted his boot on Jackson's leg and pulled the knife free. The wound bled freely. He had severed his femoral artery. It was a mortal wound.

He pushed the bloody blade up against Jackson's neck and clenched his teeth.

"If you want to live, you miserable bastard, tell me what you did with my dog—now! If you don't, I'll let you bleed to death. You have only minutes to live. We're outside the wire now and you're going to die," he said but Jackson didn't understand what the man was telling him.

Jackson held onto his leg, squirming in intense pain. He was disoriented but knew he would die if he didn't cooperate with the soldier.

"I…I don't know. I had her inside the pen out in back. Put her in there last night. She escaped somehow," he said, waving his hand in the vague direction of the pens.

"She and another dog, a black dog."

Jackson's head dropped. Dirck removed his belt and drew a tourniquet onto his leg. In the man's cabin, he found an empty pail and filled it with water.

"Drink this. It might help you live."

But Jackson's wound was grave and Dirck was doubtful whether he would make it. He ran back inside the cabin and found Jackson's cellphone on the floor. He dialed 9-1-1.

"9-1-1, what's your emergency?"

"Have a man injured badly out here. Need a response team. Now. Do you have the location from my phone?"

"Yes sir, we show it at 9380 Route 7A out west of Bingham. Are you Mr. Stoney?"

Dirck dropped the phone and returned to the stricken man. *The air temperature is low enough to slow his blood flow—he might make it*, Dirck thought.

He pushed the bloody combat knife back into Jackson's neck. This time it broke skin.

"You better tell me the truth. How long had my dog been here?" he said.

Jackson was crying. His leg burned intensely and he was dizzy.

"Since two this morning...put her in that near pen there." He gestured to the end enclosure. "Put her in the pen and closed the latch...don't know how she got free."

Dirck ran to the pens. Two of the doors were open. He walked into the first enclosure. Inside was a carrying pen and a smaller doghouse with a blanket. He picked up the blanket and brought it to his nose. *Chauncey!* Her familiar smell made his heart ache. Another pen was open with a padlock on the ground.

"What a good girl!"

He knew Chauncey had opened those pens. Her training had helped her. She had freed herself and the other dog from these men. But where was she now? He held her blanket to his face. It gave him new hope.

In the distance, he heard sirens. Medics were approaching. He walked back to the man writhing on the ground.

"You'll likely pull through. Don't care if you do, but don't move. Police on their way. You'll get a nice long sentence for stealing dogs if I don't kill you myself."

He called Dru from his own cellphone.

"Dru, we thought we had her, but she was stolen from the Bingham shelter, probably for the reward. Out here in a rural cabin near Bingham. She was locked in a pen but escaped—she opened her own pen and another with the black dog," he said like a proud father. "I think she'll find that internal compass of hers, that map she's always had in her head. She'll head north toward Vermont. We need to get the tracking team and find her." He was barking out orders as if in battle.

"Oh God, Dirck…let me think. Where are you now?"

He pulled up his phone's GPS.

"Longitude is -72.5778415…latitude 44.5588028."

"Let me get the FINDFIDO team on the phone. I know Lizzy and her group were on a job somewhere in Upstate New York. Let me coordinate and I'll call you back," Dru said.

"She can't be that far away, Dru. Looks like another dog had been in there. They must have run off together, maybe sometime this morning. Can't be too far. It's only ten now."

But after he hung up, Dirck realized the dogs had been gone three or even four hours, and they could be anywhere by now.

He sped down the driveway and careened his car left onto rural Route 7A.

A wailing ambulance sped past him followed by two state police cars.

25

The dogs moved in a wolfish pack, their brindled coats merging with the fading, dappled shadows as the winter sun sank behind the silhouettes of woodland trees.

They had slipped into a steady routine during the day, trotting side-by-side, purposeful and energized in their new freedom. At night, they hunkered low, less obvious to predators.

It had been six hours since their escape from the breeding pens of Jackson Stoney, and they were thirty miles from the Vermont border. Chauncey's internal compass had kicked in and they were headed north, in a direct line toward her home.

The wilderness had toughened her. She was determined to find Dirck no matter the costs. And she had a new companion to help her.

Jumping logs and running through thickets and brambles had greatly tired the dogs and the winterberries and roots had not sustained their strength. Chauncey knew they had to stay strong out here.

They stopped by a stand of trees that had caught the sun's warmth. Her first spring in the woods, she had watched two female coyotes catch a rabbit and several mice. In the barren winter forest, animals would be foraging. They rested by the trees, watching for movement.

An hour passed. They had fallen asleep but Chauncey was startled awake by rustling near her A cottontail the size of a cat was hopping in the nearby brush, its head down, searching for food. The rabbit moved in closer, unaware of the animal lying in wait.

At the decisive moment, Chauncey gathered herself into one violent lunge and felt the warm, pulsating prize in her mouth. Her years of training never to sink teeth into feathers or fur fell away, and for a moment she looked wolf-like as she tore into the warm flesh, taking in fur and tendon and meat by the mouthful. She let Callie eat most of the rabbit until only its bony feet were left.

The woods were full of animals. Chauncey knew she and Callie would survive.

But something unsettling was in the air. From the northeast, a storm approached. She sensed it would be large and heavy and they were in its direct path. She led her companion to a hollow under a large uprooted tree and they burrowed into piles of drifted leaves.

In the middle of the night, Chauncey woke to moisture on her face. Everything had turned white. Snow fell steadily onto the land like a large soft coverlet, obscuring the dens and burrows and hollows of hibernating animals and everything else about her—stone walls, meadows and fields, creeks and rivers, the boughs of trees adorned with plush white pillows—all becoming their one white world. Now she would have only her internal compass to guide them.

Now, their forward journey had become difficult as their legs pushed against the snow, and the dogs rested frequently in dug ruts.

By the second afternoon, they were exhausted and famished and rested in the shelter of a large fallen tree. Callie had quickly fallen asleep, but Chauncey stayed alert, watching for another meal.

For nearly an hour, she scanned the blank white forest and grew tired. She closed her eyes.

She was startled by the sound of a sudden slight shift in the landscape beyond her striking range. Then nothing. Less than a minute passed. A subtle dark shape was slinking through the white woodland forest. It was moving in.

From behind a tree only twenty feet away, an animal appeared. It was stark and foreign, like a long-legged dog, but not one she had ever seen.

It was a male timber wolf, far larger than the male coyotes she had fought last spring. The large creature smelled the dogs and turned his head. The blackness of the wolf's eyes slowly constricted to pinpoints, revealing a deep gold that seemed to glow within the shadows of his darker face. It was a wild and savage face showing no fear, only a stark hatred of the trespassers.

As the wolf crept forward, his eyes fixed on Chauncey. His sturdy, muscular legs moved fluidly through the deep snow, his thick pelt raised in defense. He stopped and crouched low, his shoulder blades protruding, ready for a strike. They were intruders in his world, and his next prey.

Callie woke and began barking at the sight of the beast. The wolf lowered his head and produced a deep, menacing growl. His wrinkled muzzle was stained with the blood of many kills. Within his own pack, the predator had taken down large bears and elk and wouldn't hesitate with two smaller dogs.

They could back away, but Chauncey knew this would only enrage the wolf. The great beast greatly outclassed them in strength and speed.

Chauncey stared at her opponent with fear but also recognition stemming from some primeval instinct that must have had its origins in the mists of time when they had shared a common ancestor.

To Callie, it looked hopeless and she began to whine in submission. She stayed behind Chauncey, shaking.

But Chauncey's imagination and intelligence along with her formidable training outmatched the primordial creature.

The wolf approached them in a straight path, a path he had been taught in his world from his ancestors, the only direction the solitary animal understood. The wolf didn't have his pack now and would have to attack alone.

Chauncey stood before the animal, half-crouched, her back hock bent, gathered, her tail stiff. Her lips drew back. Undeterred by the smaller animal's threat, the wolf crept steadily forward, keenly watching for the advantage.

Yet unexpected to the creature, the dog began to move in a wide arc to its right. Callie copied her companion, flanking toward the animal's left side.

The wolf suddenly lost its focus, looking to his right, then his left, back right. Chauncey saw the shift in the creature's eyes. He was no longer confident and moved uncertainly and nervously from side to side. He never thought he could be the one hunted. But the wolf was alone and now the one in danger.

They were four feet on opposite sides of the animal now, moving in slowly, cautiously. Callie watched her companion intently. She knew they had to work together. Chauncey lowered on her haunches and sprang into the wolf's hind leg. Simultaneously, Callie dove into the animal's left haunch. The beast screeched, snapping his razor teeth right, then left, but both dogs were just out of its lethal reach.

Against the innocent white backdrop erupted a blur of fur and fang, of blood and rage, for which neither dogs nor wolf could sense victory or defeat.

Chauncey yanked at the animal's right haunch, Callie pulling with equal fury on his left. The wolf tried to pivot but was forced onto his front paws, unable to land a strike.

But the battle was precarious and the large creature snapped viciously close to the dogs.

Chauncey knew it would be over if they let go. They had to take their opponent down

The wolf let out a threatening cry, a long high keening to alert her pack. Callie lost her grasp and went for the animal's throat. But in the second her grip shifted, the animal's right foot was freed, and he came at the black dog with great fury, nearly landing a fatal strike into her face. Callie tumbled away and whipped back to the animal's left haunch, the new strike inflicting more damage. More fury erupted in the chaos.

For a moment, a great calm settled through the white forest. Nothing moved as the ghostly breaths of the exhausted animals rose silently into the frosty air.

Then, in what seemed like long, uncertain seconds, savage cries and violent jerking spewed fur and blood into the white fury pit. Within the precarious and undecided moments, the wolf slowed and then stopped, falling back onto its mangled hindquarters into the growing pool of melting red snow.

The dogs released the great gray wolf and backed away. The animal breathed furiously, struggling mightily to get up, but could not. He raised his nose to the air and let out a long and low baleful wail of defeat. The head of the great lupine beast dropped.

By the virtue of her imagination and prowess, Chauncey had survived in the wilderness, a place where only the strong survived. Over the past weeks, her sight and smell had become acute in the wilds. Even within a deep sleep, she could hear the faintest sound and knew whether or not it signaled peril. She had learned to find food when none was obvious, shelter when there was none.

And now, the basic instincts of her breed, of her ancestors, like this wolf, had become her instinct without any effort or discovery. And Callie had now come to know the wisdom of her new and brave woodland companion, understanding the precarious balance of power in a place foreign to them both. It had been more thrilling and frightening than anything she had ever experienced in her short life.

The dogs ate ravenously, growling amicably as they feasted on the sweet, rich meat. Chauncey knew the smell of fresh blood would alert the wolf's pack and other predators in the barren forest, but for the moment, they rested in the thickening snow, their stomachs full, licking their warm, stained muzzles.

Chauncey stared into the silent oblivion. Her thoughts turned to the big man and young girl, the girl who had called her "Kady" and loved her so. When she had ran away, the young girl's desperate cries had sounded like those of a mother who had lost its child. She thought of her protectors who had saved her from the coyotes and kept her in their warm farmhouse. And she thought about the man, now so far away on the cold city street, the man she had wanted to protect, but couldn't, and he, too, was now gone.

She let out a long, whispery breath into the cold night air and closed her heavy, troubled eyes.

In the darkness, Dirck appeared. She could see him, hear him. *Chauncey, come girl, come to me*, his soothing deep voice calling to her. She could feel his strong, certain hands caressing her back. How she ached to find him!

The snow fell on her face, blurring her thoughts.

Her home was one hundred miles directly north.

26

Dirck waited along a side road as the ambulance and police sped past. They had the injured man. He drove back to Jackson's cabin to search for clues of Chauncey's direction.

Less than an hour had passed before Teri Pierce received a call from the state police.

"This is Sergeant Williams from the Bingham branch of the Massachusetts State Police. We found Jackson Stoney injured at his cabin in Stanton this morning and we see from our records that he is your employee."

"Yes, Sergeant, he was a temporary worker here. He was on duty the night one of my dogs got away. Is he okay?"

"He's in the hospital, injured from a severe knife wound. Would you know anything about that?"

Teri was trying to piece together what might have happened. She was sure Dirck had gone out to Jackson's cabin to find Chauncey.

"I'm not certain," Teri said. "We suspect he stole one of our dogs. It was a veteran's service dog. Belonged to Captain Hansen," she said. "There was an eight-thousand-dollar reward."

She wasn't sure how much information she should give him.

"Did Captain Hansen go out to Mr. Stoney's residence this morning? He mumbled something about a knife attack by someone who said they were 'outside the wire.' That's a military term for being outside a safe zone in combat. We suspect Captain Hansen may have been responsible for this."

"I can't say, Sergeant. I'm not sure of where Captain Hansen went. We had his dog here but when he arrived from Vermont, the dog had escaped, according to Mr. Stoney," she said, trying to steer the conversation away from Dirck.

"Okay. Please let us know if you see or talk to Mr. Hansen or remember anything more."

He hung up. Teri called Dirck's cellphone.

Before she could get in a word, Dirck blurted out "I'm at Jackson's house…getting some idea of where she had headed. I'm going to…"

Teri broke in.

"The State Police just called. Jackson was stabbed and they suspect you did it. They may be looking for you now."

"We need to find Chauncey, Teri. I don't give a damn about the police or some scumbag who was hurt. Our dog trainer Dru and some tracking folks are on their way out here. I'm waiting for them."

Without a response, he ended the call. He ran towards the pens around the cabin and into the woods. He thought he could see dog prints in the snow but realized the dogs had passed through the area before this new thick snow had fallen. It was early afternoon and he was about a half mile into the woods when Dru called.

"I was able to get FINDFIDO and the team with their tracker Rufus. They can meet down there tomorrow afternoon."

"No, Dru—way too late! God knows where she might be by then. Can't we get a team here now? This afternoon? Now?" he said, but realized how far he was from Dru.

"Dirck, I wish we could come out now, but it's not possible. They're coming back from another track."

He ended the call. He couldn't deal with any more bad news now, and as the minutes passed, he became less certain of where he was or what to do next.

He ran into the woods in the direction he thought the dogs might have taken but he was becoming more disoriented. He yelled for his dog but then heard voices behind him.

"Hansen," a man said. "Come out where we can see you."

Dirck pulled out his knife and hit the ground. Ambush! There were two of them, circling him at some distance. He moved behind a tree. They came into sight. Two men with guns.

"Hansen, come out now. We don't want anyone to get hurt," a man said.

He thought it odd for the enemy to know his name. He waited. A man moved five feet to his right.

Dirck sprang from behind a tree and dropped the man, bringing his knife to his throat. The trooper's partner heard him yell and raced to safety of a large tree. He crouched aimed his revolver at Dirck.

"Hansen, drop the knife. Stand up with your hands where I can see them," the one trooper yelled.

But Dirck wasn't dropping his weapon. He pressed the blade into the other man's neck. A shot rang out, jerking his arm back. The knife flew away.

Both troopers stood over the stricken soldier as he squirmed in agony, yelling for his men to disperse.

Under police escort, Dirck was taken to the Bingham hospital to remove the bullet from his shoulder. When he finally opened his eyes, he didn't know where he was. Walter Reed? He had been in another firefight. His men had not rescued him this time. He lay strapped to his bed in intensive care, delirious from drugs.

The next morning, Dru arrived at the Bingham Animal Hospital to meet the FINDFIDO team, a move coordinated by Teri, who knew about their search for Chauncey. Billy and Lizzy arrived separately with Rufus. Teri filled them in.

"Dirck is in the hospital here in Bingham. He got into a skirmish with the state police and was shot. He's okay but doesn't know where he is," Teri said. "He's under arrest because he nearly killed my worker Jackson Stoney, the night who took Chauncey. We're still trying piece that together."

To make matters worse, the search for Chauncey couldn't go forward. After examining maps of Massachusetts and Vermont and given the elapsed time and the huge area where the dogs could now be, Lizzy just shook her head.

"There's just no way Rufus could pick up her scent in this much new snow or even know which direction to start. The dogs could be anywhere by now, even a hundred miles in any direction."

At that moment, Dru lost hope that Chauncey would ever be found again.

She headed to the Bingham Hospital to bring Dirck more bad news.

27

Three days following the ordeal, the Massachusetts State Police visited Jackson Stoney at his bedside. Both Dirck and Jackson had been confined to their beds in adjoining wards, only feet apart.

"Mr. Stoney, I am Sergeant Bishop. We know you had stolen dogs, confirmed by locals whose dogs were taken. We also know you were attacked by one of the dog's owners, Captain Hansen. He's a war veteran who lost his service dog."

Jackson had been thinking of his crimes and of Captain Hansen's attack. He considered the police sergeant.

"What if I don't press assault charges against this man Hansen? Could the charges against me be dropped?" Jackson said. "I'd stop any activity with dog theft and breeding and let the whole thing drop."

The idea had occurred to him only in the past day. *Brilliant*, he thought.

"We would have to confer with the state prosecutor. And Mr. Hansen. It might be possible to work out a legal compromise, but for right now, you remain under arrest."

Later that day the police talked with Dirck. Yes, he thought the man had been punished enough and didn't want to prosecute him for his theft. For him, it was only about getting Chauncey back.

One of the state policemen he had attacked was a veteran and didn't reported the assault on him and his partner. He didn't want Dirck to suffer further after another heartbreaking setback with his lost dog.

But revenge consumed Jackson. The veteran had nearly ended his life and robbed him of his livelihood. Jackson Stoney wasn't a man who could forget something like that.

The two men's thinking was different, yet both of their worlds would soon collide.

Because Dirck was still under arrest, Dru wasn't allowed to visit. She drove back to CAS in New York. Her heart was breaking for Dirck. And she didn't believe Chauncey could ever make it back home from another state over hundreds of miles through dense forests in the middle of winter. It was a bad ending to months of hope.

The following week, the state attorney ordered Dirck Hansen to undergo psychiatric evaluation. Not unexpectedly, a psychiatrist from Veterans Affairs diagnosed him with depression and panic disorder, prescribing additional narcotics.

Every day, he was forced to sit through group therapy sessions—talk therapy—with an overly conscientious social worker. But all Dirck talked about was his dog and how it was the only thing that mattered to him. The social worker thought the veteran needed group and cognitive therapy and certainly, a dog couldn't help him. The sessions made Dirck worse.

Three weeks later, Jackson Stoney was released from the hospital. The charges against him had been dropped and he returned to his cabin a free man.

But on returning home, he found that his dog Buller had been taken from him and placed in a local shelter, the pens he had spent most of his money building had been dismantled, and he had been fired from the Bingham Animal Shelter without savings. He was left with nothing.

His phone had been returned and he had a signal. He called Ryker.

"Yeah," Ryker mumbled.

"Ryk. This is Jax. Out of the hospital…home now. Major ordeal. Had to be treated for a damned dog bite and a bad leg wound. The vet who owned the dog attacked me. It was bad. He dropped the charges so they didn't press any against me. But the bastard nearly *killed* me."

"Shit Jax, thought you were in jail or somethin'. What'n the hell happened…to our money?"

After Jackson's last call, he had heard nothing and Jackson gave him the rundown. He was free from further prosecution but no longer had a dog-breeding business.

Ryker didn't care.

"Shit man. You mean the bastard stabbed you and left you to die? And now we can't even collect our money? Shit, I was *counting* on that cash."

"Yeah, it was brutal. He's a combat vet that's messed up. All for some stupid dog, can you believe that?"

But it was just talk. Jackson honestly wished the veteran had his dog back and that he had never entered into this scheme. There was silence on the other end of the line.

"Ryk, man, you know my hand is messed up now and my goddamned leg hurts all the time. Bastard robbed me of my livelihood. They tore down my pens and on top of it all, I got fired from the shelter. No cash. Can't even pay my rent and I'm already a couple months late. Don't know where I'll go."

He certainly didn't want to live with Ryker Falls.

"Well, that bastard needs to pay for this shit." Ryker said it in a resolute, determined way. "I can find out where he lives. I have an idea on that."

Despite his angry, dark soul, Ryker was sometimes clever, a disturbing combination.

Jackson hesitated. "No, I'm not sure about that. We should leave this alone…but what were you thinking?" Another scheme in the works.

The next morning, Ryker sat in Jackson's kitchen, drinking beer, talking about calling Teri Pierce at the Bingham Shelter, how he could tell her that he knew where the dog was and that he'd return it—that way, they could get Hansen's address. Jackson dismissed the absurd idea. It would just cause more trouble.

Ryker sat quietly at the table, half-buzzed, not listening to Jackson. Without hesitating, he flipped open his phone and pushed a direct dial to the Bingham Animal Shelter. He put it on speaker phone.

"Bingham Animal Hospital. How may I help you?" a woman said.

Jackson lunged across the table to grab the phone from him. Ryker jumped up.

"Hello ma'am. My name is Michael Jenkins."

He had made up the name on the spot. Ryker spoke slowly as if to sound older, more mature. His high-pitched voice was uncharacteristically cheerful. He stared at the poster on the table.

"I'm wondering whether I could speak to a Teri Pierce. It's important—it's about that lost dog, the dog belonging to that veteran Captain Hansen," he said in one coherent string.

"Oh yes. Yes. Let me get her," the woman said and put the call on hold.

Over the mindless music, Ryker smiled at Jackson. But Jackson was pacing about the table, smoking, not looking at him. Then he remembered that he had used Ryker as a phony telephone reference a few months ago to get the Bingham job. Teri would surely recognize Ryker's voice. He waved his hands for him to hang up.

"This is Teri Pierce. You say your name is Michael Jenkins?" She was out of breath.

"Yes, ma'am. We found the dog, the one who belongs to that veteran Captain Hansen…the Golden Retriever. It's the one you had in your facility, I believe," Ryker said but wasn't sure how he would have known this and then added "I caught the news report about the dog at your facility."

"Chauncey? Oh God, where did you find her? Is she okay?" Teri said.

"Yes, ma'am, she's fine. She's even lying here by my side right now, fast asleep. She's just fine."

Ryker gave him a thumbs-up sign. Now both men were up, pacing the floor.

"I am a Marine veteran from Afghanistan. Heard that the dog belonged to a fellow combat vet. And being a vet and all, I thought it would be special to contact Captain Hansen myself and tell him we found his service dog," he said and flashed Jackson another thumbs-up sign.

Jackson smiled. It was uncommon for Ryker to sound so convincing. He had even added a hint of a southern drawl. Jackson knew the man would stop at nothing to get his money.

But Teri had become cautious after hiring Jackson and losing Dirck's dog.

"Can you give me additional details, Mr. Jenkins? Where exactly did you find the dog and how did you come upon her?"

"Sure Teri," Ryker continued. "Well, me and my friend were hunting in the woods and found her about twenty miles due west of Route 9A, out near Bingham. She was cold and hungry but okay, and she came right over to us. Sweet dog. Not a big girl, more compact."

Ryker went on to describe Chauncey in detail from the picture on the poster before him and from his memory on the night he had kicked her.

"Yes, that sounds like her," Teri said. "Was she with another dog? May have been a black dog with her."

"No ma'am, only the blonde dog," Ryker said. "I know there's a reward and all, but we mostly wanted to get the dog back to Captain Hansen. I know it would mean a lot to him if another vet connected with him."

"Yes, it surely would," Teri said. "The dog was his protector. She's been missing for well over a year and a half. I know getting her back would make all the difference to him."

But she was still skeptical. Something in the man's voice sounded familiar. She hesitated.

"Mr. Jenkins, how can I reach you? Do you have a phone number where I can call you back?" she said.

Ryker was becoming impatient with having to answer the woman's questions. Ryker eyes widened and he looked at Jackson for direction. Jackson only shook his head.

"Well, Teri, unfortunately, my wife and I are getting ready to leave town on a family vacation and don't plan to be back here for a while. We're in western Massachusetts right now and heading to Vermont on a trip with my in-laws."

Jackson looked away. Ryker with a family was laughable. Ryker continued.

"I'm using a payphone out here…don't have a phone with me to call you back. Since the owner lives in Vermont somewhere, it would be great if we could even bring the dog up to him directly. We'll be up there in Vermont in a couple days," Ryker said, but he knew he was taking too big a chance and nearly flipped the phone closed.

"You're at a payphone? I thought you said the dog was by your side."

Ryker frowned.

"Well, she is. We're now here inside a convenience store and I have her with me, brought her inside to keep her warm and all. She's resting on the floor right beside me here."

Ryker looked down, trying to think of what to say next. This was getting away from him.

"Oh. I see," Teri said. "Well, what convenience store are you calling from. I mean where are you right now?"

Now, Ryker was cornered. He looked down at the six-pack of beer that he had just opened—there was a receipt lying on top of it. He picked it up.

"Well…we're just outside Williamsberg off Route 9A. In a small convenience store…name's Cumberland Corners. Wait a second."

Ryker put his hand over the mouthpiece and mumbled something and waved to Jackson to say something back. Teri heard muffled voices over the line.

"Yes, okay, Cumberland Corners store…clerk just told me," Ryker said.

"Can you call me back in an hour? I need to find out where Captain Hansen is now. He had been in the Bingham Hospital. I want to make sure where you can reach him."

"Yes, ma'am, we'll wait an hour and get to another public phone to call you back. Thank you."

Ryker hung up and stared at Jackson in disbelief.

"Damn, man. That vet was in the *same* hospital you were at. She's checking on his whereabouts. I'll call back in an hour. Could be in the bag," Ryker said and took another swig of beer.

But Jackson thought Teri would check out the location of Cumberland Corners, which was in Stanton, where Jackson lived. Maybe she'd trace Ryker's call. She even might have recognized Ryker's voice. It didn't look good.

An hour later, Ryker called Teri back.

"Mr. Jenkins. Thanks for calling me back. I spoke with the hospital, and Mr. Hansen was released. He went back to his home. He lives at 3982 Route 44 in Glenriver, Vermont. His landline is 802-449-3393. You should call him and let him know you have his dog Chauncey. He will be most thrilled another veteran had found her. He'll arrange for the reward. I believe it's increased."

"Thank you, Teri. We will be on our way to a lengthy vacation and wouldn't have any way to cash a paper check or such. Do you think he might be able to pay us directly up there at his home?"

Jackson was now waving his arms at Ryker to hang up. He couldn't believe the risks the man was taking.

There was a pause on the line.

"I'm not sure, Mr. Jenkins. Perhaps. His colleague, Ms. Vaughan told us Captain Hansen might be able pay the reward at his home."

Ryker thanked her and hung up. He let out a long breath.

"Got it, man—3982 Route 44 in Glenriver, Vermont. Think he's got the cash at his house," Ryker said. "Could be more than the eight grand. This is *beautiful*."

Jackson opened his phone's GPS and punched in the address. Hansen's home was two hundred forty miles to the north, over four hours away.

Teri Pierce immediately called Dirck to tell him a fellow veteran had found his dog and would be taking Chauncey up there himself.

There was no answer. She kept trying. She called Dru's cell phone, but it had no signal.

28

The great snows that had blanketed the northeast had now subsided, hinting at new landmarks for the dogs as they pushed their way north through the seemingly unending vast wilderness, resting and sleeping where they could for only hours at a time.

They had now been on the run for a week and their renewed strength from the rich wolf's meat had long since faded, their sustenance coming only from roots and emerging spouts. They caught the occasional mouse, but none of it was enough to sustain them in their long, demanding journey.

And over the past days, Chauncey's initially strong sense of magnetic north had begun to fade and they had veered off toward the northwest. An hour earlier, they had unknowingly crossed into Vermont.

As was the custom, Chauncey had taken the lead and was twenty yards in front of Callie. She stopped and raised her snout, hoping for some reassurance she was on the right track.

A faint scent wafted over her, a combination of burning pine and cedar, like woody evergreens. It was familiar. This part of the woods, too, was memorable. Over a year ago, she had escaped near these woods, from that meadow in Woodsdale Corners. This was near Jake and Joannie Tollinger's cabin, the place Chauncey had spent five long months in captivity. She now knew where she. She barked at Callie in recognition and ran forward with renewed purpose.

Ahead of them lay Tuckerman's Ravine, a large, deep gorge hidden by maples and pines growing from its edges. The snow that partially covered the near and far sides of the chasm made the ground look continuous at their level.

Excited by her companion's discovery, Callie broke into a full run past her. She turned back and barked but the sound was cut short and she disappeared from view. Chauncey heard branches snapping followed by a sharp yelp.

She ran frantically about the forest trying to find Callie's scent. She walked to the edge of the ravine and looked down. Over twenty feet below at the edge of the large crevasse, her companion lay motionless.

After an uncertain minute, Callie stood. Chauncey barked, encouraging her to climb up. Callie's paws slipped on the ravine's steep muddy walls. There was no other way out. She was trapped. Would she have to leave Callie behind?

Chauncey paced back and forth along the ravine, barking frantically. Her loyalty to her companion was fierce and she was determined to get her out.

Chauncey pictured Dru and Dave Ballard standing before her in a CAS training field. They had once shown her how to overcome obstacles that had been placed in her path—how to climb a wooden platform above her using whatever tools she had been given—sticks, boards, logs, rocks, anything to create a foothold. She saw Dru standing on the platform above her, clapping her hands.

Come on Chauncey, come on girl, get up, up, on up.

She began collecting fallen branches, dropping them at the ravine's edge, but they weren't enough to help build a platform.

Farther away from the ravine, she came upon a man-made rock wall from a long-abandoned farm. She climbed on it and pushed a large boulder off, nudging it along the dirt path to the ravine. She looked over the edge. It seemed impossible to make a platform with stones and branches. She returned for a second rock.

Dru was on her knees before her, her hands out.

Come on Girl! Come on, Chauncey. Push!

The late-afternoon sun began to fade. By nightfall, she had moved over fifty rocks to the ravine's edge and lay exhausted on the pile of warm stones, her head draped over the edge.

Callie was lying at the bottom, looking up, whining. Over the unsettled night, Callie's cries grew softer and eventually stopped.

At first light, Chauncey woke and looked down into the crevasse. Callie was on her side, not moving. Chauncey barked loudly. Callie raised her head and stood, happy her companion was still there with her.

Chauncey was back at the rock-moving, stopping only to rest and drink from a nearby stream. This time of year, fiddlehead ferns and asparagus had begun to erupt from the snows. She snapped several sprouts free, dropping them into the gorge for Callie.

Callie knew her companion wouldn't abandon her.

By the following afternoon, much of the original stone wall had been moved fifty yards to the right. She looked down. Callie was standing away from the edge, her head up, waiting for something.

Chauncey! Push, girl, push.

Chauncey lowered her snout under one large rock and nudged it over the edge. It pounded down the side of the ravine, nearly hitting Callie. She knew her partner was doing something important. Another stone bounced down, then another.

Chauncey pulled several large branches over to fall in between the rocks. She stopped and looked over the edge. There was something there.

There was no stopping now. Chauncey's energy spiked as she pushed against more rocks, edging them down into the pit. As the day's light faded, over two hundred rocks had been piled along the dirt cliffs of Tuckerman's Ravine.

The stairway was built.

Callie placed her paw upon the first rock and raised herself unsteadily up, testing each new stone as she climbed. The light had gone and she was only a quarter of the distance up. Her legs burned and her side ached, but she slowly rose up, away from her dark abyss toward the bright barking of freedom above her.

From the dark edges of Tuckerman's Ravine, the black silhouette of a shaky dog appeared against the dark forest pines. Chauncey reached down and grabbed Callie's neck, pulling her up and out of the gorge.

The dog collapsed, her flanks heaving wildly, joyfully. Chauncey curled about her companion, licking her muzzle, whimpering at her hard-fought freedom.

The bond between them was now sealed. Chauncey had saved Callie's life from her captors, the men who had abused her, from the wolf, and now, this latest peril.

A cold northern wind blew over them. Chauncey pointed her snout and drew in the air. Musty smells of sandalwood and pine needles floated through the evening breeze, the smells of the little girl's bedroom. Every night since her dog Kady had run away, Joannie had continued her vigil, burning incense, keeping alive the memory of her lost dog. Then, beyond the sweet smells of incense was cooking chickens, cows and horses. The farmer's house.

They all stirred in her a deep awareness that every day, every hour, brought her closer to Dirck, to home. She knew she must be close to him, but his familiar scent was not among the others.

29

Two more days thinking through their newly hatched scheme had accomplished little. Ryker had purchased a 9-mm pistol and practiced shooting beer bottles in the back of Jackson's yard. Jackson located his old Kriegar Stiletto switchblade, a weapon he never had used. He packed several rolls of duct tape and rope that he had once used to restrain his dogs. But they weren't sure of what they'd need.

More than Ryker, Jackson thought they should prepare for anything, but in his mind, the plan was ill-conceived and vague from the outset.

He knew they would encounter a combat veteran, a man furious about the theft of his dog. And he would have weapons. God knows how many lethal weapons a veteran might have. Then there was the unknown layout of Dirck's house. How would they even get inside, and how would they find the man? What if someone else was with him?

Maybe he had even gotten another dog. Jackson thought about Arko, the big Rottweiler that had mangled his hand.

Despite Jackson's mounting uncertainty, Ryker reminded him they were both armed. But this didn't reassure Jackson, and as their morning of departure drew closer, tension between the men mounted.

"We should just shoot the bastard," he said. "Forget trying to subdue him."

"Ryker, we talked about this before. We're not killing anyone. We're just there to get the money. That's it."

Jackson wanted to execute a planned robbery, one with cooperation. But with Ryker, that didn't seem possible. He was too unpredictable.

Ryker continued shooting off his mouth.

"But what's the point of going through with all this shit unless he's taken out?"

He smiled at Jackson. His face had a blank look, no real expression in his dark eyes, and his missing teeth only accentuated his already menacing look.

He was moving his arm about as if wielding a knife.

"Okay, let me use the knife on him," he said in his high-pitched voice. It made him sound even more threatening.

But despite his tough talk, Jackson knew Ryker wasn't particularly brave when faced with a serious threat but he didn't want to have to control the man once they were inside Hansen's house.

Jackson was the bigger man and commanded respect. He walked to Ryker and grabbed his neck with a frightening grip, squeezing the air from his windpipe.

"Listen…listen carefully. You're not doing anything of the kind. You're not in charge here. If you try to kill anyone, it won't turn out well for you, I promise you that."

Jackson let go. The man sank back into a chair. There was no more talk of the plan, but again, this just filled Ryker with more rage. They both packed in silence.

The next morning, they set off early for Vermont, and by two that afternoon, had stopped at Isabell's Café, a worn-down dive that sat just across the Massachusetts-Vermont border.

They sat in a spacious curved red leather booth with ripped seams, drinking coffee, smoking, studying the local map, but it was difficult to concentrate with the afternoon sun pouring through the large dirty windows and over the buzzing conversations.

The place was packed. Jackson smoothed out the map, so thumbed through it had grown as supple as a piece of chamois. The town of Glenriver, Vermont was marked with a large red dot. It looked close.

Ryker continued on his single track about his *score*, about how when it was settled and he had his money, he would take a trip up to Canada, lay low for a couple of months in the summer, maybe a nice time of year then.

He lit another cigarette, blowing a flood of blue smoke through his nose as he continued into *no witnesses* for what seemed to Jackson as the hundredth time. It rankled Jackson, the way he said those two words. He was growing increasingly intolerant with the erratic mad-man sitting next to him.

At some old diner in some small Vermont town.

Again, Jackson thought he should call it all off, go back to his cabin in Stanton. Try to earn a living somehow, make some sense of his broken life.

They got up to pay.

To the locals walking in and out of Isabell's that afternoon, the two men wouldn't have been given a second look. If anyone had noticed Jackson sitting in the booth, he might have looked like a normal-sized man, but standing, he looked more powerful, with arms and shoulders like a weight lifter. His feet were encased in short black boots with steel buckles and he wore mismatched gray baggy pants and an undersized army-green, long-sleeved top.

Ryker projected something quite different: tall and thin and a sullen face with deep-set dark eyes. He might have even appeared sickly, like a pale teenager. A pissed-off one at that. His clothes were too big for him, hanging from him as if the man had shrunk a size.

Local men craned their necks to watch the pair at the cash register. They were clearly not from these parts. And on their way to certain trouble.

By midnight, their pickup truck was hurtling down Route 44 toward Glenriver. Ryker had dozed off. Jackson woke him to let him know they had entered Chatham County and were now close. Ryker rolled down the window and bathed his face in a flood of cold night air. Now, it was getting serious.

"We crossed over the township line a few miles back," Jackson said.

He was driving fast, maybe eighty miles an hour, at times even faster. Signs flew by, ignited by headlights: "Clark's Motel," "Nature's Playground: Birds of Prey," "Northland Motel," and finally "Glenriver Welcomes You."

Jackson slowed and skirted the rim of the town. The streets were dark. Nobody was out at this after-midnight hour, and nothing was open except the one Texaco service station. Its sign—a huge white ball with the red star and "T"—unnaturally lit the otherwise peaceful dark Vermont landscape.

He pulled in. They were just five miles to the Route 44 turnoff for Judge Benson's place and he had to have a full tank, just in case.

Jackson filled the truck while Ryker went inside to the men's room. He opened the stall and sat, pulling out a bottle of Old Crow. He took a long drink, pulled in a deep breath, and stretched out his legs. Jackson had told him they were about there. *It's about five more miles or so*, he had just said. He unzipped a pocket of his windbreaker and took out a paper sack. Inside were the thin blue rubber gloves he had bought yesterday. He inched them on but one finger tore—not a dangerous tear, just a rip on the thumb. But it seemed ominous. He wasn't even sure why he had bought the gloves. He went to the sink and looked into the cracked mirror, turning his head to one side, then to the other, looking at his long sideburns, his pale face. Ryker had always tried to make some sense of himself but couldn't. The dark circles under his eyes made him look sick, perhaps sad. Maybe that's the way he had always looked. He wasn't sure.

He walked back into the station. Jackson was paying the attendant in cash. Neither man had a credit card. Jimmy Mitch, the night attendant, straightened at the sight of Ryker, any sense of relaxation vanishing from his face.

Jimmy was a man of about twenty who lived two blocks from the station with his strict preacher father. He had never traveled more than fifty miles in any direction from here and he knew the locals, all of them, but he'd never seen these men before. And he was sure the one hadn't been in the bathroom for its intended purpose. The man's dark expression made Jimmy's heart race. Liquor was on his breath.

Ryker combed through the candy rack.

"Kinda slow here, huh?" Jackson said as he pulled out several bills.

"Yes sir. You're, uh, the only one stopped in here since three hours ago," Jimmy said as he considered the man. Jackson looked more normal than the other one but still not friendly.

"Where you headed?" Jimmy asked to break the tension.

"Goin' to Canada, up near Montreal," Jackson said.

"Up for deer?" Jimmy asked. But it wasn't deer season, not even close. He regretted asking, but it was his nature.

"Nope. No hunting," Ryker said as he eyed the candy rack. "Passin' through. Have cousins in Canada, maybe a job there."

Ryker picked up a bag of M&M's and pulled out a wad of cash, several twenties rolled in a rubber band. Locals didn't carry that much cash. Not like that.

"How much for these?" he asked.

"That's fifty cents, sir," Jimmy said.

He pulled out a twenty.

"Oh, keep it, I don't have change for that. It's okay, really."

He just wanted to get the men out of his station. Ryker looked at the young man and raised his eyebrows.

"Good deal," he said, and laughed through missing teeth.

Jackson grabbed Ryker's arm. "Let's go."

They left. In his rear-view mirror, Jackson watched the bright Texaco station disappear into the night. Jimmy Mitch was out by the pump, watching them.

A couple of days later, Jimmy would tell his employer, "we had some pretty rough customers in here the other night" but he did not think then, or for some time, to connect the strange men to what had happened in that Glenriver house, the place where that soldier lived. In fact, until that late-winter day, the world had largely forgotten about Glenriver and the veteran Dirck Hansen and his lost dog.

It was pitch-black, and Jackson sped down the two-lane road with his high beams on. Ryker stared out his window as trees flew by. He had no idea what they would encounter in that house.

And now, there were just about there.

"Let's go back," Ryker said.

30

Dru had driven to Massachusetts to take Dirck home from the Bingham Hospital, but she didn't arrive with good news.

"Dirck, the team didn't see any way to initiate another search for Chauncey. Too much time has passed and they didn't know where to start. The snow had obscured her trail and it was impossible for them to figure it out."

They drove back to Vermont in Dru's camper, a converted Volkswagen van she used for outings with her dogs.

As the camper lumbered noisily down the highway, Dirck stared out the window in silence. He had been subdued by the usual sedatives but now the doctors had added fentanyl, a powerful narcotic, to the mix. He was in a fog much of the time.

Dru told him he had suffered a severe PTSD episode and attacked Jackson Stoney, the man who stolen his dog. And the police.

"Did I hurt someone? Did I flip out? What happened?"

"You stabbed Jackson Stoney. He almost died. There was an agreement not to press charges and he went free."

"An agreement to set him free? What the hell…"

The thought of releasing the man who had stolen his dog angered him.

"Well, part of the agreement was that he wouldn't press charges against you."

Dirck's body and mind had been broken by the chronic nightmares and narcotic exhaustion. And especially from the continued disappointment of losing his dog.

Over the past months, he had come so close—the sightings near Woodsdale, in Clover, near the seed store in Hortonia, and, most recently, from the Bingham Animal Shelter. He couldn't comprehend it. Now, she could be anywhere. She seemed so far away.

"Somehow the higher powers don't want me to find her, Dru. Do you think she's still out there…out there looking for us?"

"Yes, I'm sure she's trying to find her way back home, Dirck."

But Dru didn't think Chauncey could find her way home now. She could be hundreds of miles away in the wilderness.

"There must be something more we can do, Dru. Can't we get the FINDFIDO team going again?" he said, forgetting Dru had just told him the search was impossible now. "Can't we get our veterans to look for her?"

He was striking out.

"I'll try, you know that, Dirck…I want her back almost as much as you do. I will stay with you in Glenriver and we'll put together a new plan."

There have been so many new plans, Dirck thought. They drove on in silence.

It was late afternoon when they pulled into Judge Benson's homestead. At least the weather had turned warmer.

He looked toward the field bathed in the late winter sun and thought, *the sun will warm Chauncey—life might be easier for her now living in the woods, wherever she is.*

Dirck had been gone for several weeks and the necessity of upcoming chores diverted him. This spring would bring the yearly cleanup—clearing piles of dirt and rocks that had moved during snowplowing, many windows to clean, brush to clear.

Then, there were the bears. In spring they woke, hungry from hibernation, and sought food near the house.

He went to his kitchen. He looked at his .45 pistol hanging from its holster on the corner of a door. One blast from the big gun would scare the bears from his back area, but every year, they would return, undeterred.

And then, there were the intruders. Over the past few years, kids in the area had been robbing homes for cash to buy opiates. Last year, twenty break-ins were reported around Glenriver. And now he had fentanyl, a powerful and popular opioid. He also had a substantial amount of cash in his safe.

And he didn't have his dog anymore—Chauncey would bark at anyone who came within one hundred feet of the house.

As he stared out the window, he took down his pistol and began loading the clip. He could almost see Chauncey out there, just beyond the patio, barking at intruders sneaking out of the woods. What a comfort she had been! He looked down at the gun. Dru walked in.

"Dirck, what do you need that weapon for? Shouldn't you should keep that locked up?"

"The bears. And the drug kids robbing houses around here."

But this didn't justify having such a powerful weapon. Especially a loaded one. His MK3 Navy fighting knife also hung from its holster, the knife he had used on Jackson Stoney. Dru was worried—Dirck was alone and living far from any help. The combination of PTSD, narcotics, alcohol, and weapons was lethal.

She decided she'd stay with him that week, maybe longer.

They began working on their next search strategy. Dru went out to her camper to get the notebook that contained details of

Chauncey's searches. As she passed the patio, bright lights flooded the porch and sides of the house. Dirck had installed the automatic floodlights the year he had brought Chauncey home.

Another reminder of her. But the whole house was full of reminders. It seemed like years since his dog had been home.

Dru diverted him.

"Dirck, I feel confident Chauncey is headed in this direction. Maybe the people she visited last year would have seen her. Let's get updated posters to the stores in Riverdale, Hortonia, Clover, and Woodsdale."

They had been at this point before. It seemed futile but doing nothing was worse.

The next day, Dru was on Dirck's landline with her CAS staff arranging for the updated posters.

They increased the reward to nine thousand five hundred but Dirck thought it should be higher. He'd even go to fifteen thousand if he believed that would make a difference.

The new posters were put on bulletin boards in nearby towns. They would start a new search south of Glenriver and nearby townships where the dog had been seen this past year. It was a long shot, but still, something. The long and familiar day of putting up posters exhausted Dirck.

Dirck's phone rang. He ignored it. It rang over fifteen times before it stopped.

"Sure you don't want to get that? May be important," Dru said.

He didn't acknowledge her. He sat in his kitchen with a beer, staring out the window toward the field again. Picturing Chauncey running in his field gave him a vague comfort. It was growing dark.

Dru thought it was time to let him have some peace and said goodnight. She hugged him. He stood before her like a statue. His body was warm but lifeless. Sadness exhaled from him. She pulled back and looked at him. His eyes were blank.

"We'll start our new plan tomorrow. We'll get your girl back…I will make sure, I promise. Please keep the faith. She's out there, she's safe," Dru said. She desperately wanted to believe this.

The Judge Benson place was unusually quiet that night. As spring approached, the frogs sometimes became active, but not tonight. He looked out the kitchen window toward the back of his driveway. He couldn't quite see Dru's camper. It sat at the far end of the driveway one or maybe two hundred yards from the house, hidden behind several large birches. He stared into the darkness.

His phone rang again. He ignored it.

Right now, for some reason, he couldn't take his eyes off the darkness. Something was out there, something unknown. He picked up the loaded pistol, feeling its heaviness, its lethal power. He released the safety and, almost as a joke, put it to his temple.

So quick. No more pain…just squeeze the trigger, he thought.

But this time, it felt serious, more real than it had before. His arm stiffened and he squeezed his eyes closed.

In the black void before him, Chauncey appeared. Dirck hadn't seen her so clearly, so real, not since she disappeared over a year ago. She was standing close to him in the darkness, staring up at him, her head tilted, as if asking him for something.

If he were gone now, she would be alone. And she needed him in this world.

At that moment, he knew his dog was alive. Somewhere, someplace out in that vast, dark wilderness, she was alive.

He lowered the gun and exhaled.

At that moment, he desperately wanted his dog back.

31

A checkered flag appeared on the GPS screen. Jackson lifted off his seat, looking for his destination.

"This has to be it, Ryk…we passed that school and we're at the address now." He peered into the dark landscape.

Ryker was slumped in his seat, staring blankly out the window.

Jackson inched the truck along the deserted highway. Then, he saw it—a dark lane off to the right. A driveway.

He killed the headlights. A long driveway lined with white birches sat just off the road. The moonlight lit the field in the back but he couldn't see a house.

He pulled off the road and walked down the driveway. To his right, an old sign read "JUDGE BENSON'S HOUSE 1807." He could just make out the address stamped on a side post: 3982.

This was the place! He ran back to the truck.

"We're here…careful not to make any noise," he said, but it was a preposterous thing to say. Another reminder of their ill-conceived plan. Shouldn't he be considering other things? But what?

Ryker looked at him oddly, his eyes wide. He was hesitating again.

But this was no time for second thoughts—Jackson was committed. Get the money and split. That was the plan. His plan at least.

He pulled the truck onto the driveway and cut the motor. In the darkness, he now could see a structure blocking out stars to the north and a metal roof glowing in the moonlight. The house before him loomed large against the vast sky—it was substantial, far bigger than he had imagined.

At the end of the long, snaking driveway, he saw a faint red light glowing inside a camper. A safety light. Beyond was a garage. *Why didn't he didn't park in the garage? It's winter.* His thoughts churned as he considered his next move.

"Stay here," he whispered. "I'll look for a way in."

He walked to one side of the large structure. Floodlights washed the space in front of him. He had tripped a motion detector. He backed away.

"Shit…safety lights. Have to find another way in," he said under his breath.

Ryker looked back at the porch and house bathed in bright white light. No lights came on inside.

"Get behind the wheel, Ryk. Gonna push the truck back out to the road. Don't want to start it up here."

They got the truck out to the street and Jackson drove it behind in a stand of trees hidden beyond the house. They pulled on their backpacks. Jackson looked back toward the house in the distance. At least the floodlights were off now.

"Stay here, Ryk. Going around the side." He was out of breath.

He disappeared into the darkness.

Ryker sat in the open truck. He was thinking about the money again. Half of eight thousand, maybe more. He could do a lot with that. Ryker Falls just wanted "a regular life," as he would call it, a better house (his was a rented shack), a new truck, a way to make a living. It didn't seem like much to want, really. But he didn't know how to turn money into a better life. A past littered with crime and resentments had made sure of that.

Anything, really, was better than what he had now, and he was willing to risk this little caper. *After all, we're armed, and it's only one guy and we are two*, he thought as he stared at the large forbidding structure in the distance. But he had thought this before. Many times before. There were no new revelations, nothing to strengthen his convictions. His heart began to race. Ryker didn't do well under pressure.

Jackson took a wide path around the patio and crept along the north side of the house, pulling on the first-floor windows. All locked. On the north-facing side, low to the ground, he spotted two narrow, single-paned windows twenty feet apart. Maybe basement windows. He shined his light on them. One had a broken pane.

He reached through the jagged opening and found a latch. The window loosened on one side. He unlatched the other side and the window fell free. The opening was tight, maybe two by four feet, just big enough for someone to get through sideways. He took the wide path back to Ryker.

"Found a window into the basement," he whispered. "Let's go."

Jackson tried squeezing through the small opening but his jacket caught a nail and ripped. He rolled in and fell sideways onto the floor three feet below. Now his shoulder hurt and his jacket was ripped. Not a good start.

He helped Ryker in. They were on the opposite side of the *business end* of the large house and wouldn't be detected.

He aimed his light into the basement. An old abandoned water tank and cistern was in front of them, and on the other side sat an oil tank. In the middle of the large space, a large furnace was running.

In front of them was a stairway. Jackson tried the door at the top but it was locked.

He saw the lock was an iron-slide type, common in older houses. He pulled out his knife and pushed the blade into the catch. It clicked opened—they were in.

Two floors above them, Dirck was deep in a Paxil- and alcohol-induced stupor. Dru was asleep out in her camper. They had both turned in around ten.

Jackson looked at his watch: 2:10. At the top of the stairs, they stood in a small hallway. To their right was a great room, and in front of them sat another room, its door ajar. He pushed it open.

It was an office with a large desk, a computer, filing cabinets, and drawers. Maybe an old bedroom. Perhaps the money was in there. But the vet wasn't. They'd need to get him first.

Jackson considered the layout of the house from what he had seen outside. The man's bedroom was likely on the second floor. Nobody seemed to be on this first floor and he flicked on a wall switch. Small lamps dimly lit the room.

"Get up the stairs. No lights. Slow and easy," Jackson said.

Ryker hesitated. He reached into his backpack and pulled out his pistol.

"Shit man, what if he has a weapon? Those Army guys carry weapons to bed with them, don't they?"

He didn't think Ryker would go through with this.

"We talked about this, planned this," Jackson whispered. "Don't start second-guessing this now. We're armed. You know what to do. Element of surprise. We can immobilize him."

But neither of them had ever had to subdue another man, especially a combat veteran.

Jackson opened his knife. They ascended the stairs.

The stairs of the two-hundred-year-old house creaked, each step signaling their presence. And there were twenty of them. They winced on each stair as they climbed.

At the top was a landing leading to other rooms. To the left was a small bedroom with an open door. Empty. Across the landing was a bathroom and another bedroom.

Jackson crept into the bathroom. On an old dresser sat a half-filled water glass and several prescription bottles. *The vet's bathroom*, he thought. He put a light up to one bottle: Paxil. Another read Xanax. All sedatives and narcotics. One bottle had spilled and several pills were on the counter. The man would be drugged. *This will be easier than we thought.*

From the landing, a narrow entrance led into the bedroom, which sat on another level, four or maybe five feet below them. He grabbed Ryker's arm.

"Make sure your safety's off."

Ryker's heart began pounding. His expression changed.

Jackson walked ahead through the passageway. He stepped down, but in the darkness didn't see the low overhang and he slammed his head. An audible thud and grunt. He sat to regain his balance. His head ached and it was now bleeding.

The bedroom was large and carpeted. They stepped forward in silence. Dim moonlight filled the space. They could just make out the outlines of chairs and a table beyond.

Beyond, a faint red light from a clock revealed the edges of a bed. They stopped.

In the stillness of the room, a man screamed.

32

Ambush! Take cover…" Dirck thrashed about in his bed in front of the men.

Jackson motioned Ryker to the man's left. Dirck turned to a new position on his right, facing Jackson. The intruders stood on either side of the bed. Jackson flicked on his flashlight and aimed it into Dirck's face. He pointed his knife at him.

"Stay the hell where you are," Jackson said. "We have weapons on you."

Dirck's eyes flickered. Where was he? This must be an ambush. He reached for his firearm but it wasn't there. Where were his men? He yelled out.

"Sergeant…take cover!"

The veteran's expression was stark, his piercing eyes narrowing in the light. Jackson stepped back.

"Cool down man. We have weapons. Ease yourself out of that bed," he said. "Nice and slow."

He had to stay calm but every second ratcheted up the tension.

Dirck moved to the side of the bed and lowered his legs. He sat up. He saw Ryker holding a pistol.

"Ambush!" he yelled again.

"Put your hands behind you, asshole," Ryker said. "We have weapons."

Ryker moved around to the right side of the bed, tucked the gun in his pocket, and pulled a length of duct tape. Dirck stood. He was surprised at how short the vet was, pretty average in size. *No sweat, I can take this guy* he thought. He handed his gun to Jackson.

The light from Jackson's flashlight momentarily illuminated the men. Dirck looked at the bigger man. He knew this man, but who was he?

His head was pounding from the beer and drugs. Ryker moved in front of him holding the duct tape. The expression on the man's face made Ryker stop.

"Ryk, damn it…get the man's hands taped," he urged. "You're covered. Move, goddamn it!"

Dirck's eyes remained on Ryker who had ahold of his arm. He pulled but the man resisted. His considerable strength unnerved Ryker.

"Don't make this hard, asshole. My friend here will blow a hole in your goddamn head," he said.

But just as the word *head* was uttered, Ryker flew off the ground and into Jackson. Dirck's blow had landed squarely on the side of the man's face and knocked him unconscious.

Dirck stepped forward and pressed his foot onto Jackson.

"We'll see who wins this battle," he said.

He was awake now and aware of his situation. Ryker was out cold. Dirck took the pistol from his pocket and aimed it at Jackson. He pulled his foot away.

"Get up!"

Jackson pushed Ryker from him and got onto all fours. But Dirck hadn't noticed the knife in the man's hand. Jackson sprang low at his legs and plunged the blade deep into Dirck's thigh.

As he fell, Dirck fired, the bullet ripping into the right side of Jackson's face. It was a severe wound. Dirck was on his side trying to pull the blade free but he knew he might bleed out. He tried to calm himself.

Jackson's head exploded in pain. He was dazed but managed to jump onto the freed pistol. He backed away from the wounded soldier. Dirck was on the floor mumbling something.

"Yeah—I'm the one you stabbed in the leg. You left me to die—remember that, asshole? How does it feel?" he said.

But Jackson's jaw and one side of his face had been ripped open, and he couldn't speak well. He pressed the gun into the man's head.

"Feels good, huh?"

Dirck looked up at him.

"I stabbed and killed a lot of men—you're just another piece of shit I'm dealing with."

This infuriated Jackson.

"I will kill you right here, asshole. You need to tell me where the money's at."

Dirck now knew what they wanted. To him, this was just a chess game, and he was already several moves ahead of his opponents. He thought about his next move. His weapons were in the kitchen.

"Downstairs in the safe…next to the kitchen," he said.

He tried to stand but his leg wouldn't cooperate. Jackson put his boot onto his thigh and pulled the knife free. Dirck looked at his wound. It hurt like hell but the bleeding wasn't severe.

Now he remembered. This was the man who had stolen his dog.

Dirck was trained to survive in desperate situations. He had faced deadly encounters many times, on many battlefields. He had engaged in close combat with crazed terrorists that radiated pure evil. He had stared at their heinous faces inches away and, without any emotion or hesitation, ended their evil lives.

But before him was the man who had stolen Chauncey, the only thing that mattered to him in life.

He remained still, his eyes narrowing in rage. Jackson backed away. Ryker stirred.

Inside her camper, Dru had jumped out of bed at the gunfire. The lights in Dirck's house were on. *Oh my God. Please don't have done this*, she thought. She pulled on her fatigues and boots. *Please don't have…please Dirck*. She reached for her phone. NO SERVICE.

She ran outside toward the house and, in her panic, forgot the motion detector. The porch and driveway flooded in light.

From the corner of his eye, Dirck saw the floods illuminate. His assailants did not. He knew someone was out there. Maybe Dru. Could it be Chauncey?

Then Dru realized the gunshots hadn't been from Dirck's .45—that had a much louder blast shot. It had come from a smaller weapon. *Does he have another weapon?* Dru thought as she tried the kitchen door. Locked. She looked inside. She could just see Dirck's gun and his knife still in its holster.

Inside, she could hear men yelling. She had to get to Dirck's weapons in the kitchen. But she couldn't trigger the lights again. She would have to go through the back screened porch.

Although she had been out of the service for over forty years, Dru was a Marine and her training had taught her how to eliminate a deadly threat. The assailants would have to face two trained combat veterans.

"Pull up…pajamas around wound…duct tape…to his leg," Jackson said in short gasps as he pressed the bloody towel to his face.

Ryker looked at him as if to say, *Are you out of your fucking mind?* He was sure the vet would kill him this time.

"He's wounded…have you…covered." Jackson's speech was slurred and he growing confused. And worse, he was having trouble hearing.

Ryker complied but he also taped the man's hands in back of him. His head was pounding.

"Let's go," Jackson said to Dirck.

Dirck struggled to his knees using the bed to stand. Jackson went into the bathroom to get another towel. He flicked on the lights and looked in the mirror. The entire side of his face was ripped open like raw meat and much of his ear was missing.

They need to get to the money and leave. Now.

Dirck guided himself down the stairs in front of the men. They reached the great room. Behind them was the small hallway and on the wall was a painting of Judge Benson's house. The safe was behind it. Straight ahead was the kitchen. His weapons were there. He would have to divert them.

Dirck collapsed onto the floor.

"There, behind painting," he said, nodding to his left.

Jackson removed the painting to reveal a safe.

"Okay, combination," he mumbled as he pressed the blood-soaked towel into his face.

"Don't remember it," Dirck said.

With his free hand, Jackson pressed the knife into his neck.

"You better remember it, asshole. Or you'll die right here."

"Don't remember it." His voice remained calm.

Ryker pressed his pistol to his temple.

"Go ahead, blow my head off, cut my throat," Dirck said. "But you won't get your money."

"Fine, well, you'll be dead if you don't give us a combination," Ryker said, but it sounded tentative.

Dirck had to distract them.

"Twelve left, twenty-two right, four left, back to thirty," he said.

Jackson turned the dial…12-22-4-30. The safe didn't open. He tried again. It remained locked.

"Try starting to the left," he said. It seemed like a moment of levity but more a reminder to Dirck that Jackson wasn't thinking straight.

The safe clicked opened. Jackson aimed his light into the vault. Inside were stacks of one-hundred dollar bills wrapped in marked straps and held together by a larger strap. He pulled the bundles onto the floor. The cash cascaded onto the floor.

He knelt to it. One large bundle was marked "$100,000" and a smaller marked "$20,000."

Jackson stared at the stacks. He couldn't believe how much money was before him: one hundred twenty grand! He dumped the cash into his knapsack.

But the surprise bonanza hadn't outweighed his mounting pain, and to make it out alive, they'd have to leave now. Blood streamed down his face and neck.

But Ryker wasn't ready to leave.

"Okay, let's take care of the vet," he said.

Ryker grabbed Dirck by his hair and dragged him along the floor to the basement door. He put his boot onto the man's back and pushed him down the stairs head first. Dirck tumbled down the metal stairway and slammed into the concrete retaining wall.

Ryker pointed the gun down at him but hesitated.

"Let's finish him off now," Ryker said as if asking Jackson permission.

"Are you…out of your mind? We have…money… out now."

Jackson knew now that Ryker had lost his mind. He should just take his backpack and get leave on his own. But his head was spinning and he wasn't sure he would even make it alone.

On the west side of the house, Dru had ripped open one edge of the screen and pulled herself into the porch. Before her was a glass-paneled door, the entrance to a back room off the kitchen. Locked. She bunched the small rug in front of her and punched it against a glass panel. It broke in with little noise. She unlocked the door. The kitchen was in front of her. Beyond in the great room, men were yelling.

"Let's kill him now. We don't want witnesses," Ryker said as he stood at the top of the basement stairs.

"Stop…let's *go*!" Jackson was standing holding the blood-soaked towel to his face.

Dru crawled into the dark kitchen. She could see the two men beyond. She knew Dirck was in trouble.

In the basement, Dirck came to consciousness and pulled his hands free from the tape. He looked at his wound. It was bleeding freely. The artery must have opened. He pulled off his pajama top and pushed it against his thigh. He tried to sit up but he didn't want to make the wound any worse.

Was this how he would finally die? Here, in his basement, in this way? Without his dog?

He had to make it. He closed his eyes.

Fear radiated from him.

33

The dense forests that had characterized their inhospitable world for the past week had now given way to the familiar sights and smells of the serene Vermont woods, a place Chauncey knew well. It was the afternoon of the second day after Callie had been freed from Tuckerman's Ravine.

In the past days, they had eaten only roots and shoots and they were growing increasingly weak.

They reached the edge of a field and stopped. Chauncey recognized a stand of spruce trees lining one part of the field's edge. This was where she had fought the coyotes a year ago, the field from where the farmer had saved her.

The smell of cooking chickens wafted past them. They raced across the field toward the farmer's house.

Gregory Swathe was turning the spit on a third chicken when he heard the frantic barking. From the distance, two dogs raced across the wide field toward him. One was blonde, the other black. He knelt to meet them.

The dogs knocked him to the ground, circling about him in a frenzy of barking. One was licking him. He recognized the face, that sweet face. It was Chauncey!

"Grace, Grace…come out here. Tha' dog is back, the dog belongin' to that soldier."

Grace ran out. The two dogs were now on top of Gregory, barking and whining, their tails swinging wildly. Grace ran her hands over Chauncey's body. Through her matted hair, she could feel ribs. The black dog's ribs were visible.

"Oh Greg, them poor dogs are starvin' to death…you recon' that meat's done?"

The dogs danced about the hot chickens, licking their muzzles.

Gregory pulled off one plump chicken onto a plate. The dogs were at opposite ends of it, tearing at the hot flesh, bolting down huge pieces. In seconds, it was gone. Then a second chicken, devoured. The third shredded.

Gregory watched Chauncey rip at the meat. How wild she looked since he had seen her last spring! She was fearless, bold, imposing in her movements and attitude, like a wild coyote, a wolf, yet smarter, more cunning.

Living in the wilds had taken its toll on the dog, yet despite her untamed appearance, the playfulness in her remained. She looked up at Gregory and smiled.

"Where'n the hell did them dogs come from, Greg? Haven't seen that dog for a year, since 'bout last April when you saved her from them coy-otes. Dear God, you think she's lived out in them woods this whole time?"

The dogs collapsed by the fire. Chauncey was safe and with her companion. She was happy Callie had made the journey with her.

Gregory took the dogs inside for the night.

"Grace, do we still have the flyer that fella gave us at Waterman's…what's tha' soldier's name. Dereck or Dirck or somethin'? Maybe they still have the poster up theyah."

He called the feed store.

"Waterman's Feed and Seed," Paul Waterman answered.

"Hi Paul, it's Greg Swathe. Say, do you rememba' a year or so ago the lost dog…tha' one belongin' to the war vet? Had been a flier he put out on a board there. Still have it?"

"Hey Greg. Not sure, let me look." He returned. "Nope, sorry. Took it down after the first of the year. Figured the dog was lost for good. Why you ask?"

"The dog's here. With another dog now. Damndest thing. Came outa' them same woods at my farm. It was about this time last year."

"Give state police a jingle. They might know how to get tha' number," Paul said.

Gregory dialed the number.

"Vermont State Police, Clover," a woman answered.

"Ma'am, Greg Swathe over in Hortonia way. A while back, 'bout a year ago, you were searchin' for a valuable service dog. Do you know about tha'?"

"Yes, sir, we had been dispatched to search for her a while back. Never did find the dog, but I remembered they had spotted it over your way about a year ago. Why do you ask?"

"We *found* her. She was with us last April and ran off from Waterman's out in Craftsbury. She was lookin' for her owner who lived in Glenriver or Clover. We don't rememba' his name or how to contact him."

"Hold on, Greg," the woman said. "Yes, we have the flier. Name's Dirck Hansen in Glenriver. Says here to contact him at 802-449-3393 or Drury Vaughan of CAS at 380-880-2209."

Gregory hung up and tried the first number. He let it ring—no answer. He tried the second number.

"Canines Assisting Soldiers, Michelle speaking," a woman said.

"Hello. Greg Swathe ova' in Vermont looking for someone named Drury Vaughan."

"Oh, Dru, yes. She's out of the office now. Not sure when she's returning. Can I help with something?"

"Yes, we found the dog belonging to tha' veteran. Name is Chauncey."

"What? Oh, *yes*! Chauncey is one of our dogs and has been missing for a year-and-a-half, how…where did you find her?"

"She's safe, here at our farm out here in Hortonia. Not far from where that fella Hansen lives, over in Glenriver way. It's his dog."

"Yes, sir, his service dog. Everyone has been searching for her. For over a year now. Dru is out with Dirck Hansen at his place over in Glenriver right now. I can give her a call and have her call you back."

"Sure, we're at 802-449-2297 here in Vermont. Give us a jingle. We have the dog. Came to our place with another dog, a female black Lab. We're taking care of them both."

Michelle at CAS called Dru's cellphone but there was no answer. No cell service in Glenriver—she remembered Dru telling her that. The other number just rang. She called the farmer back.

"Mr. Swathe, this is Michelle again. I can't seem to reach them. No cellphone service in that part of Vermont. The other phone is a landline, but there's no answer. We'll keep trying. We have your number. Please keep the dog safe and inside. Don't let her out of your sight."

The dogs lay by the warm kitchen stove, exhausted but their bellies full. Gregory paced about the kitchen.

"Grace, that Chauncey dog needs to get to her owner. I think I'll drive her on over to Glenriver. It's 'bout forty miles or so due north through Highway 12. Don't know about the other black dog…reckon we could just keep her here."

Grace shook her head.

"No, Greg. You don't know where he lives…rural out theyah and them dogs need to stay together. Don't know why but I can see the way Chauncey protects her so."

Gregory and Grace drank their last coffee before leaving the dogs downstairs. The dogs had fallen asleep by the wood stove.

In the middle of the night, Chauncey jolted awake. She smelled Dirck—this time, his acrid smell was strong and close. She ran to the door, frantically barking and scratching at it.

Upstairs, Grace woke. She ran downstairs and flipped on the lights. The wall clock read 1:45 a.m. Both dogs were at the kitchen door. Chauncey was pawing the door, barking wildly. She looked up at Grace, desperation in her eyes.

"Oh, dear girl, you must need to get out bad…you need to go do your business then?" she said.

She cracked the door open. Chauncey bolted past her, Callie following.

Grace watched the dogs run into the field.

"Greg, *Greg* come down," Grace yelled. "Dogs got out!"

Gregory Swathe woke and looked out his bedroom window. He could just make out the silhouettes of the two dogs as they scrambled across the field toward the far woods.

"Grace…why'n the hell did you let them dogs out?" he yelled down to her.

"That Chauncey dog was barking hard to get out, Greg. Thought she needed to relieve herself. They blew right past me. Real fast like. Must be after somethin'."

"Yeah, bet she's after her owner now. May have smelled him. He's not far. They'll go through them woods up to Riverdale Township and the back way to Glenriver. Give me that poster." He wrote down the numbers. "Dog trainin' place won't answer now. I'll call police again."

"Vermont State Police Clover Center," a woman said.

"Yes ma'am, we called yesterday. We were holding that dog, the one belonging to tha' veteran. She just escaped from our farm," Gregory said. He was out of breath.

"Yes, sir, I see you called earlier. Where did you last see the dog?" the woman said.

"Here in our house with another dog. Got out, ran north, just now…out into them woods…probably afta' her owner. He's in Glenriver town. Woman from the dog trainin' place is with him. Tried to reach him, no answer. Tha' dog knows somethin'. Thought there might be some trouble out theyah." Gregory said.

"Okay, sir. Hold on," she said.

A minute passed. A man's voice came on.

"Sir, who is speaking?"

"Greg Swathe. Called yesterday."

"How long ago did the dogs get away?"

"Couldn't be more than couple minutes ago."

"Okay sir, stay by your phone. We'll call back if we need you. We have a couple of cruisers out now near Woodsdale. I'll alert them." The line went dead.

Gregory stared out the window, the phone still in his hand.

"Oh Gracie, I hope them dogs will be all right," he said. "I'm sure she's after her owner and that black dog wants to stick with her, like you say. She knows how to get through them woods by now. Hope she doesn't run into them coyotes tonight."

He stared into the black forest, tears in his eyes.

The dogs had left the farmer's kitchen an hour ago and were now in Riverdale Township, running toward Glenriver in a direct line to Judge Benson's Place. Dirck's acrid scent was close. Chauncey could almost hear him calling for her.

They raced flat out through the woods, the moonlight guiding their paths.

Chauncey came to the far end of the forest. In front of her was a stand of six white pines evenly spaced. She recognized the unusual rows of trees—they sat just at the edge of a wide field, the field that led to her home. They crept forward.

Dirck's smell was immediately in front of her. She looked back at Callie, her eyes wide.

Through the bare branches, she saw her home.

It was 4 a.m. and the lights were on.

34

Inside Judge Benson's Place, initial uncertainty quickly spiraled into desperation and chaos. Ryker's rapidly shifting moods and anger bound them both to an uncertain end.

It looked to Ryker like his companion was on his way out. He should just grab the cash and run—Jackson had left his keys in the truck. Or maybe he hadn't. That would make his escape harder. He might have to take out Jackson. And then, the vet might live and identify him.

"I'm gonna blow that asshole away now—finish him off from the top of the stairs," Ryker said again. "We don't want witnesses to this shit."

Jackson lay on the couch, his head resting on another blood-soaked towel, trying to regain some sense of equilibrium.

In the kitchen, Dru couched in the shadows. She had the loaded .45 pistol, its safety off. Dirck's knife was slung around her shoulder. She was no more than three feet from both men.

Ryker paced in front of the couch, yelling, erratically waving his pistol. Dru waited for him to move closer but instead he walked back to the basement door and flung it open, pointing the gun down the stairs. Dirck wasn't at the bottom.

"Where the fuck is he?" he said in a panic. "I kicked that bastard down the stairs—he's not there now!"

Dru now knew Dirck was in the basement, injured.

Jackson was trying to speak. "Just…get out."

His entire head exploded in spasms of pain and he was blacking out.

There was no another way out. Ryker ran for the knapsack with the cash, passing directly in front of the kitchen entrance.

From the shadows, a gun exploded, throwing Ryker into the wall. Dru had hit his shoulder and part of his arm.

She jumped out and onto the stricken man, ripping his pistol free. She tucked the .45 into her belt and dug the knife into his throat.

Jackson lay on the couch, unable to comprehend what had just happened.

"Don't move or I'll end your life," she said.

Ryker stared up at the woman on top of him. She was older with graying hair and the veins in her neck stood out. Her flexed arms were lean but muscular. *Maybe a combat vet like her friend,* he thought.

Ryker's pain was immense—the right side of his shoulder and part of his arm was ripped open. This was exactly what he had feared from the beginning.

Dru looked over at Jackson and motioned to him to move.

"Over there, against the wall."

Jackson stumbled up, holding the blood-soaked towel to his head. She turned back to the wounded man pinned beneath her leg. Ryker screamed at her.

"Get off me you goddamned bitch! Get *off*…" She pushed the knife deeper into his throat. He cried out.

"Please don't hurt me…"

Jackson recognized the knife—it was the weapon that had nearly ended his own life. He had to calm the woman.

"Take it…easy," Jackson mumbled.

This now looked like the end of the line. Jackson had nothing more to lose. He turned to his side and slid his left hand into his pants for the switchblade. He pulled it out and hit the release. He lunged at Dru, plunging the knife into her leg. His strength was still considerable.

Dru recoiled in pain, falling from Ryker. Jackson grabbed the .45 from Dru's belt. The other pistol was not within reach. He couldn't reach Dirck's knife either.

Ryker and Dru were on the floor both writhing in pain. Jackson pointed the .45 at her. He would now do anything to stay alive and get out of this nightmare.

"Don't move, damn it!" he yelled but his jaw felt like it was coming loose.

Ryker continued to cry in pain. The man had no tolerance for pain.

"Ryk, can you stand?" he said. "Get the duct tape. Tie her hands."

Ryker struggled to his feet. He didn't see any way out of this—his fear had reached a breaking point, but so had his anger. The outcome hung in the balance, and Dru sensed it could go either way.

In the basement, Dirck had crawled away from the stairwell to the stone wall facing the low windows where the intruders had entered. He had come to consciousness hearing the gunshot and screams above him. Dru was up there, yelling. He slumped onto his side and closed his eyes.

Beyond the yelling and stomping above him, Dirck heard something else, a stirring at the windows just in front of him. He looked up.

Framed in the open window sill was the face of a dog. Dirck squinted his eyes closed and reopened them.

The dog was still there. It was blonde, like Chauncey, but its face was more sculpted, and the dirty, matted fur made it look wild. The dog squeezed through the opening and jumped to the floor. It came at Dirck, crying, shivering in excitement.

Dirck knew those sounds.

"Oh my God! Is that you, Chauncey?" he whispered. He was delirious.

He held his dog close and stared into her eyes. They were stark and wild, more alive than he remembered. But they were loving and warm, just as he remembered. He ran his hands though her dirty, twisted fur and felt her ribs.

She was a shadow of the beautiful dog he once knew. But it was Chauncey. He hadn't seen her in well over a year. She let out a low, soft moan.

"Oh my God, Chauncey! My God! Where have you been for so long, my girl? Where, my girl?"

She buried her head into his arm and closed her heavy eyes.

He whispered to her. "Be careful, Chauncey. Danger."

Chauncey's head perked. She knew this word, a training command from Dru at CAS, from the prison with Jerry.

Danger. She knew her journey was not yet complete.

Something stirred at the window. A black dog appeared, waiting outside in reverence for her companion—Callie knew Chauncey had found what she had been seeking throughout their long journey. Chauncey looked back at her. Callie jumped into the basement.

Dirck's familiar pungent odor told Chauncey he was in trouble. But other smells wafted past her, smells above her.

Upstairs, two men were yelling. Something bad was happening up there.

He held his dog close. The intense pleasure of Chauncey in his arms revived him. He knew could endure anything with her there. He looked into her steady, warm eyes.

"Girl, help us. Danger," he repeated.

He knew he must rely on his dog's skills, her intelligence, her training. But he couldn't have known how strong, how determined she had become.

Chauncey's head shifted to the noises above her. She crawled from Dirck and crept to the stairs. She had been up and down these stairs many times. She knew this house, every angle of it. It was her home, now more than ever. She was ready to face any danger for him.

Above them, a woman yelled. Chauncey smelled Dru. Then, other scents hit her—Jackson Stoney and Ryker Falls!

Then Callie heard the distinctive, high-pitched voice above them. Her head lowered and she took the lead.

The dogs silently ascended the stairs. The door was open.

Ryker had stopped screaming and stumbled to his feet, grabbing one of the blood-soaked kitchen towels for his mangled shoulder. With his one functioning hand, he reached for the smaller pistol on the floor.

"Get her tied up. We need to end this shit *now*," he screamed.

Something in the man's face told Jackson he was about to kill the woman. Ryker pushed the gun into her head.

"You are so *fucking dead*, bitch!"

He pulled the trigger. A click. Then another. The gun had jammed. He hurled it at the wall and reached for Dirck's combat knife. He drew his arm back and lunged at her.

Without warning, a black apparition filled his view as if any measure of light had been suddenly swallowed up about him. His hand was arrested and the knife flew out.

An intent and angry black dog had pinned him firmly on the floor, her mouth buried into his functioning arm. Callie's head lowered slowly into Ryker's face. She stared into the man's sinister black eyes, inches away. This was the man who had tortured her and left her for dead. A deep menacing growl resonated in her throat and her jaw tightened down on him. His arm bones began to move.

"Oh my God! Get it *off* me!"

Jackson pointed the gun at the dog, but the space immediately behind him suddenly collapsed as if some great bird were swooping in, filling the air around him. He turned and was met by the face of a creature flying silently at him, half-dog, half-wolf, its burning eyes bright and focused, its mouth agape, inches from him, in an awful, cinematic vision of the dog he had once stolen.

There was no time to react.

Chauncey slammed the man to the ground, her mouth at his neck. Jackson's mangled face pressed painfully into the floor.

In all the years she had known Chauncey, Dru had never seen her with such wildness, such determination.

"Chauncey, *hold*," she commanded but the direction wasn't necessary.

Unlike Chauncey, Callie's grip continued to strengthen.

"*Stay*," she commanded the other dog she had never seen. Callie somehow knew not to go any further.

The turn of events afforded Dru renewed strength. She ripped the duct tape from her hands, grabbed the large gun, and kicked the jammed pistol and knife across the room.

The dogs continued to immobilize the men.

"*Hold*" she again commanded.

Dru stumbled down the stairs and knelt in front of Dirck. The handle of a knife protruded from her thigh.

"Pull it. Don't think it hit artery," she said.

It took considerable strength to pull the knife free.

"Dogs saved me," she said. "A beautiful thing. Can you get up?"

He shook his head. A pool of blood was growing under his leg. She pulled her belt off and drew it onto his upper thigh. She ran back upstairs.

Chauncey continued pressing Jackson's mangled face to the floor. She remembered the wolf's bloody leg pulsing in her mouth but the predator under her now was far weaker.

Ryker's arm was still buried inside Callie's mouth.

"Get off me, you *goddamned dog*," he said and threw his leg around and kicked the dog's flank.

That was it! Callie erupted. Her head shook furiously about, instantly snapping the man's thin arm.

He screamed. It was the worst pain he had ever known.

Dru looked down at Ryker. His arm was set at a painfully odd angle. Callie held onto him firmly.

"Don't move," she said. "The dogs will make it worse if you move."

Dru knew her dog wouldn't instinctively hurt Jackson. Callie was another story. She called them both off.

Chauncey released Jackson and backed away. Callie followed and sat at attention next to Dru, ready for her next command. Chauncey scurried down the stairs to Dirck.

Outside, the deck lights illuminated. Two men with flashlights were out there. Vermont State Police. They banged at the door. Dru opened it, the gun still in her hand. One of the troopers went for his firearm.

"Drop your weapon," he said.

"I'm Drury Vaughan. Captain Hansen and I were attacked. We're injured—need medical attention—in the basement. Now!"

The troopers looked past her and saw two men on the floor. One was writhing in pain, the other was on his side, not moving. Blood pooled between them. It wasn't clear if they would survive.

Callie continued to sit at attention, looking to Dru for further direction. She liked the woman who was telling her what to do.

A trooper leaned into his shoulder mic.

"We're out at Dirck Hansen's house—3982 Route 44 in Glenriver. Need two ambulances immediately," he said. He turned to Dru. "Paramedics will be here soon."

Dru and one of the troopers went to the basement with a first-aid kit. The trooper knew about Dirck and his dog. The trooper applied another tourniquet and bandaged his wound. Dru gave him water. Throughout the ordeal, Chauncey lay next to Dirck and Dru, watching over them as paramedics treated them.

Ryker Falls died that night. Jackson survived but faced a life sentence for attempted murder. Dru Vaughan was treated at the Glenriver hospital and released but stayed behind with Dirck.

Dirck Hansen lost nearly half of his blood and had only hours to live when Chauncey had found him. During his hospital stay that spring, the dogs were taken to CAS for treatment and weeks of recovery.

By that summer, Dru returned to Vermont to stay with Dirck and his dogs. He had regained his strength and especially his mind and was finally off the alcohol and drugs.

She wanted Callie to be evaluated as a service animal, but there was no separating the two dogs. Callie eventually came to learn how Chauncey had been trained to help Dirck. She grew into an impressive and beautiful Labrador who became Chauncey's steady companion and protector.

The nation praised the two dogs for saving the lives of the veterans of two wars.

35

It was a brilliant August day at Judge Benson's homestead. Dirck was in the kitchen preparing lunch with his dogs and Dru was outside. Chauncey's attention shifted to the window.

A truck had pulled in. A large man got out and walked unsteadily toward the house. He wore an ill-fitted brown suit and his dark hair was slicked unnaturally back, giving him a forced formal air. A girl was with him, a young teenager, perhaps thirteen, holding his hand. Chauncey barked. Dru walked out from the back of the house toward him.

"Can we help you?" she said. She extended her hand but he didn't take it.

"We are looking for Captain Dirck Hansen," the man said.

Chauncey continued barking. Callie, too, was excited, but didn't know why and also began to bark.

The girl craned her neck toward the barking. Dirck walked to the patio, leaving his dogs inside.

"I'm Captain Hansen," he said. "How can I help you?"

The large man's eyes were downcast. He swayed from side to side, not offering his hand. He looked old, probably older than his fifty-one years, and despite a sobered life, his clean-shaven, ruddy face was laced with broken capillaries and set with deep wrinkles. It was a sad, uncertain face.

"Captain Hansen. Sir. My name's Tollinger. Jake Tollinger. I am also a U.S. veteran. Served in Afghanistan in the 101st Airborne Division."

Dirck grabbed the man's hand and shook it with both of his.

"Mr. Tollinger, you're in great company here. This is Drury Vaughan, also a veteran, Marine Corps from Vietnam," he said proudly.

Jake continued staring at the ground in silence. He raised his head.

"Captain. I was…I was the one who stole your dog two years ago. From that park in Riverdale. Took her for my daughter, Joannie here. But the poor dog ran off from us that spring. Probably to go find you. When I discovered it was your service dog, I tried to get the police to find her," he said, as if to somehow mitigate his crime.

Dirck's expression changed. He stared at the man in disbelief, trying to make some sense of what he had just heard.

"My daughter loved that dog," Jake said as he put his arm around her. "Named her Kady. She had lost her own dog and I couldn't keep watching her withdraw. Didn't know what else to do for her. Kady brought her so much joy. I never meant to hurt the dog…she was a very good puppy."

The girl kept looking toward the house to find the source of the barking.

"Couldn't live with myself after taking your dog, your service dog. So many of my buddies in the war had such good dogs…dogs that helped them stay alive. They just weren't the same without their dogs."

He looked down at his daughter. After Chauncey had run away two years ago, Jake had told her about stealing the dog. She forgave her father but never wanted another dog after Kady.

"Heard on the news about your dog finding her way back, how she saved your lives. I…well, we both…have wanted to come and talk to you so many times since then."

Jake tried to think of more to say but could not. Maybe there was nothing more to say.

Dirck looked at Dru, his eyebrows raised. He couldn't believe the man had taken the extraordinary effort to find him and admit his crime.

"Mr. Tollinger, Jake. It takes a lot of guts for you to come here even after all this time…but I'm glad you did."

Barking broke the tension. Dirck opened the kitchen door and the two dogs bounded out in a frenzy.

Chauncey recognized the girl's smell and immediately ran to her, her tail swinging wildly. Joannie knelt to her, hugging, crying, laughing through her tears. She remembered the young girls' touch.

But Chauncey pulled away and turned toward Jake. She recognized the man's smell—this was the man who had stolen her from that park so long ago, the man with the rope. She backed away, her ears down, a growl rising in her chest.

Dirck knelt to his dog, put his arm around her, and whispered something in her ear.

Chauncey's ears relaxed and she sat back and panted gently as she looked at Jake. The man tentatively put his hand out toward her. She stood and licked his palm in submission. The dog he had stolen and mistreated was forgiving him! Jake smiled and gently stroked her back. He had never touched the dog like this. She remembered well his mistreatment but her heart still melted at his touch. A loving touch was all it took. Chauncey looked up at him, love beaming through her eyes.

Dirck knew that Chauncey had sought love and trust from all those who had kept her. And that included Jake Tollinger. Even in her darkest hours with Ryker Falls and Jackson Stoney, she would have given her unwavering trust, but men like that wouldn't return that trust and could never have understood the unconditional love of a dog.

Dru walked over to Dirck.

"Remember me telling you about that young white Lab we worked with at CAS, the one who didn't click with any of the vets we brought through?" Dru said. "Name was Belle I think, a sweet dog, a little rambunctious. Maybe the Tollingers would love Belle. She's like Chauncey in that sweet, obedient way."

The young girl was too engaged with Chauncey to pay attention to the new possibility.

Dirck didn't remember a dog named Belle. He looked at Dru and smiled.

"I think I remember," he said and smiled in mutual understanding.

Dru would find a dog for the young girl.

Jake was dumbfounded.

"You would do this for us?" he said. Joannie smiled at her father, her face bright and open.

Dirck's attention remained on Jake. He could tell the man had led a misguided life, one that had been broken inside the ranks of the fighting and faithful men groping for survival in the blank, barren deserts of war. Young, misdirected men like Jake had been reborn inside burned-out villages scattered with death and in the terrible nights of uncertainty, reborn from having to face their own mortality in ways no man should ever experience.

He saw Jake in the same way he saw himself: brave but afraid, wanting mercy. The man before him understood that mercy.

"Jake, you and your daughter need a dog as much I. These dogs are our saviors. Chauncey, Callie, all of them, everywhere. They have been, and will always be, our protectors. Without them, we are lost. We struggle in our limited existence and they find us and teach us to love and persevere. We fail, but in their short time with us, they do not."

He wanted to say more but words didn't come.

Jake's heavy eyes lifted in understanding.

Dirck looked beyond Jake. Chauncey was in the field with Callie, running in her precious freedom, joy emblazoned on her face.

He tried to imagine what his dog must have endured in her long, uncharted journey home.

He thought of her like a wild animal, living on the wild things of the forest, traveling hundreds of miles to find him. He would never know that she had been scored by the teeth of coyotes and wolves and had lain alone in the streets and shelters to die, only to survive through her fierce determination and faith in him. She was the faithful one, uncertain in her nights of loss but singular in her life's purpose—driven to be together with him again.

He closed his eyes and could see her running, racing into the waning summer twilight, through bright and bitter winter meadows into the pale streaks of dawn, over vast, outstretched moonlit woodlands, stopping, listening to hushed forest whispers a moment before sleep, seeking, searching for that which called her.

Dru walked to Dirck and put her hand on his shoulder.

"What did you whisper to Chauncey just then?"

"I told her the man was just like me. That his love was always there for her too."

Even in the early dark hours of her confinement, Chauncey had found that love in the little girl who cherished her so. It had come through her father. Chauncey now understood that unwavering devotion and love that had always been a part of her. She could feel it in Jake's hand, see it in his eyes.

The struggles and hopelessness she had endured for nearly two years had taught her the depth of that love—it was the indestructible and unspoiled devotion she had revealed to Jerry in the prison, to her man Jimmy on the city streets, to the farmer and his wife, all those she had encountered.

It was the unwavering devotion revealed by the dog lying in torment under its soldier's casket, by the dog in the lap of a homeless man protecting him, by the homeless dog grateful to be taken in by the kindness of a stranger, and by the dog at the end of its good life, happy with its final touch.

And now, here, in the rich and heavy summer afternoon, that devotion was brightly revealed between the war-torn soldier lost to life and the magnificent, brave Golden Retriever who had rescued him.

Dirck raised his hand to the field. Chauncey raced to him with abandon.

RESCUE

A novel by
Christopher Dant

Christopher Dant is a career writer and studied English and science at Indiana University. From 2000-2004, he attended Stanford University's Creative Writing Program to study fiction and in 2001, published a collection of short stories *Appalachian Waltz*. RESCUE is his first novel. He lives in Vermont with his wife Maureen and Golden Retriever.

If you enjoyed RESCUE, please consider leaving a brief review at your online bookseller of choice.

You can find RESCUE on Amazon, Barnes and Noble, or at the Northshire bookstore at www.northshire.com

Please visit our Facebook page **Rescue, the novel** and leave a review there as well.

We welcome comments and reviews at rescuethenovel@gmail.com

CPSIA information can be obtained
at www.ICGtesting.com
Printed in the USA
LVHW020926140820
663151LV00003B/136

9 781605 714257